"I like having you here."

"I like being here," Swann answered quietly.

He thought about driving her home, and the thought seemed unappealing. He took her hand and led her through the house, flicking out lights as they went.

When they stood in his bedroom, he decided he might as well be truthful. "I'm really very tired. Exhausted, in fact. You could drive my car home, you know."

"I know," she said. She was standing very close, but they weren't touching. "I don't want to go home."

It would be very easy to loosen the bows at her shoulders, to lay her on the bed, but he was so, so tired.

"Swann," he began, his voice heavy with weariness.

"It's all right," she said softly, and then she took his hand and led him to the bed. "Remember when you said you could hold me forever? Well, I don't know about forever, but how about for tonight?"

ABOUT THE AUTHOR

Pamela Browning survived Hurricane Hugo's sweep through South Carolina in September 1989 while she was working on the outline for *A Man Worth Loving*. She decided to include some of the experiences of friends and neighbors in recovering from a hurricane in this book.

Books by Pamela Browning

HARLEQUIN AMERICAN ROMANCE

HARLEQUIN ROMANCE

PAMELA BROWNING

A MAN WORTH LOVING

Harlequin Books

TORONTO • NEW YORK • LONDON
AMSTERDAM • PARIS • SYDNEY • HAMBURG
STOCKHOLM • ATHENS • TOKYO • MILAN

For my favorite editor, Tahti Carter

Published March 1991

ISBN 0-373-16384-3

A MAN WORTH LOVING

Prologue

February, 1967

People, lots of people, pushing and shoving to reach the door to the big white building at the edge of the parking lot. The pungent odor of wet wool, and mud slipping underfoot. A woman crying in great ragged sobs, the tears coursing down her plump cheeks. A man insisting, "Let me through." He was pushing a woman in a wheelchair.

"Maybe we shouldn't have come," Swann's mother said nervously.

"Well, we're here. We might as well go through with it," her father replied.

Five-year-old Swann clung tightly to her mother's hand. She was frightened, not only of the crowd, but of her father. He seldom had time for her, and tonight he was grim. She knew that it was because of her.

She started to whimper. "Stop it, Swann," her father said crossly.

"Evan—" her mother said.

"Don't start, Mimi," her father warned.

Her mother bit her lip and squeezed Swann's hand. Swann was reassured by the squeeze although she didn't understand what they were doing here.

Her father shouldered impatiently through the crowd, pulling Swann and her mother along with him. They squeezed past others through the door of the building into a room with long rows of folding chairs, most of them already occupied.

"Down there," her father said, indicating three empty seats in the second row.

Swann and her mother followed him down the wide center aisle.

"Hurry," he said.

But Swann couldn't hurry; her feet wouldn't move as fast as her father's. Especially her left foot, which didn't bend correctly since what Swann had privately named The Badness. The Badness had happened when she fell down the stairs at their summer cottage in Maine, and her foot had hurt and hurt, and she had told Nanny that it was sore, but Nanny only ordered her to stop complaining and went away laughing with her boyfriend when she thought Swann was asleep. But Swann wasn't asleep because her foot hurt too much. It kept hurting, too. For days. And weeks. And she had cried for her mother, but Nanny told her that her mother was somewhere called France.

Now her left foot was crooked and stiff, and her father had been angry when he found out, and her mother had cried, and they made Nanny pack her suitcase and leave when they'd learned that Swann's foot had been injured months before they came back from France. And Dr. Fitz had said that she needed an operation, which sounded scary because he frowned when he said it, and he had given her a lollipop because she had been a good girl when he looked at her foot, and on the way home her mother had cried and told her father that maybe they should go to Miracle Farm.

Her father had said no at first, and her parents hadn't spoken for several days, but then her father finally tightened his lips and said, "If you're that set on trying it, Mimi, I guess there's no harm. Just don't tell anybody we know that we're going. I'd be a laughingstock in this town if anyone knew that we'd been taken in by this Child Michael nonsense."

Her mother brightened, and Swann was excited about going to a farm. She'd learned about farms at kindergarten. She was eager to feed the ducks and geese, and she thought maybe she might get to see the farmer milk the cows. Only it was night when they got to the farm, and there was no sign of a farmer or ducks or cows. All she could see were people, some of them on crutches, many in wheelchairs, one or two on stretchers.

"Look, I see him!" a woman behind her cried, pointing at the curtain-covered door to the side of the stage at the front of the building.

Swann stood up and peered around the stout man in front of her. She thought that the lady might mean that she saw the farmer, but she knew as soon as she saw the little boy dressed in a blue velvet suit that he was no farmer. Farmers wore bibbed overalls and were old like her father.

Disappointed, Swann sat down again. The chair was hard. She fidgeted. She pushed a silvery gum wrapper around on the floor with the toe of her boot. She scratched her leg.

"Don't," her mother whispered when she saw her scratching. Her father merely nailed her with a look.

The boy stood in the doorway holding back the curtain and silently surveying the audience. He was a nice-looking boy with curly blond hair tumbling in ringlets down past the collar of his suit. He seemed very solemn.

The man who stood behind him gave him a little push. Obediently the boy stepped forward, a spotlight catching him in its beam. The bright light glinted off his hair.

"It's *him!* It's Child Michael!" screamed a woman in the front row, and she ran to the stage and fell on her knees. Two men dressed identically in royal blue jackets with the letters "C.M." embroidered in gilt thread on the pockets yanked the woman to her feet and led her back to her seat. As the boy approached the short microphone, a collective sigh went up from the crowd.

"He's so *little,*" breathed Swann's mother.

"Well, that's not surprising," snapped her father. "He *is* only six years old."

The boy waited calmly at the microphone for the crowd to settle down. Disappointment washed over Swann. There was no doubt in her mind now that her parents had lied to her. This was no farm, and there wasn't any farmer. She had *so* wanted to feed the ducks and watch the farmer milk the cows.

"I thought we were going to a farm," Swann said suddenly. A teenager down the row tittered at the sound of her voice. Swann felt her cheeks turn red.

"Hush, Swann," her mother said, twitching at Swann's coat until Swann was facing front again.

"But you *said*—" she began.

Her father reached over and smacked her hard on the knee. "You heard your mother," he said.

Everything was always her fault! She could never do or say anything right. Tears stung Swann's eyes, and she blinked. When her vision cleared, she saw that the yellow-haired boy was looking right at her. His eyes were so blue, as blue as the ocean in Maine, as blue as her mother's sapphire ring. They bespoke a loneliness and a bleak kinship that told her he understood. For a long moment their eyes held, and Swann didn't care anymore that her parents had tricked her.

At that point a tall man with curly hair a lot like the boy's strode forward.

"Child Michael will begin the Help Meeting as soon as you are quiet," he said, bending over to speak into the microphone.

A hush fell over the room, and the spotlight narrowed as the houselights dimmed.

"I come to help you," said the boy in a high, light voice, and then he said a lot of other things that didn't make a lot of sense to Swann but seemed important to everyone else.

"Take off Swann's boot," her father ordered as the boy started down the steps from the stage.

Her mother struggled with the zipper and slipped Swann's boot from her foot. The sock followed, leaving Swann's crooked foot looking exposed and bare. *Like a fish washed up on the beach,* Swann thought, turning her foot this way and that and trying not to think about how much it ached.

Child Michael was now approaching the front row. He stopped in front of a young woman holding a baby.

"What is the matter with this baby?" Child Michael asked.

"He suffers from seizures," the mother said.

Child Michael placed his hands on either side of the baby's head. He closed his eyes, appeared to concentrate, and adjusted his hands slightly until he seemed more comfortable.

"Heal," he said into the air, his eyes still closed. "I ask The Power within me to make this baby well." He tensed, released his hands, and the baby began to cry. Child Michael's small hand stroked the downy fluff on the baby's head. The baby hiccuped and was quiet.

"He's well! Joey is well!" the baby's mother proclaimed tearfully.

Child Michael smiled gently and moved on to the next person, who claimed to have pneumonia, and to the next, who wore a brace on his leg.

Swann's father looked bored, but her mother followed the proceedings with avid interest as Child Michael moved slowly down the row, touching his hands to each person who claimed to need healing.

Swann curled her naked foot up under her warm winter coat and leaned her head against her mother's soft mink. It smelled good like her mother. She closed her eyes. It was late. Probably it was way past her bedtime. She should have suspected that something odd was about to happen when Miss Neville dressed her after dinner and her parents took her out into the cold. They almost *never* took her anywhere with them when they went out at night. Usually she had to stay home with Miss Neville, who had come to take care of her after Nanny had left.

Her foot began to grow numb with the cold, and Swann wished that she dared to ask her mother to put her boot and sock back on. But her mother was watching Child Michael. Swann settled more comfortably into her mother's mink coat. She loved her mother. She didn't love her father, although she knew she was supposed to. How could you love somebody if you were scared every time he noticed you?

The boy looked like he might understand. Child Michael. What a funny name! The boy's blue eyes. *So* blue. As blue as the liquid in the bottle that Rosa the maid sprayed on the mirrors to clean them. As blue as one of the marbles in the bag that Miss Neville was keeping for her to play with when she was older. As blue as—

But here was the boy. And he was looking at *her*. She sat up straight.

"Hold your foot out, Swann," her mother said gently.

Child Michael studied her with compassion that seemed far beyond his years. Looking deep into his eyes, Swann roused herself enough to extend her foot toward him. Slowly Child Michael placed his warm hands firmly on either side of it. She felt a sensation of intense heat, but oddly enough, it didn't burn. It felt good.

"Heal," the boy said softly. "Grow straight and strong. *Heal!*"

And even as he said the words, her foot began to tingle and seemed infused with a strange kind of energy. She couldn't see her foot, enclosed as it was in his small hands, but she felt as if something inside it had changed. Did that make sense? She wasn't sure, but she was well acquainted with fairy tales where fairy godmothers waved magic wands and made people or objects do things they weren't supposed to do or change into things that they weren't supposed to be. Maybe this was something like that.

Child Michael removed his hands. His eyes met hers once more, and his smile as it shone upon her was sweet and sincere and full of love. She had the brief sensation that she was floating, and her head seemed remarkably clear.

Her foot was still warm and not tingly at all. She felt cozy all over, and happy, and peaceful.

"Swann?" her mother said as if from a long way away.

She swiveled her head to look at her mother. Her mother was pretty, with long dark hair and diamonds in her earlobes. She thought that she had never loved her mother so much. Her father's forehead wrinkled in concern. For once Swann wasn't afraid of him.

"Put her boot on and let's get out of here," her father said.

"I *think* her foot looks straighter," her mother said.

Swann looked longingly in the direction of Child Michael. He was talking earnestly to the teenager, the one who had laughed at Swann earlier. Swann wished that Child Michael would come back and talk to *her*.

Her boot and sock were back on, and her mother was urging her to her feet.

"Can you walk, Swann? How does your foot feel?" her mother asked anxiously.

"It's okay," she said. Child Michael had moved farther down the row; she could hardly see him.

"Evan, maybe you should carry her," her mother said.

"Let her walk, Mimi. That's why we brought her, isn't it?"

"It's so late, Evan."

"I can walk," Swann said, eager to head off conflict between her parents, if it were at all possible. She struggled to her feet. Amazingly, her left foot didn't hurt anymore. She shifted her weight onto it experimentally.

"Are you coming?" her father said, impatience flowing from every syllable. He turned and walked away.

Slowly she and her mother followed her father up the aisle. People stared and whispered as they passed. Swann ignored everyone. All she could think about was how good her foot felt. And she wasn't limping! It *must* have been magic that the boy had done.

Outside the air was clear and cold. Stars twinkled through the blackness overhead, and as she trailed her parents past cars in the parking lot, Swann whispered to herself the little verse Miss Neville had taught her.

> "Star light, star bright,
> First star I see tonight,
> Wish I may, wish I might,
> Have this wish I wish tonight."

And then Swann wished that she would see the boy with the blue eyes again soon so they could be friends.

"Can I ride in front with you?" Swann asked as her father unlocked the door of the long black Cadillac.

"Oh, Evan, let her," cajoled her mother. Usually Swann had to ride alone in the back seat.

"Well, all right," her father agreed. He sounded less impatient, even relieved, now that they were out of the building. Swann wondered if he had noticed that she didn't limp anymore.

"I'll take her to the doctor tomorrow for X rays," her mother said as they drove out the gate. Her mother sounded excited. *She* had noticed that Swann wasn't limping; she had bent and hugged Swann, her eyes shining, before they hurried out of the building.

"That should be interesting" was all her father said.

Swann curled up inside the protective circle of her mother's arm. It was good news that tomorrow she'd see Dr. Fitz; it would almost make up for not going to a farm. Dr. Fitz would offer her another lollipop and let her choose the flavor. She'd pick a red one, and then she'd tell him about the magic the boy had worked on her foot.

Her father reached across her and turned on the radio. Soon, sinking into the fragrant fur of her mother's coat, Swann slept. She slept all the way home. And she dreamed of blue eyes, a warm tingling touch, and a look that said, *I understand.*

Chapter One

June, 1990

Someone was actually frying an egg on the pavement for the benefit of a newspaper photographer; the heat wave had settled in on Philadelphia three days ago and showed no sign of abating. Swann skirted the curious onlookers surrounding the sidewalk short-order cook and propelled herself through the revolving doors into the blessedly cool air of the hotel lobby, relieved to be out of the heat.

"Miss Triplett? Mr. Bahr will meet you in the restaurant," the concierge said from behind her desk.

Swann hesitated in the restaurant doorway, surveying the scene. Fresh vases of red and white carnations and baby's breath graced white tablecloths; the muted chime of silver and crystal provided an undertone to the soft tinkle of piano notes. As she threaded her way between the tables, heads turned at the sight of her trim figure in the pink linen dress; pearl earrings were her only jewelry. She saw Justin's snow-white mop of hair across the room only a moment before he spotted her and waved.

"Happy birthday, Swann," he said, rising as she approached. He kissed her on the cheek, then stood back to admire the way she looked. "You're as lovely as always," he said with an approving glance at her shoulder-length dark hair. "You look more and more like your elegant mother every day." Justin had been her mother's godfather, and although Mimi had been dead for fourteen years, Swann and Justin were still close.

"What on earth brings you to Philadelphia in this heat?" she asked Justin after they sat down.

"The only thing that could bring me to Philadelphia in *any* kind of weather, my dear," he said, his eyes twinkling at her. "*You*. And your birthday. I even brought you a present." He handed her a small box with a large bow.

She opened it; inside was a beautiful gold bracelet. "Thank you, Justin. It's lovely. Here, will you help me put it on?"

"This is not only a birthday present, it's to commemorate the six weeks your book made the bestseller list. I had the dates engraved inside," he said as he clasped it around her wrist. "Oh, here comes the waiter. You'd better look at the menu," he pointed out when he had finished.

"I'll let you order. You usually know my mind better than even I know it," she said with a smile. This was true. He knew her better than anyone except her best friend; Justin Bahr had taken a special interest in her from the time she was a child.

"Then we'll both have lobster salad," Justin said.

"Now," said Swann when the waiter had gone. "What really brings you to Philadelphia, Justin?"

He studied her, a small half smile on his face. "An idea. A wonderful idea. Only you can do it justice."

"Oh dear," Swann said, reaching for the bread. "It sounds like I'm about to be subjected to some heavy-duty persuasion."

"You're right. But, Swann, please take this seriously. It's an idea for your new book."

"I have my own ideas about my next project. Now that I've cut my teeth on the Winky Tapps biography, I'm ready to tackle something with more depth. You know I've always been interested in politics. How about—"

"Stop distracting me, Swann. And forget politics for now. Your sensitivity and empathy for the ordeals of a former child movie star make you a prime candidate to write a book about another personality who was famous as a child and then disappeared into oblivion. And I know the very person."

"More kiddie angst? Please, Justin. Would you mind passing the butter?"

Justin obliged. Swann buttered a roll and took a bite.

"I wish you wouldn't close your mind to what I have to say before I've even said it," Justin said with a sigh.

"My mind isn't closed. It's merely ajar."

"Thank goodness. That means there's hope. Come on, Swann. Humor me. Hear me out."

Swann turned serious. "I'm grateful to you for rescuing me from writing profiles of visiting celebrities for *Main Line Magazine,* but I don't think I have any more emotion left for writing about grown-ups who were famous as children," she said.

"Swann, I wouldn't ask you to do it if I didn't think you'd do a bang-up job."

"No, I mean it, Justin. After writing that book about Winky Tapps, I was drained, physically and emotionally. Emotionally, I hit all the peaks and valleys with her. By the time I finished writing the book I felt as though I had lived through the pain of having a relentless stage mother just as she had, and her drug use as an adolescent, and the frustration of not being able to capture any solid adult movie roles, and marriage to that washed-up jockey who walked away with most of her money, and— well, you know. *You* published the book, after all."

"I know it took a toll on you. But those feelings you're talking about—they're what came through in your writing. You're a damned good biographer, Swann. You can deal with difficult subject matter without making the reader feel as though he's wallowing in mire. The Tapps book was ultimately uplifting, you know. That's why it sold so many copies."

"And you want me to repeat that success," Swann said.

"Of course. Don't you want to?"

"Who wouldn't? But can't I write about some nice sane adults?"

"I thought you said you wanted to write about politics."

"Well, all right. A nice *insane* adult then." She grinned at him.

"You're dancing ever so skillfully away from the true subject of this conversation. Which is writing your next biography about the person I have in mind."

The waiter set large mounds of lobster salad in front of them, and they waited for him to leave before resuming their conversation.

"Promise me you'll think about it. Promise me you won't say no right away," Justin said.

"Okay, Justin, I promise. At least I think I do. How can I give my word when I don't know what I'm promising? Just tell me who it is." Swann picked up the lemon at the side of her plate and energetically squeezed it over her salad.

"It's Child Michael, Swann. Child Michael Thompson of Miracle Farm."

The juice from the lemon squirted right in Justin's eye.

"I'm sorry," Swann said shakily. Justin blotted his eye with great ceremony, then stared balefully across the table at her.

"I hope this doesn't mean you won't do it?" he asked.

"But where is he? What is he doing now?"

"That's what you'll have to find out." Justin handed Swann a piece of paper with the name of a town written on it.

Swann stared at it. "Reedy Creek, Georgia?" she asked.

"A friend of mine who vacations there from time to time thinks she saw him in Reedy Creek. Child Michael uses another name now, of course, but with a bit of work, perhaps you could find him."

"I've noticed that every year on the anniversary of his father's trial, somebody writes an article asking, 'Whatever happened to that darling little boy?'" Swann said. Her eyes grew contemplative.

"Exactly. And that, my dear, is the question that you're going to answer. A Child Michael bio would be a great follow-up for your book on Winky Tapps, and best of all, it's bound to be equally interesting to a large segment of the American public."

"If he doesn't want to be reminded of his past, what makes you think that he'll cooperate in writing this book?" Swann asked skeptically.

"Maybe he won't. That's for you to figure out. Anyway, it's worth checking. There's still a lot of curiosity about Child Michael."

"I'm sure that's true. Only—"

"Only what?"

"Only what if I can't find him? What if he doesn't want to talk to me?"

"Too many 'what ifs.' Why not go to Reedy Creek and see what you can turn up?"

"Where *is* Reedy Creek, anyway?"

"It's south of Savannah where the Sudbury River joins Reedy Creek. It should be quite pretty there at this time of the year. Trees draped with Spanish moss, a lazy little creek meandering through town, a slow-paced country life-style. What else do you have to do this summer?"

"I've rented a house on the Jersey shore with two friends. We're going next week."

"The shore is crowded and hot. And if the two friends are Gracie and Chuck—"

"Gracie and Nolan. He's a charter pilot. She and Chuck broke up."

"Haven't you done that for the past two summers? And don't you ever feel like a fifth wheel when you're with a couple? And don't you ever get tired of Gracie? She's a real flibbertigibbet, isn't she?"

"Well—"

"Go to Reedy Creek for a couple of weeks, anyway. You can always join Gracie and her pilot boyfriend later if you absolutely insist." He reached in his suit pocket and pulled out an envelope. "Here's your plane ticket. You leave next week." He presented it to her with a flourish.

For once Swann was speechless, but she reached for the ticket anyway. "It seems to me that you took a lot for granted, Justin," she said.

"Maybe, but I sense that you want a challenge. This is certainly that."

"I'll need a place to stay. I suppose there's a hotel in Reedy Creek? Or a motel?"

"Oh, I rented you a cottage. I didn't like the sound of the one-star motel they have there. The cottage is on the banks of Reedy Creek, and it has running water, an inside bathroom and everything."

"And everything," Swann repeated slowly, not sure whether she was amused or not. The very fact that he was stressing the running water and inside plumbing told her a lot about Reedy Creek.

"There's even a microwave oven. And the place is nicely furnished. Here, look at these pictures."

Swann inspected the snapshots. There were several of the town of Reedy Creek and its surroundings, a lot of blue water, wind-ruffled marsh grass and Spanish moss. The photos of the cottage showed that it was constructed of immaculate white clapboard. Two interior shots pictured a living room with plump upholstered pieces covered in flowered chintz and a bedroom of minuscule proportions but with yellow walls and lace curtains looped at the windows.

"You can set up your word processor on the porch," Justin said. "There's a wide table there, and it overlooks the creek."

"You've thought of everything," she murmured.

"Not quite. It's up to you to find and get to know Child Michael. You'll be the biographer as detective, as it were."

Swann remembered a tumble of shiny yellow curls and luminous eyes of the brightest blue. Oh, she'd know him if she saw him, she thought. His image had stayed with her throughout the years. She hadn't seen him in—how long? It must be about twenty-three years. Yet she could picture him in her mind's eye as clearly as she could see Justin, who was leaning forward in his chair watching her and waiting for her reaction.

She attempted a laugh. She didn't think Justin knew of her tie to Child Michael or of the influence he had worked on her life. He certainly had no idea that Child Michael sometimes cropped up in her dreams or that when she woke up after those dreams she always felt wistful and a little sad that she'd never seen him again.

"I guess I might as well give it a try," she said, realizing that she was outflanked.

Justin, giving free rein to his exuberance, ordered a bottle of wine and toasted her new project. And as Swann raised her glass to his, she decided that she was sufficiently interested to give the project two weeks of her time. Three, max.

The phone was ringing when Swann arrived back at her town house after lunch. She hurried to answer it, her heels clicking on the smooth marble floor of the foyer. The caller was Gracie, her best friend, and she was singing.

"Happy birthday to you, happy birthday to you—"

"Gracie, thanks, but you'll never be a singer." Swann had to laugh. Every year on her birthday, Swann was subjected to Gracie's off-key rendition of the birthday song.

"Well, aside from birthday greetings, I called to go over some details about the house at the shore. Listen, Nolan has arranged his flight schedule so he can stay there every week but the last, and he thinks—"

"Wait, Gracie. Before you say anything else, I might as well tell you that I won't be going to the shore. At least not right away."

"Not going? But Swann, Nolan has an old college room-mate who would love to meet you. He was going to come down to the shore for that very purpose."

"Well, thanks, but I'm going to Reedy Creek, Georgia. I'm starting to research a new book."

"*Georgia!* Who do you know *there?*"

"No one yet. Maybe I can finish up in a week or so and join you at the beach house."

"Nolan and I have been looking forward to this vacation so much," Gracie said in a wounded tone. "Can't you change your mind and come along with us anyway?"

"Afraid not, Gracie. Oh, my call waiting is beeping. Hold on just a minute." Swann put Gracie on hold and answered the other call, which turned out to be a salesman for a hair-loss treatment. She returned to Gracie right away.

"Sorry, but I thought that might be my father. Anyway, wouldn't you and Nolan like to be alone?"

"We're alone all the time. And you haven't heard from your father for a while, have you?"

"No. But it *is* my birthday," Swann said.

"Last I heard, your dad had a girlfriend named Tiffany. She was nineteen."

"He broke up with her on Valentine's Day. I don't know who he's dating now because I haven't seen him since Easter when he asked me what I thought of his latest love and I told him."

"Good grief, Swann, it's the middle of June. And why couldn't you have tempered the truth a bit? You wouldn't have had to be so honest."

"It goes against my grain to gloss things over, you know that," Swann said.

"Well, call me, Swann, before you go to Georgia. *If* you insist on going, I mean."

"I'm going, all right," Swann told her.

"Okay," Gracie said with a sigh.

They talked a bit more and after she hung up, Swann walked slowly to the closet where she kept her big atlas and hauled it down from the shelf.

There it was—Reedy Creek. It was the smallest of the dots on the map of the state of Georgia and only three-quarters of an inch or so from the city of Savannah.

She pushed the atlas back onto the shelf, shoving aside a large photograph album in the process. Several snapshots fluttered from between its pages.

She really should do something about that family album, she thought as she slid it out from under the atlas. She hitched up her skirt and sat down on the floor, opening the album to the first page.

There was her mother, laughing into the camera lens as she shaded her eyes from a glaring tropical sun. The picture had been taken on her mother and father's honeymoon at a hotel in Bermuda back in the late fifties. And there was one taken later of her mother and father together, her father's arm curved nonchalantly around her mother's shoulders. Her mother looked pensive, and she seemed to shrink from him. Their troubles had started early, then, even before Swann was born.

Swann appeared in the album a few pages later, a tiny baby peering up at the intrusive camera from her hospital bassinet. Her hair had been just as dark then as it was now, though her eyes had not attained their present smoky topaz shade for several months. With her dark brown hair and heart-shaped face, she'd looked like her mother even then; she'd never resembled her father.

She could recall when she was a rebellious preteen and had entertained the notion that perhaps she wasn't really her father's child at all but the product of some unknown liaison between her mother and a secret lover. Of course, it had only been a notion. There was never any doubt in anyone's mind that Mimi Triplett had been faithful to her husband. It was he who had had the affairs, many of them openly flaunted with no regard to his wife's or daughter's sensibilities.

Swann stretched and shifted the album in her lap. Here was a picture that must have been taken when she was five or six years old. She was wearing a broderie anglaise party dress, a favorite of hers. She still remembered how happy she was when her mother presented her with the dress wrapped in a silver-gilt package with a big blue bow on the day they came home from France. She had been in Maine with her nanny; it was the summer she'd broken her foot, the summer before she'd gone to Miracle Farm to be healed by Child Michael.

Funny, but that night stood out in her memory. She remembered the long ride to get there and how excited she'd been about going to a farm, and then how disappointed when she found out that it wasn't a real farm at all.

Afterward, when she'd gone back to Dr. Fitz, who had said that she needed an operation on her foot, he had taken X rays and declared his surprise that her foot had mended correctly. In fact, he couldn't believe it. Her mother told him about going to see Child Michael, and he had frowned and said that such a cure wasn't possible, that the first X rays must have been mixed up, that Swann probably hadn't needed the operation after all, and anyway, the human body had marvelous recuperative powers. Not only that, Dr. Fitz had been out of red lollipops and Swann had had to settle for grape.

Swann slid the picture of her in the pretty yellow dress in with some others taken around the same time. Someday she should arrange all the later family photos in some sort of logical order. She and her mother had begun working on the album during Mimi's long illness, and during that trying time it had helped both of them to remember their good times together. Unfortunately, Mimi had died before they finished with the album, and Swann had never had the heart to get back to it.

Now it was something she wanted to do; a labor of love in memory of Mimi. She'd stored some of the latter-day snapshots in her mother's old desk at home, and someday she should drive out there and pick them up. Finishing the album would be a good project for her to tackle while she was in Reedy Creek where she knew no one and where, she gathered, there wasn't much to do for recreation.

She could drop by the estate and get those old photographs on a weekend night when Evan was less likely to be home. Not that she was afraid of him anymore, because she had outgrown that feeling long ago. She avoided him because he never seemed to be able to resist cutting her down to size, and she refused to subject herself to his emotional abuse any longer.

Which was why she hadn't seen him in almost three months. Deep in her heart of hearts, she didn't really expect him to call to wish her a happy birthday. And as she'd expected, he didn't.

With time running short before her departure to Georgia, Swann made an effort to locate Dr. Fitz. She wanted to get those long-ago X rays and see what had really been wrong with her foot. But when she drove to the place where his office had been in downtown Philadelphia, a big, shiny, new office building stood on the spot. When she called the local medical society, she was told that Dr. Fitz had been dead for seven years and that all his old records had been destroyed.

The only person who might be able to tell her more about the injury to her foot was her father. And she couldn't talk to him about it, not the way things stood between them.

She wanted the pictures she needed for the photograph album, and after some thought she decided to drive to the ostentatious country estate where she'd grown up, on the Saturday night before she left for Georgia. A phone call to the housekeeper helped her to determine that her father wouldn't be home.

Margarita, the housekeeper, admitted her to the wide foyer with exclamations of pleasure, and half an hour passed before Swann was able to climb the stairs to her mother's old study and look in the desk where she had left the unmounted family photos.

They were gone.

Swann knew that they had been in the second drawer on the right-hand side; she had put them there herself. In another drawer, shunted to the back behind old papers, she found pictures of the ski trips she and her father had taken with a succession of his girlfriends in the years after her mother died, and there were photos of her high school commencement as well as her graduation from Bryn Mawr. She didn't care so much about these unwelcome reminders of an unhappy time in her life that she'd do well to forget. But she did want the ones of her and her mother, most of which she had taken herself with her very first camera.

She searched all the other drawers. The photos weren't there, either.

She stood indecisively in the little study where her mother had spent so much time, trying to figure out who could have moved them.

"Margarita?" she called, going to the door.

The housekeeper, who had become overweight in the past couple of years, trod heavily up the stairs. Swann waited patiently.

"Yes?"

"Those pictures that were in the second drawer of Mother's desk—do you know where they might be?"

"No, I don't disturb."

"One of the help, perhaps?"

"No, no, I always say to leave Mrs. Triplett's study alone. I dust it myself sometimes."

Margarita had idolized Mimi Triplett and had made a shrine of her study. Swann believed her.

A door slammed downstairs, and Margarita jumped. "It is Mr. Triplett," she said, looking apprehensively over her shoulder. "He told me not to expect him until tomorrow."

"Margarita?" he called. "Any messages?"

"A few," Margarita replied. She headed down the stairs.

"Is that my daughter's car outside? Where is she?"

"She is upstairs in Mrs. Triplett's study," Swann heard Margarita say, and she steeled herself for a face-to-face meeting with her father.

He came up the steps, taking his time. He was a big man, broad-shouldered, with the heavy eyebrows that characterized the Triplett side of the family. Now those eyebrows met in the middle of his forehead in an expression of distaste. Swann thought he looked older and more tired than he had when she saw him a few months ago.

"Hi, Dad," Swann said as optimistically as possible.

"Swann. You're looking well." He didn't move forward to embrace her, only stood looking her over in that critical way of his. She tried not to cringe under his gaze.

"Thanks. Dad, I stopped by to pick up some old photographs I left in Mother's desk. They're not in the drawer where I kept them. Do you know where they could be?"

"If you're talking about an old plastic bag full of snapshots, I threw them away. I needed the room for some papers of mine." His tone was expressionless.

Swann felt a rush of blood pounding in her ears; she stared at him in disbelief. "You threw them away?" she repeated.

"Years ago."

"But—but they were a record of the last three or four years before Mother died!"

"There's nothing to be done about it now," Evan said brusquely. He pushed past her and strode down the hall toward his room. Swann followed him, walking as fast as he did. He would have closed his bedroom door if she hadn't been hard on his heels.

"Why, Dad? Why didn't you ask if I wanted them first?" she said.

"I was cleaning out her desk. I saw no reason to keep old pictures."

"How about sentimental reasons?" Swann said heatedly. It had always upset her that Evan Triplett had tried to obliterate all signs of Mimi from his life as soon as she had died. The study had been allowed to remain only because both Swann and Margarita had been so vociferous in their objections to his plan to convert it into a closet during the year after Mimi's death.

"You should know by this time that I'm not the least bit sentimental. Now if you'll excuse me, I'm late for a dinner engagement this evening." He waved in dismissal.

"Every time I see you, you have something better to do," Swann said, half to herself. She turned to go.

Evan caught her arm. He glared at her. "It's not as though you ever give me adequate notice when you decide to drop in. Can't you call first?" he said.

"If you must know, I didn't intend to see you tonight. I thought you'd be out." She yanked her arm free of his grasp.

"Sorry to spoil your plans," he said. The tone of his voice was in direct contradiction to the conciliatory words.

"As for the next time, I'm leaving town in a few days. That should make you happy." After this parting shot, she walked out. She wasn't surprised when, behind her, Evan closed the door firmly, putting an end to the exchange.

As soon as the door was shut between them, Swann's shoulders sagged. She always swore that every confrontation with her father would be her last. And it was—until the next time.

Swann stopped briefly in her mother's study to close the desk drawer where the photos should have been. She felt sad, not only because the pictures were gone but because no matter how hard she tried to get along with her father, it was never going to work. When he wasn't reproving her, he was distant. Whenever she tried to get closer to him, he only shut her out. She had recognized the problems in their relationship long ago, of course, but deep in her heart she couldn't help wishing that they could have a normal father-daughter relationship. And every time she saw him, she had to admit to herself that it could never be. Maybe someday she'd wise up and stop trying.

When she left the study, Margarita was hovering in the doorway. From the pitying expression on her face, Swann could tell that the housekeeper had heard the exchange between her and Evan. Margarita had always been kind in the years after Mimi died, and her kindness was always welcome, especially during Swann's turbulent teenage years when living with Evan had come close to breaking her spirit.

"You come back when he is not here, won't you? We will sit and have a nice cup of tea in my room," Margarita said.

"I'll call you," Swann promised.

Margarita patted her shoulder. "I will look for the negatives of those pictures. Maybe I can find," she said.

"Thanks, Margarita. Maybe you can."

Margarita walked her to the door of the big house. "You drive carefully home," she called to Swann from where she stood in the circle of light in the driveway.

Swann waved as she drove away. As much as she wanted to see Margarita, she wouldn't come back for that cup of tea; she'd invite Margarita to visit her in the city. At that moment she felt that if she never laid eyes on her father or this place again, it would suit her just fine.

Chapter Two

Well, here I am, Swann thought to herself as she drove past the bright green welcome sign at the edge of town. *Reedy Creek, Georgia.*

She had arrived in Savannah last night, rented a car at the airport and driven south the next morning through marshland golden and glimmering in the hot sunlight. After taking the Reedy Creek exit on I-95, she'd found herself on a short stretch of narrow two-lane road. Nothing marred the watery landscape on the way into town except a lone gas station and a fifties-era motel.

Reedy Creek turned out to be a dusty, drowsy village where traffic trickled past a bank, a newspaper office and a nondescript string of shops. Vaulting moss-hung oaks spread a protective leafy canopy over narrow brick streets; the town's tallest structure was the pristine white steeple of the First Baptist Church. After a quick look around, Swann stopped at the local real estate office to pick up a key to the cottage. She followed Justin's careful directions to the winding creek road.

On this narrow track, houses were smaller and far between, some no more than tar-paper shacks where chickens pecked and scratched beneath chinaberry trees coated with roadside dust. Finally, after she passed a small pecan grove, she spotted a tilting rural mailbox almost grown over with weeds, sentinel to a driveway composed of crushed oyster shells. Nearby a spindly peach tree bore abundant fruit. Up ahead she saw the cottage, property of an absentee owner. A few dandelions dotted the untended lawn, which sloped through a grove of pecan trees to the shimmering creek.

The cottage was adequate, even charming, with a cubbyhole of a kitchen and a wide glassed-in porch. The yellow bedroom seemed as cheerful as sunshine. After a cursory inspection, the first thing Swann did was to open all the windows to let the gentle breeze dissipate a slightly musty odor, and the second thing she did was to cart in her suitcase and several boxes of books.

That done, she stopped to massage her aching back and went out on the porch. The air seemed scented with several flavors of green from creek, grass and trees; leafy domes cast cool shadows on the ground. The grass grew long and lush, and Swann could hardly wait to walk barefoot in it.

Yes, she could be happy here for a couple of weeks. Or maybe even more, although she had warned Justin not to count on her writing the book. Whether she would do so or not depended on whether she had any luck finding Child Michael. Or whatever he was calling himself these days.

THE TEMPERATURE SOARED into the high nineties the next day. In downtown Reedy Creek, men wiped the sweat from their faces with large handkerchiefs and passersby scurried from one air-conditioned shop to another complaining about the heat. To Swann, this southern air seemed softer and fresher than the concrete-baked heat of the northern city that had always been her home. She began her detective work with a spirit of optimism.

Swann showed the young girl at the drugstore cash register a picture of Child Michael taken when he was about twelve years old.

"Have you ever seen a man who resembles this picture?" she asked.

"Is this one of those missing child searches?" the girl asked curiously.

"Not exactly. The boy is grown now."

The girl narrowed her eyes. "You trying to find him to make him pay child support or something?"

"No, no," Swann said hastily. "I just want to talk to him."

"Well, I've never seen him," the girl told her firmly, turning away to ring up the purchases of the man who stood in line behind Swann.

Swann couldn't figure out if the girl was telling the truth or not, but she left the drugstore anyway.

She inquired the same thing of the town real estate agent, who smiled regretfully and told her that he hadn't seen anyone who looked like the boy in the picture. She asked his pleasant-faced secretary and got another negative answer. She walked down the street to the town's only liquor store and asked the man behind the counter, and she stopped a few people on the street and questioned them. No one seemed to recognize the boy in the photograph as Child Michael, and no one answered in the affirmative when she asked if they'd ever seen a man who looked remotely like him. She began to wonder if Justin's tipster had been imagining things.

Idly, trying to figure out whom to ask next, Swann dropped a dime through a slot in a newspaper box outside the offices of the *Reedy Creek Gazette* and tucked the paper she bought into her purse. In the sweltering heat of midafternoon, the streets were almost deserted. She decided to call it quits for the day so that she could think about making a new game plan. This one certainly wasn't producing results.

It wasn't until after her solitary supper of a bacon, lettuce and tomato sandwich that she read the newspaper that she'd bought earlier. And then she saw a picture that made her do a fast double take.

The picture was three columns wide and it was of a paramedic with the local emergency services rescue squad who also worked as a Red Cross instructor in CPR, cardiopulmonary resuscitation. A new class was starting that week, and in the caption underneath he was quoted as saying he hoped to see a large enrollment.

Swann, perhaps because she was alert to the possibilities, saw a marked resemblance to Child Michael in this man. She laid the two pictures, one of the child and the other of the man, out on the table, side by side.

"It's him," Swann murmured to herself. "It's got to be."

The man in the *Gazette* picture had curly hair, although it appeared darker than Child Michael's. His forehead looked higher than the boy's, but Swann noted a similar distinctive shape to the jaw. Both the boy and the man had fine, even features. The man in the newspaper wore glasses, but it was the deep-set eyes behind the lenses that drew Swann's attention. The newspaper photo was black-and-white, but she could identify them by their shape and expression, and had a pretty good idea that they would be blue.

The man's name was Paul Thompson. Child Michael's surname had been Thompson.

With rising excitement, Swann knew that she had found Child Michael. She was sure of it.

Swann almost phoned Justin to tell him. He would be as pleased as she was.

But she didn't call. She would wait in case she was wrong.

SWANN SPENT the next few days setting up her word processor, arranging her books in the bookcase, and stocking the cottage's small refrigerator with food. She learned to enjoy walking along the creek early in the morning, inhaling deeply of pungent salty water, of sun-warmed dew, of green growing things. Pelicans, their bills filled with fish, flapped their wings overhead, and fish glinted with silvery light as they leaped in shining arcs from the water before falling back with a sharp slap.

She found an old push lawn mower under a tarpaulin beneath the roof overhang, and she made an attempt at cutting the grass, although in a way she hated to do it. It felt so soft against the soles of her feet, and yet she was afraid that the overgrown grass and shrubbery would engulf the cottage if she didn't deal with them soon.

She labored at cutting the grass all of one day. Afterward it didn't feel as gentle against her feet, but the new-mown smell was heavenly. She sat outside and sipped a glass of lemonade, wishing she could find a pair of clippers with which to cut the shrubbery away from the back door. On the porch was a door that appeared to lead to a utility room where she thought there might be clippers, but it was locked and she could find no key.

The shrubbery would have to wait, but that was okay. She had plenty of other things to do. And one of them was going to be enrolling in Paul Thompson's three-hour CPR class.

ON THE NIGHT of the class, Swann showed up along with a number of other people in a classroom at the local elementary school where she took her seat beside an older gray-haired man and his wife. The man had smiled at her as she'd walked down the aisle of school desks.

"Hi, I'm Swann Triplett," she said.

"My name's Hunter Epling," he said when she sat down. "And no, it's not a disease."

"Oh, Hunter, hush," said the sweet-faced woman beside him.

"This is my wife, Mary the contrary," Hunter said.

"Isn't he a pain?" Mary said, but it was clear that she enjoyed her husband's teasing.

"Better to be a pain than have one, I always say," Hunter said firmly.

"I'm taking CPR because of Hunter's heart condition," Mary volunteered.

"Oh, Mary, you worry too much," Hunter said.

"Just the same, it's something I need to know," Mary told him. She turned to Swann. "Did you fill out a registration form, dear?" she asked.

Swann shook her head, and Mary passed her a form. Swann spent the next several minutes filling in the blanks.

Soon a few more people filed into the classroom, among them two women in their late teens. Swann looked up as they sat down in front of her. They quickly filled out their registration forms and picked up a conversation that sounded as if it had been previously interrupted.

"Paul Thompson's not teaching this class. I know he's not teaching it. You've dragged me down here for nothing," fretted one of them. She bestowed a few self-conscious pats on her elaborately styled frosted hair.

"He is, too. The Red Cross lady told me so," insisted the other, who nonchalantly took out a bottle of fingernail polish and painted orange enamel on her long fingernails as they waited.

Swann sat back in her chair, becoming increasingly amused as she learned that neither of them had an apparent interest in learning cardiopulmonary resuscitation. No, the reason they were here seemed to be the instructor.

She grew more curious about Paul Thompson as she listened to the two women whisper. They giggled behind their hands and slid archly hopeful looks toward the door from time to time. When he finally hurried into the room wearing his white paramedic uniform, they poked each other in the ribs and smothered their giggles.

"Welcome," he said easily, tossing a briefcase on the desk. "Sorry I'm late. As most of you know, I work for emergency services, and we had a slight emergency. Not a medical emergency—a lost-paperwork emergency. I'm happy to report that the paperwork has been found, and so have I. We'll get started with our class right away."

"He could get me started, all right," Fingernails whispered to Frosted, who convulsed with laughter.

If Paul Thompson noticed this byplay, he gave no sign. He surveyed the room and greeted a couple of Swann's classmates, including the Eplings, by name. His gaze lingered on Swann with a degree of puzzlement; he was clearly trying to place her. She returned his gaze steadily, objectively, and with interest, studying him carefully as he walked to a closet and removed a dummy that was to be used in his CPR training.

Paul Thompson was tall—over six feet. His curly hair was not yellow but golden. His eyes were a startling blue that stood out in his tan face, and he had an easy smile. For the informed person, his face held clues to the child he might have been; the distinctive jaw, the even features, the merest suggestion of a cleft in the chin. Although he'd worn glasses in the newspaper photo, tonight he did not, making him all the more recognizable as long as you knew what to look for. At that moment, Swann would have bet her life that he was Child Michael.

But to the locals attending this class, he was Paul Thompson, emergency paramedic and CPR instructor. As he continued, the members of the class began to concentrate on what he was saying. So did Swann. He had a pleasant deep voice, and he spoke with an air of authority.

"Cardiopulmonary resuscitation is the most effective lifesaving technique available to us without using a lot of equipment that most of us don't happen to have around when someone has a heart attack," he said seriously, walking around to the front of the table that held the dummy. "Now, there are two important stages of CPR. Compressing the chest to move blood through the heart, and blowing in the victim's mouth to inflate the lungs."

He spoke for a while longer before circling to the back of the table and demonstrating how to clear the victim's airways preparatory to ventilating the lungs. As he bent over the dummy in order to commence rescue breathing, Fingernails whispered to Frosted, "He could do that to me any old time," and Frosted erupted into silent mirth.

Hunter Epling took that opportunity to pin them with a stern look, which only sent them off in new gales of laughter. Swann, in the meantime, was paying attention to Paul Thompson's demonstration. He placed his mouth over the dummy's, blew two breaths, lifted his mouth and carefully placed his hands on the dummy's chest over the heart.

"Woo-woo," Frosted said under her breath with a meaningful look at Fingernails, and they jabbed each other's midriffs. Both of them had flushed bright red.

Paul, unflappable, continued to teach the class. One by one the students practiced giving CPR to the dummy under his direction. When it was her turn, Swann felt a bit self-conscious bending over the dummy until Paul gave her an encouraging smile. Afterward, she returned to her seat near the Eplings. Frosted and Fingernails were still snickering behind their hands.

By the time the three-hour class was over, Swann felt that she had learned something worthwhile; she wasn't sure what Frosted and Fingernails had learned unless it was that they preferred kissing men to dummies.

"'Course, sometimes you can't tell the difference," Frosted had commented under her breath, a statement that Fingernails seemed to find particularly entertaining.

"If you'll all complete one of these cards," Paul said toward the end of the class as he distributed them around the room, "you'll soon receive a genuine certificate in the mail. It will tell the world that you're a real, honest-to-goodness graduate of CPR training."

They filled out the cards and passed them forward.

"And that's the class," Paul said with a smile. "Thank you for taking the time to learn CPR. If you have any further questions, feel free to ask."

As they stood up and began to file out of the classroom, Hunter Epling touched Swann's arm. "Some of us are going down the street for a cup of coffee and maybe a bite to eat. Want to come along?"

"Well, I—"

"Did I hear you say you're going to the Little Bit? Mind if I come, too?" Paul Thompson smiled at them from behind the desk.

"Of course not," Mary Epling declared. "We don't see enough of you, Paul."

"Just don't bring your date," Hunter said, gesturing at the dummy.

"Hey, she probably wouldn't want to come anyway. Go ahead and I'll meet you there after I finish up here," Paul said with a grin as he snapped his briefcase closed.

Swann walked with Hunter and Mary to the Little Bit, a small restaurant that she'd noticed on her first day in town.

It was a tiny hole-in-the-wall café with walls painted peach and booths with tables of black Formica. Evidently the place was the town hangout, because it was packed.

They slid into a booth being vacated by some people. Swann recognized three or four others from the CPR class who were already there sitting on stools at the short counter. She was relieved that Frosted and Fingernails were not among them.

Swann barely had time to order a cup of coffee before Paul Thompson arrived.

"Paul, sit with us," Hunter called. "We have an extra seat right here next to Swann."

Paul pushed his way through the crowd and sat down beside Swann, and she tried not to look too interested. He chatted with Hunter and Mary until a friend of theirs stopped by the booth and began an earnest conversation with Hunter about a pair of coon dogs. Swann toyed with the paper packet of sugar, unsure of how to begin a conversation with Paul. She was saved from having to do anything when he turned to her and said, "Would you like something to eat? A piece of pie? Cake?"

"No, thanks," she told him, wondering why he was blinking so rapidly.

"New contact lenses," he explained in answer to her questioning look.

She thought, *So he usually does wear glasses.* It was another reason why people here might not have recognized him from the picture of Child Michael at an early age.

Paul signaled to the waitress, who delivered a piece of pecan pie to their table shortly thereafter. Paul had barely begun to eat it when Hunter and Mary slid out of the booth.

"We don't like to run off, but Mary needs her beauty sleep," Hunter told them with a wink.

"Oh, you're such a tease, Hunter," Mary said. "Come and see us, Paul. And it was nice meeting you, Swann." They made their way out of the restaurant, and Hunter winked and waved at Swann as they went out the door.

"I think I'll sit over here where I can see you better," Paul said, getting up and moving to the other side of the booth so he was sitting where Hunter and Mary had been. The crowd was thinning out, and it was much less noisy now.

"I should be going, too," Swann said, although she had every reason not to. His frank appraisal of her from across the table made her slightly nervous, and she told herself that she'd have to get over this feeling that he knew what she was up to, here in Reedy Creek. He had no way of knowing, she was sure of that, but nevertheless, the feeling persisted.

"Pennsylvania," he said after a moment. "What part?"

"I beg your pardon?"

"You're not from around here. I can tell by your accent."

"Philadelphia," she said.

"I almost guessed that," he said, focusing those remarkable eyes on her. "So," he said, studying her carefully. "What brings you to town?"

"It's a quiet place," she said.

"That's for sure. We don't have many visitors."

She sipped her coffee. "I think it's a pretty town," she ventured.

"Prettier than where you're from?"

"Philadelphia has its moments," she said. Then she grew more serious. "I needed a change of scene," she said levelly. "I'm writing a book." She'd prepared a cover story in advance. She knew that if she were to gain his confidence, she couldn't tip her hand right away.

"A book? Sounds interesting. What's it about?"

She was prepared for this question, too. "It's a biography of my father."

"*He* must be interesting."

"He's Evan Triplett, founder of Triplett Airways. And Triplett Freight. And Triplett Van Lines."

She was familiar with the long appraising look he gave her. She'd seen it so many times before when she told people who she was. First came the assessment, then the realization that she probably didn't have to work for a living. She had grown weary of it long ago.

"What's he like?"

Swann shrugged. "It's hard to explain," she hedged.

Paul's eyes crinkled at the corners. "In other words, I'll have to read the book, right?"

"Right," she answered, glad that he'd given her an out. Her ruse wouldn't stand up to close scrutiny, she was sure of that.

Paul snapped his fingers all of a sudden and leaned back in the booth. "I should have recognized your name when you told me! I've read your book about Winky Tapps. I found it one of the most engrossing biographies I've ever read. You must have spent a lot of time with Winky Tapps. Did you like her?"

"She was pathetic at times and egotistical now and then, but mostly she was charming."

"Is she still selling used cars at a lot in San Bernardino?"

"She's their number-one salesperson."

He smiled thoughtfully. "Well, well. The former Little Miss Happiness selling used Fords and Chevys. How strange."

"Strange?"

"Life, I mean." Before Swann could comment, he beckoned the waitress. "I'd like a refill, LaRue. How about you, Swann?"

Swann shook her head.

He turned back to her. His eyes were friendly. Her gaze fell inadvertently to his mouth, and she thought about the way Frosted and Fingernails had giggled when he placed his lips on the dummy's. She felt her face turning pink.

She began talking in order to distract him. She was surprised to learn that Paul was extremely well-read and informed. His insight into political situations matched hers, and he was vitally interested in what was going on in the world—he faithfully followed the changing situations in Europe and China. Sports were not his thing, he said, and she admitted that they didn't appeal to her, either.

Something clicked shortly thereafter, and she found herself relaxing and telling him more about herself than she usually revealed during a first encounter with a new person. She told him that she liked Marx Brothers films, and so did he. He said that he liked the Rolling Stones, and she did, too. She mentioned that almost nothing made her happier than curling up with a good book, and he smiled and said that if she needed any books to read, she could feel free to borrow some of his while she was here. Of course, he said, there was the public library over on Oglethorpe Street, but then he wouldn't get to see her. It was clearly a blatant invitation for more contact.

The conversation paused for the length of a heartbeat, and in that moment she knew that she liked him a lot. She was disappointed when he glanced at his watch and said, "Finished with your coffee? I'm on duty later, and I'd like to walk you to your car."

Quickly she drained her cup, thinking that they had barely scratched the surface of subjects she'd like to discuss. She hadn't expected to feel attracted to him as a man, but that was definitely what she was feeling, and she had an idea that she could make this attraction work in her favor.

In the parking lot he said, "I don't suppose you have a phone yet?"

She blessed Justin's foresight.

"Oh, but I do," she said. "It was already there when I moved in."

"I'd like to call you sometime," Paul said. "If it's all right with you, I mean."

She pulled a pad and pencil from her purse and scribbled her phone number on one of the sheets of paper. He looked pleased when she handed it to him. He was still standing beside his car gazing after her as she drove out of the parking lot.

Swann left her car window down and turned the radio volume up. She sang all the way back to the cottage.

Everything was wonderful, everything was fine. She had found Child Michael. And she had him right in the palm of her hand.

PAUL THOMPSON WENT HOME to his solitary house and checked the messages on his answering machine. His friend Bo was going to Savannah for several days and had left a message asking Paul to pick up the newspapers from his front yard; Paul's ex-girlfriend Linda had called to ask if he wanted to come to a cookout at her house on Saturday night.

First he walked down the street to Bo's house and picked up the newspaper from the front porch, carrying it home to read. Then he called Linda, prepared to decline her invitation, but instead she tried to talk him into accepting.

"Nobody's seen you in weeks," she complained. "What have you been doing lately?"

"Playing pool with Bo and the guys, and I went deep-sea fishing last week," he said.

"You sound depressed. Are you?"

That was the trouble with Linda; she was always trying to psychoanalyze him. He knew from experience that the best thing to do in such a situation was to head her off.

"Who wouldn't be depressed, Linda? You ran off and married another guy. One of my best friends, in fact." He said it teasingly because making light of the situation was all he could do. Linda's demands on him two years ago had been excessive, and he'd needed some space; it was his own fault that *her* space had been eagerly filled by his buddy Rick.

"That was a long time ago, and anyway, you and I had decided together that we'd see other people. Say, does it really still bother you?"

"Only when I drink a cup of your coffee. You make the best cup of coffee I've ever tasted."

"Paul, dear, you may drink all the coffee you want at our party," Linda said.

"Is that a promise?"

"Absolutely. Please come. The party won't be any fun without you."

"Well," Paul said, unsure that he wanted to obligate himself.

"Come on, Paul. We want to show off our new swimming pool. The whole gang will be here."

"Okay, okay. I'll do it."

"Good. I've never had so much trouble trying to get someone to come to a party. It starts at seven. And bring a date, Paul."

"Hmm. I'll see what I can do."

"We'll see you Saturday night," Linda said. She sounded pleased with herself.

Well, thought Paul as he prepared to go to work, she probably *was*. One thing about Linda—she had a healthy self-concept. She'd bounced back from his semirejection, rebounding right into Rick's arms. Paul had missed her, but she and Rick were one of the happiest couples he knew. And he, Rick and Linda were still good friends.

But this party—he really didn't want to go. The Reedy Creek young couples' social scene wasn't exactly his bag. He had his buddies, he went out with women occasionally and he always felt out of place at parties. Yet he had more or less obligated himself to show up.

One of the problems was that all his friends here had grown up together. Chased each other around the playground in grammar school, passed notes in junior high and made out in the back seats of their cars on the weekends during high school. He was the only "new" member of their group.

Speaking of new, he wondered about Swann Triplett. She was something different for Reedy Creek. He'd had her pegged right from the moment he spotted her in his CPR class—she was too sleek, too svelte and too polished to be from around here. Hair like that had to have been styled in an upscale salon in a big city; clothes like that were straight out of a trendy boutique. Everything, from her pearl earrings to the understated gold bracelet on her wrist, bespoke quality. She was beautiful. And intelligent. And, probably lonely.

He'd definitely give her a call, but maybe he'd wait until this weekend. By that time she'd be wondering if he'd lost her phone number.

SWANN COULD HAVE SWORN that Paul Thompson would call her, but the phone didn't ring. In Philadelphia she had many friends and there were always lots of phone calls. Here she knew no one, and she hadn't realized how empty her life would seem once she was away from all that was familiar. She spent most of her time these days sitting on one of the spindly kitchen chairs and reading old newspaper and magazine articles about Child Michael. Photocopies had been thoughtfully provided by Justin.

Child Michael had been a real phenomenon, the likes of which hadn't been seen since. He seemed to rocket to fame at the age of four when his father Mac, a former carnival barker, used a series of slick public relations maneuvers to shove the boy into the limelight. Media flacks, sick of reporting the war in Vietnam, turned to promoting an endless number of features about the photogenic child and his

Help Meetings where he practiced the laying on of hands, thus healing the sick people who flocked to him in droves.

Of course there had been much skepticism and doubt about whether Child Michael was really healing anyone, but even his critics were charmed by the boy. Swann knew from experience that his cures had been real; otherwise, she didn't think she could have stomached writing a book about a boy who had been so exploited by his own father.

Child Michael had disappeared from sight shortly after Mac Thompson had been arrested for income tax evasion and sent to prison. One day he was America's darling, and the next day, he ceased to exist. And now, here he was in Reedy Creek where he had managed to keep his secret very well. Apparently no one around here recognized who he was.

Except Swann. And she wasn't telling. At least not yet.

By SATURDAY AFTERNOON, Swann was going stir-crazy in the little house, and she decided on the spur of the moment to take the dust-coated rental car to the car wash.

It was a coin-operated kind where the customer does the work with the aid of long nozzles that spray soapy hot water and then clear water over the car. Swann had to study the actions of the previous customer to find out how to operate it. She wasn't accustomed to washing her own car; at home, she always paid someone to do it. Now she found something soul-satisfying in squirting a froth of bubbles on the shiny metal and watching the road dust swirl away into the drain.

She had almost finished when Paul drove up beside her in his dark blue Honda coupe. Rolling Stones music blared from the car radio's speakers. He cut the sound when he saw her and rolled down the window.

"Need some help?" he asked.

At that moment the nozzle automatically cut off, leaving the air suddenly quiet except for the sound of dripping water. She was embarrassed that she was wearing what she had begun to think of as her working clothes since she had come here—her oldest pair of jeans and a baggy T-shirt bearing the childhood likeness of Winky Tapps.

Before she could answer, Paul was out of his car and wadding up old newspapers that he pulled from the back seat.

"Newsprint is the best way to polish windows," he said, vigorously attacking the front windshield. His arms were long and lean.

He stepped away when the front window was sparkling. "There," he said with satisfaction. Today he wore sunglasses, which obscured the expression in his eyes. He was wearing a pair of white shorts, and his legs were tan and corded with muscles. Swann looked away, secretly embarrassed by her own sudden fascination with his body. Frosted and Fingernails had nothing on her.

"Now the back window," he said.

"Let me," she said.

"I've got the longer reach," he told her, swabbing at the wet glass until the window sparkled. While he worked he was thinking, *now that I've ingratiated myself with her, would she object to eating lunch with me?* He swung his head around to look at her. Her face was inscrutable. But the way she was dressed was so much more casual than it was on the night of the CPR class. She seemed approachable and almost ordinary.

He decided against a prolonged play. Better to be straightforward; he had an idea she'd find that infinitely more reassuring than light, slightly sexual banter.

He pushed his sunglasses to the top of his head and grinned at her over the wet expanse of the car hood. "I'm a nice guy. *So* nice that I'm going to offer to share my Super-Double-Bubble submarine sandwich with you. It's too big for one person to eat. How about it?"

She would have liked nothing better, but her mouth felt dry and it was all she could do to answer. *This is business,* she told herself. It was important to get close to him, to get to know him, to wedge her way into his confidence so that she could eventually reveal her real purpose in coming to town. Except that right now it didn't feel like business. Gazing into his eyes, those bright eyes that she had never forgotten after that night at Miracle Farm, it felt like pure pleasure.

"That sounds good," she heard herself saying.

He beamed at her. "Want to park your car over there? Then we can take mine. I had in mind a picnic up on the bluff. Have you ever been there?"

She shook her head.

"Then it's about time," he said, tossing the heap of damp newspapers into a trash bin.

She parked her car as he had suggested, then slid into the Honda. They stopped at a convenience store on Liberty Street to buy two canned soft drinks. Afterward they turned left at the small Reedy Creek cemetery onto a winding road that led to a sandy promontory overlooking the Sudbury River.

Spreading live oaks shaded a wide concrete picnic table from the hot afternoon sun; gray Spanish moss swayed in the breeze. Paul opened the bag containing the sandwich while Swann popped the tops off the soft drink cans.

"This is a pretty place," she commented.

"It's one of my favorites around here," he told her.

"Do you come here often?"

"Every now and then."

It was quiet as they sat down to eat, except for the scolding of a blue jay in a nearby tree. Swann longed to ask him something, anything, about himself, but she didn't wish to appear to pry.

"Have you lived in Reedy Creek long?" she ventured finally.

"For four years. It's a great little town."

"How'd you get your job?"

"I saw an ad in the Savannah paper. But I'm not that interesting, Swann. Emergency paramedics and CPR instructors are a dime a dozen. I'd like to know more about what you do.''

She shrugged, wishing he'd go on talking. But perhaps if she revealed some things about herself, he'd do likewise.

"I met Winky Tapps at a party, and I wrote a profile about her for *Main Line Magazine,* the upscale magazine in Philadelphia where I worked at the time. Soon after the profile was published, Winky called me and asked if I'd be interested in writing her biography. I have an old friend who is an editor for a major publishing house, and he jumped at the chance to publish it, so that was that,'' she said.

"I suppose your father was a natural for your next subject,'' he said.

"Yes,'' she agreed. It was hard to lie to him; she hadn't expected to be pricked by her conscience every time it became necessary to repeat or elaborate on her falsehood.

A jet zoomed over, so low that the ground vibrated. She looked up quizzically.

"There's an air-force base ten miles away,'' Paul explained.

Swann absentmindedly folded the paper that the sandwich had been wrapped in and put it in the bag.

"Don't pack up yet,'' he objected. "I thought we could go for a walk along the river. As your Reedy Creek tour guide, I recommend that you take the five-dollar tour.'' He grinned at her, and she grinned back.

She quickly drank the last of her soda and followed him down the steep embankment to the sandy beach. Someone was sailing a small sailboat in midstream, and they stopped to watch until the bright red sail disappeared around a curve in the river.

"Do you plan to stay in Reedy Creek long?'' he asked her as they began to walk.

"Until I get far enough along in my first draft that interruptions will no longer disrupt my work,'' she said evasively.

"Don't you miss home?'' he asked.

Swann thought about her professionally decorated town house in the Society Hill section of the city; she thought about the cultural events for which Reedy Creek offered no substitute.

"In some ways I do," she admitted.

"Do you have family there?"

"Just my father," she said.

"Is he retired or is he still working?"

"Oh, he goes to his office every day. I can't imagine Dad retiring."

"No other family?"

"My mother died when I was a teenager."

The conversation paused for a few beats. She shot him a look out of the corners of her eyes trying to judge whether this statement hit a nerve. Child Michael had been separated from his father when he was fourteen.

"That's a tough time to lose a parent" was all he said, and if he felt any emotion, he didn't show it.

She was about to reply when she heard a faint mewing noise. *A sea gull,* she thought at first, but then she heard it again and knew she was mistaken.

"Do you hear that?" she asked.

"It sounds like a cat," he said.

"Stop," she said, because the sound of their footsteps crunching on sand made it hard to hear the faint mewing.

"Over this way," Paul said, scrambling up the incline. His foot caught in a vine, and he stumbled. After he recovered, Swann caught his hand, and he hauled her up after him.

A cardboard box lay on its side under a willow tree at the top of the bluff, and as they approached two kittens tumbled out.

"Are they hurt?" Swann asked, all concern.

Paul picked up the two animals, one in each hand. They were tiny, and he judged their age at about five weeks old— hardly old enough to be taken away from their mother. Both were gray tiger cats with white feet, stomachs and masks.

"They're so little!" Swann exclaimed, holding out her hands. Paul gave her one of the kittens, and it mewed plaintively. She cuddled it against her chest and stroked the tiny head.

Paul held the other one gingerly as if it might break. "Someone left them here to die," he said.

"Oh, but how could they?" The one she held climbed tenaciously up her shirt and nuzzled against her neck. Its nose was moist, and it tickled.

"Maybe they intended to drown them but didn't have the heart to go through with it," Paul said grimly.

"Wouldn't somebody who had unwanted kittens take them to the animal shelter?"

"We don't have an animal shelter here, Swann. And they may have thought it was too much trouble to take them to the shelter in Savannah."

"We can't leave them," Swann said, looking into the tiny face. The eyes were gray, the nose a soft pink, the ears small and set well down on the side of its head. Like every kitten she had ever seen, it was adorable.

"No, we certainly can't leave them, Swann. But I can't keep them."

"Why not?"

"I've never wanted a pet," he said.

"Oh, but yours is so sweet!"

Paul's kitten was attempting to suck on his finger. It would have been comical to watch if it hadn't been so sad. "They're hungry," he said.

"We should feed them."

"If you feed an animal, it's usually yours," Paul said.

"They don't look old enough to eat solids. Maybe they're still nursing."

Paul peered into the underbrush. "I don't see any sign of the mother," he said doubtfully.

Swann stood up and started down the slope to the beach.

"Swann, wait!" Paul said, scrambling after her.

"Cats make good pets," she said when he caught up to her. Her kitten's head bobbed when she walked.

"I don't *need* a cat," he said.

"We could give them to someone."

"Who?"

"Someone who wants a cat. *Two* cats."

"I can't think of who that could be."

"I don't know anyone in Reedy Creek. You know lots of people."

Paul thought about it. Bo? No, Bo's constant companion was a black Labrador retriever who would no doubt hate relinquishing his position as top dog around that household. Linda and Rick? No, Linda was allergic to cats. The Eplings? Maybe, but he thought they already had a lot of cats. Really, Swann was the one who should keep them— look at how much she liked them.

"For now, we can take them to my place and give them some milk," Swann was saying.

"They're probably starving," he agreed. Both kittens were nothing more than skin and bones.

"I feel so sorry for them," Swann murmured.

Paul glanced in her direction. The kitten had hooked its claws into the fabric of her shirt and was clinging to it for dear life. He wouldn't have pegged Swann Triplett as a motherly person, but there was certainly something maternal in the way she was looking down at the kitten.

In the car, he said, "Where to?"

Swann, who was cradling both kittens in her lap, stared at him blankly.

"I don't know where you live," he reminded her.

She had almost forgotten that. She felt so comfortable with him, in fact knew him so well from reading about his remarkable childhood, that she had begun to believe that he knew as much about her. She told him how to get to the cottage and hid her embarrassment in her concern for the kittens.

At the cottage, she led the way inside and let him hold the kittens while she poured milk into a cup and warmed it in the microwave oven.

"We'll see if they can lap from a saucer," she decided, and she set the saucer on the floor before guiding the kittens to it.

They sniffed at the milk, then dunked their noses in it. Swann's kitten looked so funny with milk bearding its chin that she laughed out loud.

"Mine's drinking," Paul observed from where he knelt beside them.

"Mine, too," Swann said.

"I think they're going to be all right, Swann," Paul said with some relief.

Something suddenly occurred to her. "We'd better go get my car at the car wash," she said.

"You know, I'd almost forgotten about it!" Paul replied, and they laughed together.

They left the kittens sharing the saucer of milk in Swann's kitchen. All the way back to town they carried on a good-natured argument about what to do with the kittens. Paul insisted that Swann should keep them, and Swann denied that she wanted them. Just before she got out of his car at the car wash she extracted a reluctant promise from him that he would survey his friends and acquaintances to find out if anyone wanted a cat.

"I really don't understand why you don't keep them," she said. She turned to him, her forehead slightly wrinkled in a frown.

How to tell her? How to explain that he didn't want to share his life right now, even with a pet? He didn't need someone—or *something*—around all the time. He didn't like being accountable.

He mumbled a few words, all the time thinking how pretty she was. When she got out of the Honda, he watched her walking back to her car. Her hair swayed when she walked. Suddenly he knew that he wanted to see her to-night.

She was in her car and sliding the key into the ignition when Paul surprised her by tapping on the closed window. She hadn't realized he was standing there; he startled her. She thought maybe he had changed his mind about taking the kittens.

She rolled down the window, and he smiled.

"Swann, my friends are having a cookout and pool party at their house tonight. Would you like to go?"

"Well, I—"

"Please say yes. I've had a good time today."

She gazed into his face. It was an earnest face as well as a handsome one. And it hid a mystery, an enigma.

"I'd like that," she said slowly.

"Good. I'll pick you up around six-thirty." He wheeled and walked away as she busied herself with backing out of the parking space, and when she sneaked a look at the Honda before driving out onto Liberty Street, he waved. She waved back.

She couldn't have planned things better if she'd tried. He liked her. She liked him. Now all she had to do was to get him to admit that he was indeed the famous Child Michael.

Chapter Three

Swann couldn't recall a social situation in recent years at which she hadn't felt adept, but she was surprisingly ill at ease as she and Paul walked up the path in front of the small brick house situated in a quiet neighborhood not far from the bluff.

"This is an easygoing crowd," Paul said, smiling down at her. "They'll like you a lot."

Before Swann had a chance to reply, the door opened, and a petite redhead, presumably their hostess, threw her arms around Paul.

"Paul's here!" their hostess announced, and conversation in the living room was immediately suspended.

"I'm Linda," the redhead said to Swann. "Come in." She swept Swann forward for introductions.

Music began to play from somewhere in the back of the house; the relentless bass beat was loud enough to vibrate the floor. A stocky man appeared and put his arm around Linda.

"My husband, Rick," Linda said.

"I'll get you both a drink," Rick said. "Beer for you, right, Paul? And Swann?"

A quick glance around the room at Paul's smiling circle of friends told Swann that beer was the preferred drink, so she asked for one, too. Paul introduced her to the other couples, then disappeared into the kitchen with Rick, leaving Swann on her own.

Glancing around at the group, Swann felt overdressed in her silk blouse and slacks. The other women wore simple cotton shorts or shifts. The men sported T-shirts or polo shirts with Bermuda shorts or jeans. The male members of the group had all drifted into an adjoining den, and suddenly Swann realized that the attention of the women in the room was riveted on her.

"How did you happen to come to Reedy Creek?" Linda asked with purely candid curiosity. It seemed to be a question everyone asked.

"I needed a quiet place to work on my book. And so—"

"You're a *writer?*" asked a round-faced woman with lips set in a perpetual pout.

"I wrote a biography about Winky Tapps," Swann said.

Utter silence greeted this statement. Finally a woman in the corner said timidly, "I've seen you on television, I think. Weren't you on Johnny Carson's show?"

Swann barely had time to answer in the affirmative when the woman, whose name was Shannon, said, "I just love Winky Tapps. I watch all her old movies when they come on TV."

A chorus of agreement greeted this statement, and then came the inevitable question: "What was Winky Tapps *really* like?"

By the time Swann had given her stock answer, Paul reappeared and handed her a plastic cup containing beer. Swann took a deep swallow, and the conversation veered into another topic.

The summer light wouldn't fade for another hour or so, but tall torches were lit on the concrete patio surrounding the glimmering new swimming pool in the backyard. Smoke from a portable barbecue wafted upward. Swann watched it, thinking that the setting was so normal, so middle-class. She sneaked a look at Paul through the door of the den. Did he fit in here? On the surface, perhaps, but she had the feeling that he was as much of an outsider as she was.

The men in the den laughed loudly over the sound of a baseball game playing on TV. After a while Paul left the group and stood looking out at the swimming pool. She remembered that he didn't like sports. Observing him, Swann thought, *I was right. He's different from his friends*. Swann wished he'd join the women in the living room, but once, when he caught her eye, he only smiled.

Soon Rick announced that the hamburgers were done, and everyone moved to picnic tables outside. As darkness fell, Linda became more vivacious, Rick became more garrulous, Shannon pouted, and Kathy's hilarity reached new peaks. A recently arrived engaged couple, Sue and Howard, danced in a quiet corner of the patio, their bodies throwing wavy shadows on the high cypress basket-weave fence. Johnny talked with Paul and Swann about his pet project of restoring his '52 Dodge, and Swann, bored by the conversation, began to wish that she were back in Philadelphia.

That was when Linda, fully clothed, dived into the pool.

"Gee, Linda, you really know how to liven up a party," Johnny called. He ripped off his shirt and followed her. Rick threw Kathy in, provoking a new wave of laughter, and Shannon, Sue and Howard ran into the house to avoid being thrown in themselves.

The swimmers splashed water at Swann and Paul.

"You're next!" they called.

Paul pulled Swann to her feet. "We were going to dance," he said, taking her in his arms.

Swann relaxed and leaned into him. He was a good dancer, graceful and lithe. She had been feeling awkward, listening to Johnny talk about his old car and realizing that she was completely out of her element. Now she felt drowsy, as though she had drunk too much beer. Probably she had, since she hadn't exactly felt like joining in the talk; drinking had been easier to do. Isolated from the others, her closeness to Paul felt full of possibilities, expectant. The feelings tingled a memory of her adolescence when boy-girl interaction had been new territory. This felt that way, perhaps because Paul and this setting and these people were new.

Their shadows on the fence merged into one shadow with two heads. She giggled, and he looked around to see what she was giggling about. When he saw, he held out his hand and pantomimed a barking dog, wiggling his little finger up and down. Then he laughed and pulled her closer so that her head rested against his shoulder and their shadow looked like one person.

"Better," he said, and she nodded, the smooth cotton of his shirt brushing her cheek.

The summer night hung heavy with humidity, and the voices from the pool sounded muffled with her one ear pressed to his chest. Someone turned up the music, and Howard and Shannon appeared. They began to dance nearby.

Paul caressed her back so that her cropped blouse hitched up. He touched her skin, a sensation so electrifying that her eyes flew open. He went on stroking the soft skin of her back until she relaxed again.

I shouldn't mislead him, Swann thought, but then she realized that perhaps she wasn't misleading him at all. She readjusted her thoughts; not only was she here to draw him out about himself, she was also here because she liked him. And she especially liked what he was doing right now, holding her so close, and she didn't want him to stop.

For many people, the inevitable conclusion of such an evening might be making love. Was that what she wanted? Even though she knew a lot about this man's background, she really didn't know him very well. Child Michael had once been the world's darling, but Paul Thompson was an unknown quantity.

Jed had roused himself from a lounge chair to dance with Sue, and they waltzed around the others, clearly mimicking them in a way that was supposed to be funny. Rick climbed out of the other end of the pool and stood dripping in his clothes.

"Think I'll put on my swimsuit," he said. As he turned, he bumped against a picnic table and knocked two beer bottles to the concrete patio. They shattered.

The sound stopped the party, except for the stereo which continued to blare.

"I'll get a broom and clean this mess up," Rick said, disappearing into the utility closet.

Kathy climbed up the pool ladder and heaved herself, heavy with water, onto the edge of the pool.

"Careful, Kath," Linda cautioned.

"I'm okay," Kathy called back, but she spoke too soon. As she was pulling herself to her feet, her hand slipped on the wet metal pool railing and she fell headlong into the broken glass.

"Oh!" she cried as Linda screamed, "Kathy!"

Jed ran to his wife's assistance, and by the time he reached her, blood was running in rivulets down her arm.

"She's hurt!" he said.

Paul stiffened momentarily and released his grip on Swann. In an instant he was running to Kathy's aid.

Swann was right behind him, grabbing a handful of napkins from the buffet table as she ran. Kathy bent over her arm and moaned.

Paul took charge immediately, urging the others to stand back and easing Kathy onto a nearby lounge chair. Moving carefully through the shards of broken glass, Swann handed him the napkin and he applied it to the wound as he located the pressure point.

"Linda, get a blanket," he ordered. Linda, dripping wet, ran into the house.

Paul knelt at Kathy's side. It was clear to Swann that the cut on Kathy's wrist was deep. She had had a better view of the injury than the others because she had been closest to Paul when he reached Kathy. The blood from Kathy's wound soaked through the napkin, and Swann silently handed Paul another one.

"I feel sick," Sue cried. Howard led her away into the house.

"Where is Linda with that blanket?" Jed wanted to know. He looked jittery and white. Someone turned off the music.

Swann glanced at Paul; he was tight-lipped and silent. He had moved so that his body shielded Kathy and her wounded arm from the view of the others, except for Swann, who was on the opposite side of Kathy's lounge chair facing them.

"The bleeding doesn't seem to be stopping," Swann murmured under her breath. Kathy lay back against the woven plastic of the lounge chair with her eyes closed, her face ashen.

"I know," Paul said. He tossed the second napkin away and reached for another. Swann saw the neatly sliced cut on Kathy's wrist. It was deep.

"Paul—" she began. Then she saw the look in his eyes.

It was a look of utter concentration and intense will. He stared at the cut on Kathy's arm and placed his hands on either side of it. Swann herself could almost feel the vibration, just as she had all those years ago at Miracle Farm. Perspiration broke out on Paul's forehead, and Swann held her breath. Kathy moaned. And then it happened. Blood ceased to flow before Swann's very eyes.

She couldn't be mistaken. She had been watching intently; she doubted that she had even blinked.

Paul shuddered slightly and removed his hands. Swann shot a look at the others, but clearly they hadn't noticed. Paul picked up another napkin and held it to the wound, only now there was no need. The napkin remained white. Hot beads of perspiration broke out on Swann's forehead as she realized what had happened.

Paul himself appeared stunned. After a moment Swann reached out and touched his arm.

"Shh," he said with a warning look, and she drew back. Kathy opened her eyes and sucked in her breath with a sibilant sound. Color flooded back into her cheeks.

Linda and Jed arrived with the blanket and draped it over Kathy's supine figure.

"I have a first-aid kit in my car," Paul said. "Rick, would you get it, please?"

"I'd better call an ambulance," Rick said uncertainly.

"It's only a surface wound," Paul said.

"I'm fine," Kathy said, speaking her first words since she'd fallen.

"But—"

"I'll clean this cut and apply a bandage. That should take care of it," Paul said.

"Paul *is* a paramedic," Shannon said.

Johnny picked up the broom and began to sweep up the broken glass. Rick brought the first-aid kit, and Swann fell easily into the role of assistant, handing Paul gauze pads and ointment when he asked for them. She got a good look at Kathy's wound, and she was not surprised that it was now little more than a scratch.

"Well," Paul said, helping Kathy to her feet. "How do you feel?"

"I feel very well," Kathy said with some surprise. "In fact, I feel wonderful. Relaxed."

"Are you *sure* you're all right?" Jed asked anxiously.

"Of course I am," Kathy said, leaning over and kissing him on the cheek. He regarded her doubtfully.

"I'm taking you home," he said.

"I think we'll shove off, too," said Shannon.

"Gosh, what a way to end a party," Linda said in a mournful tone.

"Hey, it was a great cookout. And we love the pool," Howard said, putting one arm around her and one arm around his fiancée.

"We'll do this again soon," Rick promised as they all flocked toward the door.

"Soon," everyone chorused as they headed for their cars, which were parked along the street.

Swann said her thank-yous and goodbyes and silently got into the Honda with Paul. He was quiet as they drove through the all-but-deserted streets of the town and headed out the dark creek road to the cottage.

"That was a bad cut," she ventured when Paul didn't speak.

"Not so bad," he said. He sounded tired.

"I saw it," she said. "I reached her when you did. It was a serious injury."

"I see worse than that all the time."

"Of course. You're a paramedic. But this one—"

He swiveled his head to look at her. Shadows from the trees on either side of the road hid the expression in his eyes.

"Swann, it was nothing. And I *did* nothing except what I'm trained to do. Okay?"

She understood from the tone of his voice that he didn't want to be challenged, and she shifted uncomfortably in her seat. She knew what he had done, and he knew she knew, and yet he wanted her to act as though nothing out of the ordinary had happened.

If she refused to accept his explanation, he might cut her out of his life. And she was just getting to know him. She couldn't lose him, not now. It would be a defeat on two levels, the professional and the personal.

The shells of the driveway crunched under the tires, and as soon as they reached the cottage, Paul jumped out of the car and came around to her side to open the door. She preceded him to the porch, where she had left the outside light on. She unlocked the door and turned to face him.

"Um, I had a good time," she said.

"I did, too. I'm sorry it had to end on the downside."

"It was okay," she said uneasily.

He ran a hand through his hair, making it seem even curlier. She had a fleeting memory of his hand on her bare skin beneath her blouse. She thought for a moment he might kiss her.

He moved away, stepping backward down the steps. "Thanks for going to the party with me," he said.

"I'm glad you asked me," she said.

He nodded, a curt silent little nod, and before she knew it, he had fled toward his car, leaving her standing there in the midst of the moths and mosquitoes swarming around the light. He started the engine of the car before she was even inside the house. She listened to his retreat, and it seemed as if she could hear his car for miles and miles after he was gone.

PAUL COULDN'T SLEEP when he got home.

He tried to read or watch television, but it was impossible. His mind kept flashing back to Kathy and the cut on her wrist.

It had been a bad one, that was for sure. He'd known as soon as he'd seen it that it was serious. He'd shifted into gear right away, applying pressure, ready to call the ambulance. Swann's face across from him had been white and tense; she'd realized the seriousness of the injury, too.

And what had made him try for what he had always called The Power? Why was it there for him now all of a sudden?

He hadn't used The Power in a long, long time. He'd thought he was unable to call on The Power anymore. He had seen a lot of bad accidents when it would have come in handy, but he'd never been able to find that high-tension frequency in his head that meant that The Power was going to come through. He himself hadn't been sorry to see The Power leave him all those years ago. He did regret, however, his inability to help others.

Swann knew. Of all people, why did it have to be Swann Triplett? He'd wanted to impress her, but not that way. He remembered her look of stunned comprehension in her eyes when she realized that The Power had healed Kathy's cut.

Well, maybe she wasn't sure what she'd seen. Maybe he'd convinced her that what he had done for Kathy fell within the realm of the medical, not the inexplicable. Maybe.

He walked into the kitchen and took a bag of pretzels out of the pantry. He ate them while leaning against the sink and staring out at the night. He had hoped that his evening with Swann would end differently. He had enjoyed being close to her, and she was a good dancer. It had been a mistake to take her to that party; she didn't quite fit in, although she'd tried.

So much for Swann Triplett. He wouldn't call her again. There was no future in their relationship, and he didn't want her to ask questions that he couldn't, wouldn't answer.

THE NEXT MORNING when Swann awoke, she knew that she was being watched.

She hadn't drawn the curtains fully across the little bedroom window, and she felt someone's eyes upon her as she lay staring up at the ceiling trying to assess the events of the previous evening.

She raised herself up on one elbow and peered at the window. Untrimmed shrubbery reached halfway up the glass, and she thought she saw a flicker of movement. She leaped out of bed and threw open the sash.

"Hey, you!" she called when she saw the small boy running into the woods.

He stopped and threw her a terrified look.

"Come back," she called, amused. "I'm not angry with you."

When he didn't answer, she threw on a robe and ran to the porch in time to see a pair of pumping legs disappear in the direction of the creek. She went outside, pushing away the big bushy branch that always blocked the opening of the back door. Really, she'd have to do something about that plant before it took over the whole patio. The boy didn't reappear even though she waited for a few moments to see if he would.

"Kids," she said musingly as the two kittens bounded outside. They skidded to a stop as soon as their feet hit the dewy grass.

She took both kittens back inside and ground her favorite special blend of coffee beans in the electric grinder. Savoring the fresh coffee aroma that permeated the air, she plugged in the coffee maker and poured the kittens a saucer of milk.

"What am I going to do with you?" she asked out loud. She sat down to await her coffee and pondered her course of action for today.

She should call Justin and tell him that she now was positive that Paul Thompson was Child Michael of Miracle Farm. She could call Gracie and tell her that this project was going to take longer than she thought. Should, could...shouldn't, couldn't. If she called Justin, he'd get excited and give her a pep talk, which she didn't think she needed. Her interest was already sufficiently aroused. And Gracie would try to talk her into coming to the New Jersey shore regardless of what she needed to do in Reedy Creek, because Gracie usually thought of her own selfish needs first.

She couldn't go to the shore now. Paul Thompson was just beginning to get interesting.

The kittens stopped drinking milk and began to roll around on the floor together. Swann watched them play as she sipped her coffee. Last night when she had asked at the party if anyone wanted a kitten or maybe two, she had found no takers. She still hoped that Paul would manage to find someone who would accept them.

The kittens followed her into the bedroom and watched solemnly from the foot of her bed as she dressed in slacks and a blouse, which she tied above her waist, leaving her midriff bare. She went out onto the porch and began organizing her papers preparatory to writing down her impressions of Paul's extraordinary healing of Kathy's wound.

She was finishing up when she saw a twitch of blue denim out of the corner of her eye. It was that boy again; she'd caught a glimpse of his mischievous face.

She bounded out the porch door and chased after him. He crashed through the underbrush near the creek, and, panting, she caught up with him.

"Wait," she called. "I won't hurt you."

He hid beneath a tree trunk, peering cautiously around it. Freckles covered his whole face, and he was missing two teeth.

"I just wanted to know your name," Swann wheedled. She leaned against a tottering old fence post to catch her breath.

"Mott," he said in such a soft voice that she could hardly hear.

"Well, Mott, do you live near here?"

Warily he pointed to some indefinite place behind him.

"Is it far?"

He shook his head.

"I have a candy bar in my pocket. I'll share," she offered. She took it out and dangled it in his line of vision.

"My mother won't let me take candy from strangers," he said, coming partway out from behind the tree.

"Oh. That's very wise," Swann said.

"Maybe if you asked her," he said hopefully. He looked longingly at the candy bar.

"Maybe," she agreed. "You'll have to take me to her."

"You'd come to our house?"

"I'd like to," Swann said. So far she had met no neighbors. In fact, she hadn't thought there were any within walking distance.

"Okay," he said, scampering away so fast that she could hardly keep up.

"Wait," she called, and he slowed his steps.

They walked along the bank of the creek on what was no more than a cow path before Mott turned abruptly and held up the barbed wire of a fence so that she could crawl under it.

"I thought you said it wasn't far," Swann said, huffing and puffing in his wake.

"It's right here," he told her as they rounded a pine-and-palmetto hammock, and Swann saw a tiny wooden house with peeling white paint. The front porch leaned sideways, and one window was covered with plastic sheeting. In a clearing was a small vegetable garden.

"Ma? I've brought our new neighbor!" Mott hollered, holding the front door open for Swann.

Swann heard quick footsteps. At first she thought that the person standing in the doorway to the kitchen must be another child, perhaps Mott's older sister, but when she stepped forward, Swann realized with astonishment that this must be Mott's mother. She was a mousy little thing and so thin that she looked as though a stiff wind would blow her away.

"I'm Angelyn Soames," she said, ducking her head as though she were embarrassed. Wispy blond hair fell across her cheeks.

"Swann Triplett," Swann said, extending her hand. "I've met Mott, and he wouldn't let me give him a candy bar until I'd asked you."

"I told him—"

"Oh, I understand. But may he have it?"

"Why, why—"

"Do you have a candy bar for me, too?" said a small voice from under the table, and Swann looked down and saw a tiny round-faced blue-eyed sprite of about five or so who must be Mott's sister.

"Carlie, that's not mannerly! Mott will share with you," Angelyn Soames said.

"Aw, Ma," Mott said.

"Here," Swann said, handing over the Snickers snack bar. The little girl scrambled out from under the table, and Mott went to cut the candy bar in two with a table knife.

A wail went up from an adjoining room, and Angelyn said, "Oh, that's Rhonda, she's waking up. Please set down a bit while I go get her."

"Oh, I didn't mean to stay," Swann said hastily.

"I'd be much obliged if you would," Angelyn said, hanging her head in that funny little way of hers, and so Swann sat down in the living room while Angelyn tended to the baby, who turned out to be a toddler somewhere between the ages of one and two.

"Now," Angelyn said, sitting down on a slat-back rocker and matter-of-factly unbuttoning her blouse so that Rhonda could nurse, "I hope you don't mind if I pick peaches off that tree near your driveway. The owner said I could."

"Of course not," Swann said. "Help yourself."

"How do you happen to be here in Reedy Creek?" Angelyn asked.

"I came here to work on a book," Swann said reluctantly. So far she couldn't even begin to count how many people she had told; soon the whole town would know about the nonexistent book about her father.

"A book! You're a writer!" Angelyn's eyes lit up, and then, as though embarrassed to have been so impressed, she lowered her eyes to look at the baby, who was sucking greedily at her breast.

"I don't plan to stay long," Swann said. "Just long enough to get a good start on the book."

"And then will you go back where you came from? Where is that?"

"Philadelphia," Swann said, thinking that the woman had all the natural curiosity of a child. In fact, there was something childlike about her—a kind of naïveté, an enthusiasm not yet reined in. Swann wondered how old she was. Surely she could be no older than twenty-three or twenty-four. Younger than Swann, and with three small children to care for.

"Philadelphia," Angelyn breathed in wonder. "I've never been there. Or anywhere."

"You've always lived here?"

"Right here in Reedy Creek all my life. In this house, even. It was my mama and daddy's house, and after they died, Bobby and me lived here."

"Bobby is your husband?"

"Was. Ran off with my sister over a year ago, and no one's seen them since. Now it's just me and my kids."

"I'm sorry," Swann said. She had noticed how threadbare the little rug under her feet looked, and certainly the furniture was falling apart.

"It's okay. Mrs. Dawson, the social worker from Family Services, said maybe I should put the kids in a foster home, but I'd never let us be split up. Never. Welfare takes care of me and the children," Angelyn said. She pronounced it "chirren."

"Anyway," Angelyn went on, "as soon as Rhonda here gets a little bigger, I'll get me a job. At least I hope I will," she said, frowning slightly. Then she grinned. "We get by with fish from the creek and vegetables from our garden. I get lonely, though, with only the kids to talk to all day. Bobby's family, they don't have nothing to do with me these days, and anyway, there's only his uncle and aunt. My family is all gone. So I'm happy to see you. I hope if you get lonesome you'll come by sometimes. If you'd like, I mean."

The torrent of words took Swann by surprise. "Why, of course I'd like that," she said slowly, warming to Angelyn's gentle smile. With those freckles and that soft pale hair, Angelyn must have looked a lot like Mott and Carlie when she was a child.

Deftly Angelyn buttoned her blouse. She stood up when Swann did, shifting the baby to one hip. "I'm going to hold you to that, now," she said.

"You come and see me, too," Swann said impulsively.

"Oh," Angelyn said with a sigh. "I can hardly do that. There's the kids, you know. No, it'd be best if you'd come here. I know it's a lot to ask, but—but I'd be so honored."

She gazed at Swann with an expression that could only be described as pleading.

"I'll come tomorrow," Swann promised, although she had intended to do no such thing.

"Thank the nice lady for the candy bar," Angelyn said sternly to Mott and Carlie, and they chorused their thanks.

"You're welcome," she told them.

Swann stepped out into the bright sunshine and headed toward the creek path.

"'Bye!" called Mott and Carlie.

"'Bye!" called Angelyn.

Rhonda clapped her hands and laughed.

Swann turned and waved when she reached the edge of the pine-and-palmetto hammock, and then continued on her way.

She hadn't intended to be here long enough to get to know any of her neighbors; she was thinking ahead to the day when she would leave Reedy Creek, and it would be harder if she left friends behind.

Yet she sensed that Angelyn needed a friend, and maybe they could be company for each other, if only for a limited time. The children were cute and well mannered, and if she could help them, she would.

Why, maybe they would like to have a kitten! She should have asked Angelyn if it was all right.

Of course, she couldn't very well give away what she really didn't consider hers; she had hoped that Paul would take at least one of them and find a home for the other.

When she let herself inside the cottage, the kittens ran to meet her at the door, mewing for something to eat. She opened a can of tuna and broke up the fish into tiny pieces, offering the kittens tidbits on her finger. Before long they were gulping down the tuna, so she sat back and tried to figure out what to do about them. Should she give them away without Paul's consent? But what if he'd found a home for them, too?

The kittens had barely finished eating when she picked up the phone and dialed Paul's number.

"SWANN?" PAUL SAID. The phone's ring had awakened him abruptly from his nap; he had been trying to catch up on the sleep he'd lost the night before. He sounded confused.

"Swann Triplett," she said.

"Sorry if I sound, uh, a little vague," he said, pushing himself to a sitting position. He had fallen asleep on the floor, believe it or not, when he'd been watching an old movie on TV.

"I didn't wake you, I hope," Swann said.

"No, well, as a matter of fact I was snoozing. I was watching this old Marx Brothers movie and drifted off."

"Sounds like the Marx Brothers must be losing their touch."

"No, it was *Duck Soup,* my favorite. Maybe I've just seen it too many times." He pictured Swann in his mind, and the thought of her lightened his spirits. It was easy to forget that he was never going to see or talk to her again after last night. He hoped she wasn't going to open up the subject of what had happened with Kathy.

"I called about the kittens," she said.

"Kit—? Oh, the *kittens,*" he said.

"It's just that I thought of a good home for one of them, at least, and I wondered if you had any objection."

"Me? Of course not. I didn't want them in the first place. I figured they'd be good company for you."

"I can't keep them, Paul. I won't even be here long. And I can't take them back to Philadelphia with me. The city is no place for them."

"Don't lots of people keep cats in the city?"

"Yes, but I've never liked the idea of a litter box in my town house, and they can't be allowed to run free."

"Hmm. I see. Certainly if you've found a home for them—"

"Not *them.* Just *one.* I'd like to give it to the family I met today. It's Angelyn Soames and her three kids. Do you know them?"

"I think I know who you mean. A small woman with straight blond hair? A towheaded boy and girl who look just like her, and a baby about a year and a half old?"

"How do you know them?"

"Oh, I've seen them around town like I do everybody else. Also, I heard she has been having a rough time since her husband left."

"I gathered that. She seems lonely."

"She probably doesn't get much company out there on that lonely road."

"Exactly. So I thought I'd go over there tomorrow and offer them the kitten."

"Good idea. She'd probably welcome you with open arms."

"She already has. Well, thanks, Paul. But I wish you'd keep your eyes and ears open for a home for the other kitten. I really can't keep it."

"I'll do that. By the way, I bought a huge bag of dry cat food for the kittens. Mind if I bring it over?"

She sounded delighted. "When can you be here?" she asked.

"Oh, a couple of hours?"

"That's fine," she said with a lilt in her voice.

After he hung up, he rubbed the stubble growth on his chin and stared at the phone. He hadn't really bought any cat food. He'd have to stop at the supermarket on the way to her place.

He was finding that it wasn't so easy to shut Swann Triplett out of his life. Maybe it was the veneer of the big city that clung to her even in out-of-the-way Reedy Creek. Maybe it was her considerable sex appeal. He hadn't meant to see her again, but it was almost as if he couldn't help himself.

If he were lucky, maybe she wouldn't mention last night's incident. If he talked enough, maybe she wouldn't get a chance to bring it up.

Chapter Four

She came to the door before he knocked, smiling at him through the screen.

"Come in," she said, and as he walked in he caught a whiff of her perfume—a light scent that put him in mind of jungle gardens where banks of night flowers shone in the moonlight.

"What do you want me to do with this?" he asked. He held out a large bag of kitten chow.

"My goodness, we only have two kittens. That's enough food for a whole—a whole—say, what do you call a bunch of kittens?"

"A kaboodle?" he suggested, and she laughed.

"Put it in the corner for now. And thanks, I'm glad you brought it. I used up the only can of tuna fish today."

The two kittens ran around the edge of the door, and one of them arched its back and hissed at Paul's foot.

He bent over and picked it up. "I saved this animal from starvation, and it treats me like the enemy. Cute little thing, isn't it?"

"So cute I don't see how you can resist taking it home with you. By the way, I'm awfully tired of referring to them as 'it.'"

He checked. "One male and one female," he announced. "You can tell them apart at a glance if you'll remember that the female has a bit of white on the end of her tail and the male doesn't.''

''Maybe the Soames family will take both of them,'' she said doubtfully.

''I wouldn't count on it.'' He set the kittens on the floor and they scampered away into what he supposed was the bedroom.

Swann wore her hair pinned to one side with a tortoise-shell barrette; it exposed the slender line of her jaw. Her yellow blouse accentuated the golden flecks in her eyes, and she wore a pair of flowing cropped trousers cinched at the waist by a paprika-colored belt. He liked the way she dressed. She projected a certain sophistication and an appreciation of color and line.

He supposed he should leave, since she hadn't asked him to stay as he'd anticipated. He hesitated, unsure of himself, and suddenly he realized that she didn't know what to say to him, either. Considering what had happened last night, he supposed that wasn't so surprising.

''Is that where you work?'' he asked, sauntering toward the porch where a table holding a word processor was pushed to the far end.

To Swann, it was not the most reassuring question he could have asked. She'd decided she couldn't risk his seeing her books and papers and all the articles about him, and so she had packed everything up and stashed it in the file cabinet when she found out he was coming over.

Somehow she must try to get him to talk about his past. She struggled to think of an opener and failed. The next best thing would be to lure him away from her work space. Just watching him near it made her nervous.

''I made fresh lemonade this afternoon,'' she said, trying to keep the uneasy edge out of her voice. ''Would you like some?''

She was rewarded by his smile. ''That sounds good,'' he said.

The lemonade lured him to the much safer territory of the living room couch. "Your father must be an interesting man," he said once they were seated. "Tell me about him."

She blinked, then glanced off into the distance, then back at Paul. "He's just . . . my father," she said.

"Was he one of those rags-to-riches types?"

"He inherited a small, down-at-the-heels trucking company after World War II. He drove trucks, learned the business, fought tooth and nail to survive. He made a lot of money and used it to acquire a small airline. In a few years, he was rich."

"Money was never a problem around your house?"

"I can't remember it ever being discussed. We had maids, I had nannies and governesses, I went to the best schools. It's only since I've been grown up that I've appreciated the advantages."

"Any disadvantages?"

She thought about the fights between her mother and father, and she thought about being left with servants while they were out of town.

"A few," she admitted.

"Like what?"

"The poor-little-rich-girl syndrome," she said reluctantly.

"It can't be *that* bad," he said.

"It's hard to describe to anyone who hasn't lived through it," she admitted. "Anyway, what about you? What kind of upbringing did you have? I don't detect a Southern accent."

"I grew up in Ohio and Pennsylvania," he said carefully.

She waited to give him time to elaborate, but he didn't.

"That's my neck of the woods, more or less," she said after a moment.

"I've never spent any time in Philadelphia," he said. "I used to eat at a restaurant near my home where they advertised real Philly steak sandwiches. They were good, but I'll always wonder if they were anything like the real thing.''

''Your home? Where was that?'' she asked, holding her breath.

''A little town near the middle of the state. No one's ever heard of it. Say, is that a boat I see over by that pile of bricks?''

He was looking out the wide porch windows toward the edge of the property where he had discerned the outlines of an old wooden skiff overturned there.

''I don't know. I haven't paid much attention,'' she said.

''Mind if I take a look?''

''Well, no, but—''

Before she could finish the sentence, Paul was on his feet and out the porch door. All she could do was trail after him, seething inwardly at her inability to keep him on track now that she had managed to get him to touch on the subject of his childhood. Miracle Farm had been located outside of Montberry, a small central Pennsylvania town, and she'd thought she had him. Well, more fool her. He was full of surprises.

She followed Paul to the edge of the creek where vines threatened to envelop the small boat. After a few minutes' study, Paul wrenched it free of them and flipped it right side up.

''I wonder if she floats,'' he mused as he walked around it.

''I have no idea,'' Swann answered. She wasn't the least bit interested.

He poked experimentally at the bottom. ''Hey, she looks like she could be made seaworthy. We're in luck.''

''I don't know anything about boating.''

''I do. You'd enjoy floating down the creek on a lazy afternoon. Maybe I could get this thing back in shape for you.''

''Maybe,'' she said doubtfully.

"I'd scrape the barnacles off, recaulk it, and get you a couple of oars. In fact I have some that no one is using. They were in my carport when I moved into my house."

"Why don't you bring them over sometime?"

He smiled at her. "I will," he said.

A lizard scurried over the boat's gunwales, and she jumped. "That scared me," she said.

"It's getting dark. We'd better go back inside," he said with obvious reluctance.

Behind them in the square of the window shone the glimmer of the light Swann had left on in the kitchen; the creek with the rustle of reeds and the occasional grunt of a bullfrog. A fresh breeze wafted the sweet water scent over and around them, and she was overly aware of Paul beside her no more than an arm's length away.

"We'd better go," he said again, but his arm brushed hers, whether by accident or design she couldn't say.

They turned and walked slowly up the bank. He held the door to the porch open for her, and, as usual, the branch of one of the overgrown shrubs flanking the steps caught in the space between the door and jamb. He stopped to free it.

"This shrubbery hasn't been cut back for a long time," he said. "It needs trimming."

"Do you know anyone I could hire to do it for me?" she asked. Her heart was beating so fast that it seemed out of control. He was standing so close, his face shadowed in the dark.

"I'd be glad to do it for you. I have an electric trimmer that would get the job done fast."

"Oh, I couldn't ask you to do that."

"I wouldn't mind."

"But—"

"I said I wouldn't mind, okay?"

She smiled up at him and, suddenly self-conscious, she went into the living room and switched on a lamp. She jumped when the telephone rang. Still more aware of him than she should be, she turned her back to Paul as she lifted the receiver off its hook.

"Swann? Is that you?"

It was Justin; she shot a quick surreptitious look at Paul out of the corners of her eyes.

"Yes," she said cautiously.

"I haven't heard from you. I've been worried."

Paul appeared in her line of vision. "I'm going," he said in a low tone. "I didn't mean to stay so long." It was obvious to him that this was a phone call she'd rather not share with him. The thought that the caller was someone important to her, perhaps a *male* someone who missed her, had occurred to him when he heard her cautious tone of voice.

She covered the mouthpiece with one hand. "But—" she said to him.

"No, really, I'll call you sometime." He tried to be gracious; quickly he let himself out the front door. Of course she would have someone else, he told himself. Women as attractive as Swann always did.

Swann watched him go, her heart plummeting.

"Swann?" Justin said in her ear.

She sighed and removed her hand from the mouthpiece. "It's okay. He's gone," she told Justin. She heard the Honda's engine spring to life in the driveway.

"I hope I haven't interrupted anything," Justin said.

Justin could be exasperating at times.

"No," Swann said. "Child Michael was standing right here in my living room, that's all."

"In your *living* room?" Justin said.

Swann sat down, prepared for a long chat. "That's right. You wouldn't believe how easy it was to meet him." She quickly related how she had seen his picture in the *Reedy Creek Gazette* and had attended his CPR class.

"Don't keep me guessing, Swann. What's he like?" Justin asked with the avid curiosity of a natural busybody.

"Oh," she said, wondering how best to describe Paul Thompson.

"What does that mean?" Justin asked when no explanation seemed forthcoming.

"He's different from what I expected."

"A good ol' southern boy?"

"Not exactly, although he has friends like that. I met some of them last night. And Justin, I saw the most amazing thing. At the party we went to, a woman cut her wrist on a piece of glass. He stopped the bleeding, Justin, just like that!"

A profound silence greeted this remark.

"It happened, honestly. And afterward, he told me I hadn't seen anything. In other words, I was to act as though nothing out of the ordinary had happened!"

"Not that I doubt your powers of observation, dear dear Swann, but are you positively sure?"

"Yes. Kathy was practically going into shock from what appeared to be a severe wound, and he pressed his hands to either side of the cut. The bleeding stopped immediately."

"And nobody thought this was unusual?"

"I was the only one who saw how bad Kathy's cut really was. The rest of them had their view blocked by Paul."

"Do you suppose this guy is still going around healing people? And if he is, why isn't anyone talking about it?"

"You tell me, Justin. I can't figure it out. Unless, of course, he only practices on friends. But then why would he give me the distinct impression that he didn't want me to say anything about it even to him?"

"Hmm, that's a good question. I must say, Swann, that I'm proud of you. Less than a week in that town, and you produce not only Child Michael, but a first-person account of a healing."

"Keep it to yourself, please. I still need an admission from Paul that he actually is Child Michael, and after that, I'd better get his cooperation in my writing his story."

"Think he'll cooperate?"

She thought about his eagerness to repair the skiff and his willingness to trim the shrubbery around the cottage.

"He's probably one of the most agreeable men I've ever met," she said truthfully.

"You like him, don't you?" Justin demanded.

"Yes, I like him very much."

"Do I detect a hint of something more?" he asked slyly.

"Don't be silly, Justin," she said as indignantly as she could. "He's interesting to me, yes, but only in a professional way." For some reason, a disconcerting and totally absurd mental picture of the groove between Paul's nose and upper lip sprang into her mind. She closed her eyes, willing it to go away. It didn't.

"I'm glad you're not bored with him, at any rate. Well, Swann, keep me posted on your efforts to win his cooperation. That's the key to the situation. Remember, I'm always available to discuss the project."

"Thanks, Justin. I'll call soon."

They hung up, and Swann made her way slowly and reflectively through the cottage, plumping the pillows on the couch, putting dishes in the dishwasher. Finally she undressed, showered, and climbed into bed to read. The kittens curled up at her feet, purring and pressing their claws in and out of the bedclothes.

It was a cozy feeling, just her and the cats; when she turned off the light, she should have drifted easily off to sleep. And yet she didn't. She had too much to think about. *Entirely* too much.

THE NEXT DAY, Swann trudged along the trail beside the creek carrying the two unprotesting kittens. They huddled against her shirt, blinking in the bright sunlight.

Angelyn Soames met her at the door of their house, the baby balanced on her hip. She was immediately joined by both older children.

"Swann's got a kitten—no, two kittens," shrieked Carlie.

"Are they for us?" Mott asked.

Swann smiled at Angelyn. "They're mine," she said. "I thought you might like to play with them for a while."

Angelyn held the door open for Swann, and after they dropped the kittens off in the kitchen where Mott found a ball for them to play with, she led Swann into the living room.

"I hope you don't mind the cats," Swann told her. "They were abandoned down by the river, and I found them. I'd like to find homes for them."

"Why, I'm glad you brought them. The kids love animals."

"Would you like to have them?"

"Oh, I—"

"They're really not any trouble. And a friend of mine gave me a huge bag of cat chow you can have."

Angelyn glanced through the kitchen door at the two older children, who were twitching a piece of twine across the kitchen floor.

"The kids do like them," she said. "But feeding two cats—I don't know, it might get expensive."

"Then just take one," Swann said impulsively. "I can keep the other, I suppose."

"One wouldn't be so bad," Angelyn conceded.

"Then you'll keep it?"

Carlie, standing at the door, heard. She ran to tug at Angelyn's skirt. "Please, Ma, say yes," she begged.

"Please, Ma," Mott chimed in. "Anyway, there's mouses under the house. The kitten could catch the mouses. And cats like fish—I'd catch fish for it."

He was so engaging in his eagerness that Swann could see Angelyn relenting.

"Please, Ma," Carlie added softly.

"Oh, all right," Angelyn said with a smile. "Kids should have a pet, I guess. But only the one. Swann says she'll keep the other."

"Yippee!" shouted Mott, and he and Carlie scampered off toward the bedrooms with the kittens in hot pursuit.

"I hope you don't mind," Swann said belatedly. She had never thought about a pet being an economic burden.

"Won't you please set down with me for a while? I made peach cobbler this morning. Would you like some? The peaches came off your peach tree." Angelyn seemed touchingly eager to make Swann welcome.

"That would be lovely," Swann said, giving in to Angelyn's palpable loneliness.

"Maybe you could hold the baby," and before Swann knew what was happening, Angelyn had deposited Rhonda in her lap.

Swann blinked down at the small face, and, after staring at Swann openmouthed for a full minute, Rhonda puckered up her eyes and let out a wail.

"Now, now," Angelyn soothed from the kitchen, but this had no effect. Rhonda continued to cry, much to Swann's consternation.

Angelyn brought two small dishes of cobbler and a pitcher of iced tea, which she set on the table.

"I'll pour tea if you'll take the baby," Swann said. She had to raise her voice to be heard.

"That's fair," Angelyn told her. She held out her arms and Rhonda practically launched herself off Swann's lap. Once in her mother's arms, she immediately stopped sobbing.

"I haven't had much experience with children," Swann said apologetically.

"Never mind, I guess a lot of people haven't. Now me, that's about all the experience I've got," Angelyn said, settling comfortably on her chair.

Swann stood up. "If you'll tell me where the glasses are," she suggested.

"They're in the cabinet to the right of the sink," Angelyn said.

Swann went into the kitchen. The linoleum was worn and patched, the paint on the metal cabinets was chipped, and the curtains above the sink were limp with too many washings. Still, she noted how clean everything was, and on the windowsill a red geranium in a clay pot added a brave touch of color.

After Swann returned with the glasses, Angelyn put the baby on a blanket on the floor with some toys. She bent over to wipe the baby's nose. "Rhonda has hay fever," she explained. "It's really bad this summer."

Angelyn pocketed the tissue and accepted her glass of iced tea from Swann. Swann thought briefly that the two of them had almost nothing in common. She knew little about children.

"I was wondering," Angelyn said dreamily, staring out the window where flies buzzed against the screen. "Wondering how come someone like you would want to come to a place like this. I mean, it must be fun living in a big city."

"I like the city," Swann admitted.

"Do you live in an apartment? Or is it a house?"

"It's a town house. Three stories tall, and overlooking a bridge across the river."

"I bet the view is real pretty."

"It is, but I like having the creek right outside my door here."

Angelyn brightened. "It's nice, isn't it? I like to walk down there in the morning before the kids wake up. Just for a minute all by myself with the mist curling up into the trees.... Oh, but you'll think I'm silly." She reddened and looked down at her hands. They were spare and work roughened.

Swann was touched by Angelyn's embarrassment. "I don't think you're silly at all," she said quickly. "In fact, I like to walk beside the creek in the morning, too."

"There's a family of otters living on the creek bank in front of the house," Angelyn said eagerly. "I could show you sometime."

"Would you?"

"Yes, but we'd have to go early. Right after dawn if you could. 'Cause the children would still be asleep then. They'd just make noise and scare the otters if we took them. Would you like to go tomorrow?''

''Yes, if you could.''

''Oh, I'll be there anyway. It's my quiet time. It's the only time I get to be by myself and think. The rest of the time the kids keep me real busy.''

''I can imagine,'' Swann replied as Mott and Carlie came laughing into the room, each one carrying a kitten.

''We have to decide which one we should keep,'' Angelyn said.

''No, they're twins. They're almost exactly alike. The kids may choose the one they like and I'll take the other one home with me.''

Mott and Charlie sat down on the floor.

''I like this one,'' Carlie said, cradling the female kitten close to her chest.

''She's the one that climbed in my dresser drawer. I think she wants to sleep there,'' Mott said.

''Then she's yours,'' Swann told him. She picked up the male and held him in her lap.

''What should we name her?'' Carlie asked. She was clearly entranced by the kitten.

''Stropstripe,'' said Mott.

''Stropstripe? Why in the world?'' Angelyn asked.

Mott caressed the soft belt of white fur on the cat's stomach. ''This is her strops, and this,'' he said, pointing to the gray tiger stripes on her back, ''is the stripes.''

Carlie made a face, and Swann laughed. ''Stropstripe is a fine name. Since you're so good at picking out cats' names, what shall I name mine?''

Mott looked at Swann's kitten for a long moment. ''Joe-the-Cat,'' he said at last.

Carlie rolled on the floor, laughing. For some reason she found the name really funny.

''Joe-the-Cat?'' Swann repeated.

''Joe-the-Cat,'' Mott verified without cracking a smile. ''Why?''

"He looks like a Joe, and he's a cat. Besides, I like it," Mott said with an indignant look at the still-mirthful Carlie.

"Then Joe-the-Cat it is," Swann said, privately glad that she hadn't ended up with the one named Stropstripe.

She stood up to leave. Amid the chorus of goodbyes, Angelyn bent close and whispered in her ear. "I'll meet you at the curve in the path tomorrow. Early, now, and don't forget."

"I'll be there," Swann promised.

On the way home, Joe-the-Cat squirmed up the front of her blouse and lay like a fur collar around Swann's neck. When she emerged from the woods into the clearing, Swann recognized Paul's car in the driveway. He hailed her from the creek bank as she headed toward the house. He had stripped to his waist, revealing a chest matted with curly blond hair.

The old boat rested on a pair of sawhorses, bottom side up. He thumped the side of it with the palm of his hand. "This is going to be a fine vessel," he told her, his eyes sparkling.

"That's hard to believe," she said. To her it looked impossible to restore.

"You wait and see." He watched as Swann unwound the kitten from her neck. He said, "Say, did you manage to give away the other kitten?"

She nodded. "The Soames family took it. The kids were delighted."

"How about their mother?"

"Oh, she seemed happy about it. They named it Stropstripe," and she told him about how Mott had named the kittens.

She held the kitten toward him, and Paul paused to scratch it lightly behind the ears. "So this is Joe-the-Cat, huh? Well, that's a good name. And you're planning to keep him?"

"It looks as though I have no choice, unless you've had a change of heart." She moved away, holding the cat close.

"He'll be good company for you out here in the boon-docks."

"Maybe so. I'm worried about what will happen to him when I go back home."

"He'll travel, I'm sure. Or maybe you can find a home for him between now and then." Paul resumed scraping barnacles off the bottom of the boat, using the blade part of a shovel with a broken-off handle. His torso was sheened with sweat; it made every ripple of his muscles noticeable.

"It's awfully hot out here," Swann said. "Not a breeze anywhere. I think I'll go inside."

"Good idea. I'm warning you, Philly heat waves are nothing compared to what you're in for, down here." He grinned at her as she turned toward the house.

Inside, she set Joe on her bed. He immediately curled up, tucked his nose under his tail and went to sleep. Well, she thought, he looked as if he belonged there. And yes, maybe she could use the company.

Swann went out on the porch and pulled her notebook from its drawer. Down by the creek, Paul continued to scrape barnacles from the bottom of the boat. He seemed totally absorbed in the task, which he accomplished with the grace of movement that she had come to identify with him. He seemed supremely competent at what he was doing; even from here she saw the way his hands firmly gripped the handle of the old shovel so that the skin was taut and sinews stood out in relief in the bright sunlight. Such hands, she thought musingly. Even if they weren't healing hands, they would be remarkable in their strength.

She rested her gaze on her notebook, looking over what she had written about him. She'd begun to keep detailed notes of their every encounter. Her observations and insights might prove useful later on.

She couldn't keep her eyes on the paper because the words kept blurring together. And she kept looking up so that he would be within her field of vision. The sun, sinking lower in the west, shot golden sparks off his pale hair.

She bent her head over her notebook and began to write.

Paul stopped by after work today. He was here when I returned from Angelyn's house. He is scraping barnacles from the bottom of the boat. Seems to enjoy the physical labor. He—

She stopped writing at the sound of the distinctive *whap!* of the overgrown branch hitting the back door as Paul opened it. He stuck his head inside. "I could sure use a drink of water," he said.

Swann snapped the notebook closed and tried not to look as flustered as she felt. What if he had seen what she was writing? He hadn't, she was sure about that; but what if she had been so absorbed that she hadn't closed the book in time?

"Come in," she invited, her heart pounding with her own knowledge of her duplicity as she shoved the book into a file drawer. Paul stepped inside and followed her into the kitchen.

She handed him a glass of ice water and he drained it in one gulp. She wished she'd thought of offering it before he'd had to ask.

"That was good," he said. He hesitated, and she didn't know where to look. He filled up the tiny kitchen, blocking her exit.

"I was wondering if maybe you'd like to come over to my place for dinner tonight," he said slowly. "I've got a buddy who owns a shrimp trawler. I passed him on the way out here, and he says he had a big catch today. We could boil a couple of pounds of shrimp, and I've got some cabbage slaw."

"Well, I—" This was totally unexpected, and she already felt off balance because he'd almost caught her at work.

"I figure I can call it quits on the boat, go home, take a shower and come back and pick you up in an hour and a half or so."

He looked so expectant, so eager, so invested in her answer. Something about his expression reminded her of Mott when he was begging Angelyn to let him keep the kitten. Swann found herself reluctant to hurt Paul's feelings. After all, she remembered what he'd looked like as a boy, and although he was no longer a child, that little boy, the one who had made her feel so good by offering a smile of understanding at a time when she'd needed it, was hidden deep inside the man.

She'd meant to guard against getting emotionally involved with him. After the Winky Tapps experience, she'd had no intention of being caught up in any more emotional maelstroms. But then she hadn't known Paul Thompson, hadn't realized how the considerable presence of a handsome and very virile male could work on her resolve. And she had also underestimated her ties to the boy within.

"Shall I pick you up at—oh, seven o'clock?"

"Yes," she said, and was rewarded with his radiant smile.

Chapter Five

After Paul left, when she was no longer under the influence of his considerable charm, Swann wished fervently that she had thought about his invitation before accepting so readily. She admitted her own jitters as she walked aimlessly around the cottage, Joe-the-Cat at her heels.

Had she agreed to see Paul because she wanted to, or was it only that she couldn't bear the hurt in his eyes if she said no?

Come on, she chided herself. *He's a grown man. He knows how to handle rejection.*

Yet she couldn't get the picture of the young Child Michael out of her head. She recalled exactly the way he had looked that night when he'd happened to see her father slap her on the knee. His empathy had been real enough; he'd known how miserable that physical rebuke, which was only one of a multitude of slaps and spankings she'd received during her childhood, had made her feel. Only Swann knew what an uphill battle it had been to regain her self-esteem after her father's severe disciplining, and she still had a hard time dealing with rejection. Judging from what she knew of Paul's childhood, maybe he did, too.

Joe-the-Cat pounced on her shoelace as she passed the refrigerator, then circled around and attacked her again from the bathroom door.

"So why reject the man?" she said aloud. She liked him and she enjoyed being with him. She only wished that she could separate her professional feelings from her personal ones. Also, what if she slipped and said something that revealed her true reason for coming to Reedy Creek? At this point, that would certainly toll the death knell for the biography Justin wanted her to write. She'd be better off to keep her relationship with Paul a casual one, which meant that the wisest thing was to avoid intimate little dinners on his turf.

Swann walked into the bedroom and sat down on the edge of the bed, staring at the telephone. It offered her an easy way out. Why not take it? Impulsively she picked up the receiver and punched in his number. His answering machine answered her call.

"Paul, this is Swann. I won't be able to come for dinner tonight. Something important has come up." The lie did not spring easily to her lips, and immediately she felt guilty. She hung up quickly in case he was monitoring his calls and decided to pick up the phone.

After she replaced the receiver on its hook she sat for a moment, drumming her fingers indecisively on the nightstand. Now the challenge was to find something else to do. But what was there to do in Reedy Creek?

There wasn't a movie theater or even a bowling alley; no skating rink, no miniature golf course and no shopping mall. For everything except the pure necessities, one had to take a road trip to Savannah.

That was it, then. Savannah was only an hour's drive away. If she stayed home, Paul might hop in his car and ride out to see if she was here, and she'd rather not be faced with her own bold-faced lie. *Another* lie, she corrected herself. Almost everything the man knew of her was based on falsehood, and she, who could be painfully honest at times, couldn't feel good about that.

So instead of spending the evening with Paul, she'd walk around one of the malls in Savannah, maybe take in a movie. She'd never been to a movie alone in her life, but there was always a first time.

She heard the phone ring as she stepped outside and locked the front door behind her. She hesitated on the steps for a moment as it rang three times, then four, then five. It was still ringing when she turned her back and strode resolutely toward her car.

PAUL SLAMMED THE PHONE down after calling Swann and wondered first of all what he was going to do with several pounds of fresh shrimp.

Well, he could throw the shrimp in the freezer, although frozen shrimp never tasted as good as fresh. Anyway, he wasn't hungry now. Who did that woman think she was?

Her bad manners surprised him. She'd seemed happy enough to accept his invitation when he was standing in her kitchen. And he was smart enough to know that nothing had come up; she'd merely decided for some reason that she didn't want to see him.

Why?

He might as well boil the shrimp and eat them. Still, a solitary meal didn't appeal to him.

He put the water on to boil, then took the pot off the burner.

He wasn't hungry. He wanted to see Swann.

He wrapped the shrimp securely in a plastic bag and tossed them into the freezer.

She hadn't answered his phone call, but that didn't necessarily mean that she wasn't home. In fact, he was willing to bet that she'd be there. He was going out to her place and find out what the hell was going on.

PAUL APPROACHED the creek road from a crossroads and stopped at the stop sign. Not so surprisingly, he recognized Swann's rental car as it barreled past.

So she *was* going somewhere.

Since she wasn't at home, he saw no point in going to her place after all, so he turned and followed her back toward town.

He kept pace with her car as it negotiated the twists and turns of the creek road. She drove fast. He didn't intend to follow her, at least not at first. Whatever it was that she'd found to do that was so important, it was none of his business.

He continued to follow her unnoticed, and once they were in town, a pickup truck turned onto Liberty Street and blocked her rear view of him. She didn't stop at the bank or the car wash, and she sped right through the business section. He should have turned off on his own street, but for some reason he didn't. It looked as though she had decided to head toward the interstate highway to Savannah.

What business she could have there, he didn't know. And it wasn't as though he expected to find out as he continued to trail her along the highway leading to I-95.

He knew a woman in Savannah who would be glad to see him. Maybe he'd drop by her place and ask her if she'd like to go out for a few beers. He'd stop at a gas station up ahead; no sense in making the trip with a tank less than half full.

One thing for sure: Swann Triplett wouldn't be hearing from him again. Let her scrape barnacles off the old boat herself, and let her trim her own shrubbery. He had better things to do than to allow himself to be snubbed by some high society dame who evidently considered spending time with him to be slumming.

AT FIRST SWANN THOUGHT there was something wrong with the car's engine. Then she felt an ominous tug to the right, and immediately afterward her teeth rattled with the rough ride that meant a flat tire.

She steered carefully off onto the shoulder of the interstate highway and eased to a stop before climbing out of the car. Grass and weeds reached almost to her knees and tugged at the hem of her skirt as she walked around it. A truck roared by, stirring up little whirlwinds of dust. Grit flew in her eyes, nose and mouth. A rapid inspection told her that she had no choice but to change the tire, a prospect that she certainly didn't relish.

Swann straightened, heaved a sigh and wiped the perspiration from her forehead with one hand. It was hot, even though the sun was about to disappear into the rim of the marsh. She wondered how far it was to Savannah from here. She hadn't thought to keep track of the mileage.

She found instructions about how to change a tire in the glove compartment, and, feeling encouraged, she traipsed around to the back of the car and opened the trunk. The spare was located in a well underneath the felt liner, and it took some doing to heave it out and onto the ground. She fumbled underneath the matting in the trunk, trying to find the vinyl case containing the necessary tools for changing a tire, but they weren't there.

"Great," she muttered under her breath. "Just great." The vinyl case contained the tool for tightening the lug nuts as well as the jack.

When further searching revealed nothing else that looked as if it were remotely connected to the task of changing the tire, Swann swore and sat down on the back bumper of the car to catch her breath. The trouble was, this wasn't helping matters. Reluctantly she scrambled to her feet and tried to look helpless. Maybe some kind passing motorist would come to her aid.

She waited hopefully as a Trailways bus swept past, followed at great length by a brown sedan trailing plumes of black smoke. The man driving it didn't stop, but she could hardly blame him. From the looks of the smoke billowing from his exhaust pipe, he had his own car problems.

She had the idea that the back seat of her rental car might be removable and that the necessary tools could have been stored underneath, so she opened the back door of the car and began to tug at the seat. It refused to budge. She wedged herself firmly between the back of the front seat and the back door and expended a mighty effort. The seat moved a bit, which encouraged her. She was just mustering her strength for an all-out effort when a car lurched to a stop in front of hers. The driver, who was unrecognizable due to the glare of the setting sun on the glass of the back window, appeared to do a quick double take. Then the car slowly backed up.

She couldn't believe her eyes when Paul Thompson got out of his Honda.

PAUL HAD STOPPED for gas before entering I-95. He had drunk a Coke from the machine outside the station and had chatted for a few minutes with the attendant. His spirits bolstered by the caffeine and the banter, he'd headed toward Savannah.

And then he'd come upon Swann and her incapacitated car on the side of the road.

He was alarmed because he didn't see her at first; most of her was folded into the back seat. The spare tire was lying in the weeds behind the car, and when he slowed to a stop, he saw that her right front tire was flat.

She emerged from the back seat of her car, looking disgruntled. When she saw him, she looked even more so.

He grinned at her, almost laughed. She looked guilty, like a kid playing out of school.

"Have you been following me?" she demanded.

He hadn't expected to be put on the defensive right away. "Not exactly," he said.

"What does that mean?"

"I was on my way to Savannah, and I was aware that you were in front of me. In fact, that's one reason I stopped back there at the gas station to get gas. I wanted you to get a lead. I didn't want you to think I was checking up on you." *Even though it started out that way,* he thought but did not say.

"Mmm," she said, appearing to think this over.

"Looks like you need help," he said in deliberate understatement.

"I can't find the jack that's supposed to be in the car," she said.

He walked around to the trunk, checked for the jack, and couldn't find it.

"I thought it might be under the back seat, but I can't move the seat," she explained. There was a smudge of dirt on one of her cheekbones and he fought the urge to wipe it off.

He picked up the spare. "Your spare's too flat to use," he said. "A jack won't do you any good anyway."

She pushed a finger into the side of the spare. It was decidedly flabby. "Fine," she said, "wonderful, great and groovy. I can't believe the rental company would let me take a car with no jack and a flat spare tire."

"Looks like you'd better believe it," he said mildly.

She sank down on the back seat of the car and stared disconsolately at the spare tire.

"How about giving me a lift?" she said finally and reluctantly.

Paul was enjoying this. "Into Savannah?" he asked.

"You could take me to the airport and I'll tell the rental-car people what happened. I can probably pick up another car while I'm there."

It was ironic, he thought, that he was going to spend time with her this evening anyway. And she, like it or not, had little choice but to spend time with him.

"All right," he said. He picked up the flat spare and shoved it down into the trunk, slamming the lid after it. Swann locked the car and waited for him at the side of the road.

They got into his car, and he shot her a look. She seemed edgy and wary of him, and no wonder. She probably thought he was going to ask her what she had planned to do in Savannah.

He started the car and turned the wheels back onto the highway, smiling to himself. Swann kept her head turned away, looking out the window. Water glittered between the reeds on both sides of the highway, and they passed an old man and a boy fishing in one of the channels running through the marsh. Overhead a jet from the nearby air-force base had left a white contrail; it disappeared into the fiery red sunset. Paul increased his speed and glanced at Swann.

He caught her looking at him. She tried to cover up the fact that she had been studying his profile, and this amused him. He considered starting a conversation before he thought better of it. He decided that he'd see what she'd say.

The trouble was that she didn't say anything. The miles flashed by, and she sat there with her head slightly angled away from him as if there were something to look at out there besides miles and miles of marshland.

Traffic picked up as they drew closer to Savannah. He took the exit leading toward the airport, wondering if the whole ride was going to be accomplished in dead silence.

Finally, when he couldn't stand it anymore, he slid a tape into the tape deck; it was Mick Jagger singing "Satisfaction." Swann looked slightly startled, then eased back in her seat. After a while, and to his surprise, he noticed that she was tapping her toe to the music.

"We're almost there," he said when the airport directional arrows appeared on signs at the edge of the road.

"I—I really appreciate the ride," she said stiffly. "I don't know what I would have done if you hadn't come along."

"You were lucky, all right," he agreed, keeping his eyes front and center.

For a moment she looked as though she might speak, but then she appeared to catch herself at the last minute. He drove up in front of the airport and stopped at the curb.

She looked straight at him. Her pupils were dark, and he sensed a rip in her self-composure.

"Thank you, Paul," she said.

"I'll wait until you talk with the rental-car people," he said.

"Oh no, that isn't necessary," she said firmly. She sat half in, half out of the car.

"I'm not going to leave you here. What if their office is closed? You'd be stuck at the airport with no way home."

"I'm sure everything will be all right."

"I'll wait," he insisted, settling back in his seat.

He watched her walking into the building, her hair flouncing around her shoulders. More than one guy turned to look at her. She was a beautiful woman and he was attracted to her, but there was something strange about the way she acted around him, something he had noticed from the beginning.

Paul waited five minutes, then ten, and there was still no sign of her. He began to worry that the airport security guard who kept strolling by would ask him to move his car from the passenger unloading zone to the parking lot. He craned his neck, trying to spot her inside the building.

After another five minutes, he saw her approaching the glass doors from the inside. She walked as though she was angry about something, and when she emerged from the building, two spots of color burned high on her cheeks.

He leaned over and opened the car door for her.

"Any problems?" he asked as she sat down beside him.

"I'll say. They don't have any more cars. Can you imagine that—a car-rental company with no cars to rent? Evidently there's a medical convention in town this week, and they've had a big demand. The agent said they should get some cars in by Thursday, but that's six days away! He's going to go out and get the car I left on the side of the road and get the tires fixed. I should have it tomorrow."

"So, what next?"

She closed her eyes and rubbed the bridge of her nose between her forefinger and thumb. "This is such an inconvenience. I suppose I'll have to get a taxi or something."

"A taxi all the way to Reedy Creek?"

"It's all right, I don't mind," she said wearily. She took a deep breath.

"Swann, don't be ridiculous. I'll take you home," he said.

Her eyes flew open. "Oh, I couldn't—" she began.

"I said, I'll take you home." He reached across her and yanked the door shut. His upper arm brushed hers briefly and he felt a tingle, like a current of electricity. He had thought such things happened only in books. He was attracted to her, but *electricity?* It was doubtful. *Very* doubtful.

The airport security guard appeared in his rearview mirror and scowlingly waved him out of the way. Paul started the engine and pulled away from the curb.

"We could," Paul said, testing the water, "stop for a bite to eat."

She knew what that would mean. He'd want an explanation for her cancellation of dinner. She stared out the window, wishing that she could be anywhere but in Paul's car, a captive to his earnest goodwill. She had no idea how to regain control of the evening other than to tell him what was on her mind, and things had already gone too far for that.

"I know a quiet place where the seafood is good. What do you think? Unless you don't like seafood," he said, mindful that her reason for ducking out of dinner at his house tonight could have had something to do with not liking shrimp.

"I like it," she said, resigning herself. She had never expected to have to explain anything to him; she hadn't given a thought to being caught in her fib. Her most recent fib, that is. If only she hadn't agreed to eat dinner with him in the first place, she wouldn't be in this situation. If only the spare tire had had air in it, if only— But what was the use? Here she was, caught in a web of her own weaving, and here she would stay until he decided to take her home.

He drove to the restaurant, which was located adjacent to a commercial fishing dock where water lapped at the bottoms of the deserted trawlers and seabirds spiraled over-head in search of part of the day's catch.

After they were seated at a small table overlooking the water, they ordered drinks.

"Now," he said. "Something is on your mind. What is it?"

You, she wanted to say, but she couldn't. His expression had softened, and his eyes invited intimacy.

She couldn't tell him everything, because she didn't want him to hate her. Not that she thought he would, but he'd certainly be angry, and she didn't want to risk even that.

Her eyes searched his. *Oh, boy within the man,* she thought, *I felt a bond with you all those years ago. And heaven help me, I still feel it even now.*

The boy had been compassionate, kind and empathetic. The man was no different. The bond she'd always felt so strongly had strengthened in these past few days, had become something important in her life. It was no longer possible to ignore the way she was beginning to feel about him, yet she was afraid to admit it even to herself.

These were the things that were on her mind, but putting them into words wasn't possible. She stared at him blankly, wondering what to say.

He leaned across the table. "Why did you leave that cowardly little message on my answering machine? It's pretty clear to me that you didn't really have anything important to do."

"Oh," she said, and stared off into space.

"I like being with you. Unless I'm misreading the signals, you feel the same way about me."

She felt suddenly breathless, and she inhaled deeply.

"This is the part where you're supposed to agree with me," he said, the suggestion of a smile touching his lips. "Unless, of course, you don't feel that way."

She shifted uncomfortably in her chair. "Oh, I do. It's just that...that..." and she found herself at a loss for words. She couldn't possibly tell him that she needed to get to know

him for the sake of the biography she wanted to write and
that the way she was beginning to feel about him posed a
threat to that project. She didn't like feeling deceitful; she
wished everything could be out in the open. But how could
it be when he never mentioned anything about his childhood as Child Michael?

Their dinner arrived, saving her from explaining. They
had both ordered the swordfish, and for a while Swann
picked at her food. Their discussion seemed not to have affected Paul's appetite at all, and he appeared to have
dropped the subject. When the waiter removed their plates,
Swann's had barely been touched.

"Dessert?" Paul asked.

She shook her head, and he paid the check.

Stars were beginning to wink through the darkening sky.
The scent of brine and tar wafted upward from the docks.
Swann seemed troubled, and Paul wished she would open up
and talk to him. If he took her home as she'd requested,
there was little chance that this would happen.

"Let's go for a short drive before we go home," he said.

When she didn't object, they got in his car, and he headed
downtown. They passed the Savannah City Hall, its silvery
dome towering over the surrounding trees. Behind the city
hall, old warehouses on the Savannah River had been re-
furbished into shops and stores. A bumper-to-bumper line
of cars clogged River Street, young people out cruising for
the evening.

"We should get out and walk," he said, and without
waiting for her reply, he pulled into a parking space. She
made no objection when he hurried around and opened the
door for her. She felt leaden and zombielike in his presence. She wished she'd never started this; she wished she
were back home in Philadelphia. All she could hope was
that he'd get tired of her near-catatonic state and find it so
disagreeable that he'd take her home.

They entered the throng surging along River Street, stopping from time to time to look in the windows of the

boutiques along the way. They passed a coffeehouse where a man was playing a guitar.

"Shall we?" he said, and he held the door open for her. With a sense of impending doom, she preceded him inside. They sat at a tiny table, their knees touching because it was so crowded. They both ordered espresso, and they watched the couples dancing on the floor. It reminded Swann of dancing with Paul at Linda and Rick's party; they had moved so well together as though they were practiced partners.

"Let's dance," he said, his hand on her arm, and before she knew it they had moved effortlessly to the dance floor and he was holding her in his arms.

Within his embrace, the misery she felt at her own deceit dwindled and lost importance. What was important now and what filled her whole consciousness was Paul—the reality of him. She relaxed, felt fluid, followed his lead. Paul's arms around her seemed to shut out the rest of the world, making them a magical unit unto themselves in the crowded, smoky little coffeehouse. Nothing else, nothing at all, mattered now.

Usually when she danced, Swann kept track of what music was playing, but tonight she didn't care. She barely noticed the strumming of the guitar or the others on the tiny dance floor. She looked up at Paul once to see that he was gazing down at her, a look of quiet pleasure on his face. His eyelashes were tipped in gold and cast feathery shadows on his cheeks when they briefly danced into the path of a spotlight.

Her heartbeat quickened, and she looked away. He tightened his embrace and pulled her closer, and she felt her body ease intimately into the contours of his. His left hand brought her right hand to his chest and placed it there so that he could briefly drift his fingertips along the softness of her cheek in silent communion. She lifted her face to his, and she knew that if they had been alone, he would have kissed her.

"Let's get out of here," he said, his voice rough in her ear.

He tossed a bill down on the table, and they hurried out. Swann felt numb; she had never felt so ready to be kissed.

Outside, the heat and humidity washed over them in a wave. People hurried past, and the raucous music from a bar down the street assaulted their ears.

Paul groped for her hand and found it. He pulled her along after him.

"Paul?" she said, scarcely feeling the pavement beneath her feet.

They stopped amid the swirling pedestrians.

"I had to get out of there," he said, though there was no need to explain.

"I know."

"I never knew dancing could be so intimate."

"I know that, too."

"Over here," Paul said, pulling her into a space between two buildings. It was shadowed and dark, but they were in view of anyone who chanced to look in their direction. His heart beat beneath his skin, she could feel it, and the wind rushed in her ears, although the air was calm and still.

He lifted her chin with the tips of his fingers and gazed deep into her eyes for a long time. She knew his eyes; they were the ones she had so often seen in her dreams all these years since the night at Miracle Farm.

His lips descended to hers, and his kiss was warm. It suspended time and space and sharpened the longing deep inside her. He lengthened the kiss, then deepened it, and she clung to him while the world spun around them.

When he released her lips, he stroked her hair thoughtfully, then kissed her lightly above the ear.

"We can't stay here," he said.

"Where do you suggest we go?"

"Back to Reedy Creek. We can talk along the way."

She felt anticipation and excitement swirling in the pit of her stomach, and for a moment—only a moment—she longed for the return of her own good sense. It seemed to have evaporated when Paul Thompson pulled her into his arms back there on the dance floor. It wasn't as though she didn't know what she was doing. They were both adults, and as sure as spring followed winter, she knew what would happen if they spent any more time together.

The lights from the restaurant next door cast a pink glow on his face. She reached up and wonderingly traced his eyebrow, his cheekbone, the line of his chin.

"What's happening to me?" she whispered, half to herself.

He caught her hand and pressed it against his cheek. "The same thing that's happening to me, lady. And whatever it is, I like it. I like it a lot." And he kissed her once more, this time with ineffable tenderness.

Chapter Six

Traffic on the interstate highway was light, and Paul kept his arm around her as he drove. Lights from oncoming cars illuminated their faces, and talk seemed unnecessary. But after they left I-95, Swann realized that some things needed to be said before they reached her house, and it was going to be up to her to say them. Paul seemed thoughtful as he drove, but at last she felt at ease with him as she never had before.

"I've only known you for a couple of days," she said, but as soon as she said it she regretted the statement. In reality she had known him ever since she was five years old. How could she explain that long-ago rush of emotion, and even if she did, was there any validity to a five-year-old's feelings?

"You don't want to rush things. Is that what you're saying?"

"When we were dancing..." she said, and then didn't know how to finish the sentence.

"Ah, when we were dancing," he agreed as if that explained everything.

And maybe, she thought, it did.

When they arrived at the cottage, she was still trying to figure out whether or not to invite him in. If she offered him, say, a cup of coffee, he could very well construe that invitation as a come-on. Yet she didn't want the evening to end. She also didn't want him to expect to spend the night. It was going to be hard to find the middle ground.

He stopped the car at the edge of the driveway, out of the direct glare of the porch light. As the engine died, he reached out and pulled her closer. For a moment he gazed down at her, a quicksilver half smile illuminating his face, and then he scattered a line of tiny kisses along her cheekbone. Her breath caught in her throat, but she was melting against him. Her breasts pressed into his chest, and she was instantly aware that this would arouse him. She pulled away, but he caught her face between his two hands and lowered his mouth to hers.

His tongue traced her lips lightly, and then he pressed his lips to hers. His mouth was soft, soft and wet, and she lost herself in the sweet sensations. Her hands slid tentatively to his shoulders, then went around his neck as he clasped her to him. Her head whirled; she was growing dizzy.

He made himself pull back from the situation and look at it clearly. It wasn't easy, since kissing her was something that he had been longing to do ever since this afternoon. Or longer, really. Since the night he'd sat with her in the Little Bit after the CPR class.

But he sensed she didn't want to rush things. He had to respect that because he respected her.

"Swann," he said. She rested her head on his shoulder. He felt her heart beating erratically against his chest.

"I'm not going to pressure you," he said softly against her hair. "I mean, this isn't going to go any further until and unless you want it to. I can't have you leaving messages on my answering machine, running away because you think I'm a threat."

She stirred against his shoulder and sat up. Her eyes were wide in the light from the porch.

"Paul, I won't do that again. It's just that there are— there are so many things to think about."

"For instance?"

"Where we're headed. What's happening. Why we're doing this." *And who you are, and why it matters,* she thought, but she didn't say it.

He laughed low in his throat. "Why we're doing this? That's pretty obvious, isn't it?"

"Chemistry, you mean?"

"I used to be pretty good at chemistry," he said, kissing her eyelids.

"You still are," she murmured.

He kissed her again, and she sighed against his lips when he released her.

"You'd better get inside. It's starting to rain," he said softly.

She looked at the windshield. It was starred with tiny raindrops glinting in the light from the porch.

"I'll walk you to the door," he said.

"Oh, there's no need," she said. Her lips felt the way they did when she drank champagne.

"But I want to," he told her. She opened the door on her side of the car, but he jumped out and hurried around to hold it for her. He slid his arm around her shoulders, and after a moment's hesitation, she put hers around his waist. They walked slowly through the falling splinters of rain, matching their footsteps along the damp path.

"I'll see you tomorrow," he promised as she fumbled with her keys. Finally he took them from her, found the right key on the first try, and slid it into the lock. Then he kissed her lightly on the forehead and loped down the porch steps and back to his car. His hair was misted with raindrops and stood out from his head in a golden aureole.

"'Bye," he called before driving away.

Swann watched him from the door, wondering what effect, if any, having a love affair with her subject would have on the biography of Child Michael that she now wanted to write more than anything in the world.

SO SHE HADN'T HAD TO FACE the issue of inviting him in after all, Swann thought as she turned on the lights inside the cottage. She should have felt relieved, but at the moment all she felt was a kind of letdown.

Joe-the-Cat twined around her ankles mewing for food. She should have saved him some of the swordfish from dinner, but she hadn't thought of it at the time. She hadn't been able to think of anything but her burgeoning relationship with Paul, and now that she was at home, it was no different. She had an idea that he'd be on her mind a lot from now on.

The telephone rang after Swann finished pouring kitten chow into the dish for Joe. The sound jarred her to reality. She hurried into the bedroom and snatched up the receiver on the second ring.

"Swann? Hi, it's Gracie. Where've you been? I've been calling for hours!"

Swann sank back onto the pillows and swung her legs up onto the bed.

"Oh, I went to Savannah," she said.

"By yourself?"

"Well, no, actually I went with, um, a friend."

"Good—I'm glad you've made friends there. Did you do anything interesting?"

"Sort of."

"Sort of? Must you sound so mysterious? Who was this friend?"

"He's the subject of the biography I'm going to write."

"Going to write? Since when? I thought you were merely there to check it out. You didn't seem particularly interested in the guy before you left here. Who is he, anyway? Some kind of psychic?"

"No, it's a man named Paul Thompson," Swann said.

"Gosh, I've never heard of him."

"You might know him as Child Michael."

"Child Michael, Child Michael. Oh, sure, seems to me I do recall something about him. He was a healer of some sort, wasn't he?"

"Yes. The prospect of writing his biography is more interesting than I thought."

"Who would have guessed that you'd be gung ho to write about the life of some old geezer like that? Honestly, Swann, I thought you wanted to write about politicians."

"I did before I met Paul Thompson, and anyhow, he's not an old geezer. He was only a kid when he conducted those healings. And Gracie, he doesn't know that I know who he is. He's never once mentioned anything about his childhood."

"How old is he, anyway?"

"He's thirty. And nice."

"Nice? And only a year older than you are? Say, Swann, exactly how nice *is* he?"

"I like him."

"Now that's a fine how-do-you-do. I called to tell you that Nolan's college roommate is here, and I showed him your picture. He's terrific, Swann, and he wants to meet you. I was hoping you could fly up here for a weekend."

"Oh," Swann said. The prospect was unappealing. Another weekend, and she might be able to draw Paul out enough to talk about his childhood. Another weekend, and perhaps she could reveal her true purpose in Reedy Creek, ending the subterfuge between them once and for all.

"Well? Take it from me, Nolan's friend is charming. And lonely. He hasn't had a relationship with anyone in a while, so he's available."

"I'm sorry, Gracie, I don't think so. I need to stay in Reedy Creek and get to know Paul. You see, he doesn't suspect that my reason for coming here was to check him out as a prospective subject for my next biography. Somehow I need to make him open up to me, and I'm just getting to know him. It wouldn't be a good idea for me to leave now."

"I see," Gracie said slowly. Swann could almost hear the wheels inside her brain churning out speculations.

"I promised Justin," Swann said too quickly.

"Swann, my inborn fib detector just set off an alarm. What's going on between you and Paul Thompson?"

Swann stared at the ceiling for a long moment.

"Swann?"

"I don't know what's happening with us," she admitted finally. "There's an undeniable physical attraction, and he's different from the men I usually go out with. Also, I can't figure out what he's doing in Reedy Creek. He's working as an emergency paramedic, but I have an idea that he's capable of so much more. I like his friends, but they seem settled into the most mundane kind of life here, and I can't imagine Paul getting into backyard barbecues or buying bunk beds for the kids. In that crowd, he seems like he's on the outside looking in."

"Hmm," Gracie said. "You sound intrigued by him."

"I am. There are so many things I want to know about Paul. For instance, what has he been doing in the years since he left Miracle Farm? And how did he end up becoming a paramedic? And why is he in Reedy Creek?"

"I can see that you're going to be busy prying those secrets out of him," Gracie observed.

"I don't want to pry. I want him to *want* to tell me."

Gracie laughed. "If you make him fall in love with you, he certainly will. In fact, you probably won't be able to stop him from talking about himself. You know, men are so narcissistic. They all actually seem to think that we *want* to hear about the time they built a science project out of 3,526 Popsicle sticks and shellacked it and left it lying on the dining room table so that it ruined the varnish and their father came home and sent them to bed without any supper. I mean, with the men I've dated, I've heard dozens of similar stories, haven't you?"

"I suppose so, but that's the strange thing about Paul. He *never* tells stories about himself. Never," Swann said.

"Well, your strategy should be to make him fall for you and fall hard."

"It would be different if I didn't care anything about him, Gracie, but I like the guy. I couldn't deceive him," Swann said unhappily.

"You told me a few minutes ago that he doesn't know the real reason that you're in Reedy Creek. If that doesn't qualify as deception, I don't know what does."

"I know," Swann said with a sigh. "I've been feeling guilty about it ever since I met him. Yet I don't see how I can tell him, since it would almost certainly mean that he'd run as fast as he could. He seems to have guarded his true identity so carefully that no one knows who he really is."

"All I can say is that you seem to have your work cut out for you. And I did hope you'd come to the shore so you could meet Burt. That's Nolan's college roommate's name."

"Thanks for asking me," Swann said lamely.

"Oh, well, maybe you'll catch up with him later."

"Maybe," Swann said, but she doubted it.

"Swann, before I forget. Your father called."

"He did?" This was a surprise; her father never called.

"I wasn't here, and Burt answered the phone. You know I'm having my calls forwarded from Philadelphia, don't you? Your dad wanted to know your Reedy Creek telephone number."

"Did you give it to him?"

"Like I say, I didn't talk with him. Burt didn't know your Reedy Creek number, so he asked him to call back later. He never did."

"Was it an emergency? Some kind of problem?" Visions of an automobile accident or a fire at home popped into her head.

"No, I don't think so. I quizzed Burt pretty thoroughly. He said your father just sounded like a lonely old man."

"Lonely? Dad? That's ridiculous. He's always got a girl hanging on his arm."

"If he calls back, I'll give him your number unless you'd rather I didn't. In the meantime, you could call him."

Swann was doubtful. Chances are if her father had called her, he only wanted to chastise her for something.

"You can tell him where I am if you like, but I have no intention of phoning him. Every time I try to make contact with him, it ends in disaster."

"Suit yourself, Swann. Oh, did I tell you that Nolan took Burt and me up in a Cessna the other day? We flew out over the ocean," and Gracie was off on another tangent leaving Swann to wonder what on earth her father could have wanted.

She and Gracie chatted for a few more minutes before they hung up. As she prepared for bed, Swann shut Evan's puzzling phone call out of her mind and wondered what Paul was doing now. She tried to picture what his house was like; she kept trying to imagine a setting that was suitable for him. Did he live in a small house or a big one? Was it tastefully decorated? Did he live with rental furniture, Salvation Army thrift store gleanings, or something more substantial? The way he lived would provide her with even more clues to his character.

She set her alarm for early the next morning because she had promised Angelyn to go see the otters with her. But she didn't fall asleep for a long time because she was reliving the evening with Paul.

AT THE SOUND of the alarm, Joe-the-Cat leaped onto the bed and marched straight to Swann's pillow where he sniffed at her eyelids and batted at her mouth with one paw. Swann brushed him away and buried her head under the pillow, whereupon the kitten uttered one plaintive mew.

Swann shot out an arm to silence the clock's annoying beep. She slid from under the pillow and sat up, regretting her promise to Angelyn to go with her to see the otters. Still, she had given her word, and after a moment she peeled back the covers and reached out one hand to part the curtains at the window.

The creek was shrouded in pearly gray mist, and the sun had not yet risen over the opposite bank. Dew glittered like jewels on the grass, and the birds were waking noisily in the tall pine trees in the woods.

Later, it would be hot, perhaps unbearably so, but now the air was cool and sweet-scented. Swann slid out from under the covers and pulled on jeans and a T-shirt as quickly as she could, forgoing breakfast in favor of a quick glass of orange juice. Then, leaving Joe on the porch, she slipped out of the house and set foot along the path to Angelyn's.

Her clothes were damp with mist and dew by the time she rounded the curve, but she felt the spirit of adventure as she saw Angelyn tiptoe quietly out the front door of her little house. She waved, and Angelyn smiled and warned her with a forefinger to her lips not to speak.

Swann caught up with Angelyn near the creek..

"I didn't want you to wake the kids," Angelyn whispered when they were out of earshot of the house.

"What if they wake up while you're gone?"

"We'll be close by and I'll hear them, but they'll sleep for another half an hour or so."

They walked quietly along the creek bank. The mist had lifted slightly, but bits of it hung in the treetops like trailing scarves.

"Hush, now, we're almost there," Angelyn whispered. She held back the damp undergrowth so that Swann could step through it into a small clearing in sight of the house. Swann's sneakers sank almost to the canvas in mud, and by this time the legs of her jeans were soaked with dew.

"Over here," Angelyn beckoned, and at her direction they crouched down behind a fallen tree.

"Watch," Angelyn said, pointing at the opposite bank.

At first all Swann could see was the sluggish water of the creek purling around the reeds at the bank. Beneath the encroaching shrubbery, the water was shadowed and dark.

Then, suddenly, she saw a slight disturbance of the water, and a sleek pointed head appeared momentarily before slipping beneath the surface. Angelyn shot her a look of pure delight, and Swann nodded to let her know that she had seen.

There was another flick of the water, so brief that it might have been the creek shifting in its course, but Swann spotted what might have been a carefree fillip of a tail, and then a svelte shape arced above the water, slipping back into it again just as quickly. Now there were lots of shiny sleek bodies swirling over and around each other; bright eyes darted, small heads swiveled and the rays of the rising sun glinted off shiny brown fur as the otters gamboled together in their water games.

"They're beautiful," Swann mouthed silently to Angelyn, and Angelyn nodded happily.

If they noticed the intruders, the otters gave no sign. They seemed intent on their amusements. Swann was reminded of Stropstripe and Joe-the-Cat at play; only, this frolic of the otters was much more intricate and engrossing.

Swann and Angelyn continued to watch unobserved as the sun peeked over the trees and began to cast dappled rays across the otters' playground. At last Angelyn gestured that it was time to go, and Swann followed her as she led the way back to her house.

"I'm so glad I went with you," Swann said softly as she prepared to bid Angelyn goodbye.

"Me, too. Oh, I hear Rhonda—she's ready for her cereal. Would you like to come in?"

Swann hesitated. She was reluctant to intrude, but a cup of coffee would taste good after crouching in the damp mist near the creek, and she wasn't eager to hurry back to her own cottage where whatever breakfast she managed to throw together would have to be eaten alone.

"I'd like that," Swann replied and was rewarded by Angelyn's brilliant smile. She had realized before that Angelyn was hungry for adult company, but perhaps she hadn't fathomed the depth of this woman's loneliness. Swann's heart went out to her, and she followed her up the steps, thinking that there must be something more useful that she could do for Angelyn besides present her children with a kitten.

She watched while Angelyn efficiently prepared breakfast, and she even lent a hand by pouring the kids' milk and supervising their feeding of Stropstripe. Afterward, she and Angelyn lingered over coffee, although Swann only accepted one of the homemade biscuits Angelyn offered. She gave Angelyn the excuse that she was dieting, but her real reason was that she now realized that food in this household was a precious commodity, and she didn't want to be the reason that any of them did without.

Swann left the Soames house around nine o'clock after extracting assurances that the Soameses would visit her tomorrow for lunch.

Back at the cottage, Swann spent most of the morning noting last night's impressions of Paul on three-by-five-inch cards, omitting what Gracie would have called "the good parts." She certainly saw no reason to detail the moments when he had kissed her, but she carefully included the information about how he had stopped to lend a hand when he saw her stranded at the side of the road, how he had seemed to enjoy the guitar music in the coffeehouse, and she noted that he was a good dancer.

That afternoon she ran out of things to write on note cards and looked around for something to do to fill in the time until Paul arrived—something that would do nothing to raise his suspicions.

Her eyes fell on the photo album she had brought from home, and she decided that she might as well start working on it. She pulled it out of the file drawer and began to organize the pictures of her family in an orderly sequence.

There was the picture of her and her mother on a trip to Niagara Falls; it was the last trip they had taken together before her mother's illness. And this one—it was of Margarita, who had not been so plump in those days and had laughed when Swann wanted to take her picture. "Oh, I am sure you can find someone else to take pictures of," Margarita had said, but in any case, she had posed beside a rosebush in the garden.

Swann became so absorbed in her task that she missed the crunch of Paul's car wheels on the driveway and didn't realize he had arrived until she saw him at the door.

"Hi," he said, when she looked up, and at the sound of his voice her heart flipped over. She stood up, heedless of the photos on her lap, and they slid to the floor, fanning out in a swirl around her feet. He saw it happen, and he said, "Sorry if I startled you."

"Come in," she told him.

"I'd better help you pick these up," he said, bending over and scooping up several of the pictures.

"I'll do it," Swann said as their hands met in a moment of confusion when she didn't know whether to let the snapshot go or to tug it from between his fingers.

"Hey, let me see that," he said.

She relinquished the picture and proceeded to gather up several others.

"This is you, isn't it? How old were you?"

"Oh, thirteen or so," she said. The picture was one that her mother had taken of her. She was standing in front of Niagara Falls, smiling into the sunlight.

"You were just as pretty then as you are now," he told her.

"Thank you," she said, wondering if he were only being polite; she'd been a pale stick of a girl at that age. Something in her voice must have communicated this uncertainty, because he sat down on the couch beside her and said, "No, I mean it."

He picked up another picture and laughed. "Now that's an interesting variation of the old bearskin rug," he said.

Swann saw that he was holding a picture of her naked six-month-old self sprawled amid a profusion of flowers. No background, no toys—just flowers.

She felt her cheeks redden before she snatched the picture and buried it between the pages of the album.

"Baby pictures by that particular photographer were all the rage that year," she explained. "He went out and bought fresh flowers and arranged them so that they looked disarranged, then plunked the baby down in the middle of them and snapped away. My mother always regretted having that picture taken. I got some kind of terrible rash from the plants."

"What's that one?" Paul asked.

"This is a picture of our house. It's an estate outside Philadelphia."

"It's a beautiful house," he said.

Swann supposed that other people would consider the house beautiful, and perhaps it was, but her judgment of it was clouded by her feelings. She had never been happy there, and so the vast gray limestone edifice with its slate roof, long windows and porticoes had only seemed oppressive to her while she was growing up. Still, it had been her mother's dream house, and Mimi had had impeccable taste in everything except husbands.

"Who's this?" Paul asked, holding out a picture of her father.

"My dad," she answered.

"Oh, I see a certain resemblance. You must be very close to him."

"Not exactly," Swann answered. She took the picture of her formidable father from him and closed the album with what she hoped was finality.

"Are you close to your father?" she asked, hoping to trick him into revealing something about his family situation.

"He died," Paul said. He stood up and walked to the porch. "I'd better get started on the boat," he said.

Paul had given her no opening to ask any further questions. She followed him out onto the porch and stood close behind him. "If you have another scraper, I'll help," she offered.

He turned, smiling. "Are you sure you want to?"

"Of course. *If* you can promise me those shrimp I missed last night."

He casually draped an arm over her shoulders. "It's a deal." He took his arm away and headed out the door. "I'll get a scraper out of my car trunk," he called over his shoulder.

They worked on the boat for the rest of the afternoon. The sun disappeared behind thunderclouds rolling in from the west, but the clouds passed to the south and did not threaten the town of Reedy Creek. Nevertheless, the humidity was high, and by the time Paul called a halt to the work, Swann felt sticky with perspiration. She held her hair up with one hand and fanned her neck with the other.

"Hot, isn't it?" Paul sympathized.

She nodded and kept on fanning.

Paul tossed their scrapers on the grass. "I know a remedy," he said. Quickly he stripped off his shirt and, wearing only his shorts, waded into the creek. He glanced at her over his shoulder. "Come on in," he said.

"I didn't think it was okay to swim in there," she said. "I mean, aren't there leeches? Snakes?" She felt like Katharine Hepburn in *The African Queen,* recoiling from the very thought of swimming in this semitropical creek.

"Not a leech in sight," he told her, walking in deeper. The water was only as high as his waist.

"I should put on a swimsuit," she said. She stepped gingerly onto the sandy shore and touched a tentative toe to the water. The temperature was tepid, but it was so much cooler than the air that it felt wonderful.

"A suit's too much trouble. Just roll up the legs of your jeans."

"Too bad I didn't wear shorts," she said as she followed his suggestion.

Paul privately thought so, too, but he held his tongue. He splashed water on his chest, then cupped his hands and brought a handful to his face. When he looked up, Swann had waded in almost to her knees.

"How would I know if a leech were on my leg?" she asked with a grimace.

Paul laughed. "I promise that there aren't leeches. The most you should watch out for is the sharp points of branches or perhaps broken glass under the water," he cautioned.

"Ugh, that might be worse," she said, making a face.

"Don't worry, I'm a paramedic, remember?"

She studied him enviously. "I wish I were you," she said. "You look so comfortable."

He submerged to his shoulders. "The water *does* feel good," he told her.

"Oh, what the heck," she said, and, surprising him, she plunged into deeper water, sending a spray of water flying. She had decided to join him fully clothed.

"That's the spirit," he said approvingly. "Although swimming in the creek does seem incongruous for a society girl from Philadelphia."

"Society girl? Is that what I am?" She lazed backward in the water, letting it buoy her up.

"Aren't you?"

"I work for a living," she said.

"Your father is one of the most-admired businessmen in the United States. Everyone knows he's amassed a fortune."

"That's true. I admit that I have a trust fund. Would you believe me if I told you that I haven't touched the money since I got my advance for the biography of Winky Tapps? I'm able to live on what I earn."

Paul's eyebrows lifted. "Why? You could live very well on the money from the trust fund, I should think."

"I could and I did, but I always knew that once I could pay my own way, I would." She didn't tell him that she loathed the idea of living on her father's money.

"What happens to the money?"

"It accumulates. I donate some of it to worthwhile causes."

He turned his head to look at her. "That's unusual, I'm sure. Most people in your situation wouldn't feel so strongly about supporting themselves."

She shrugged, but the effect of the gesture was somewhat diluted by the water flowing around her shoulders. "I've always worked, first as a staffer on a short-lived regional magazine, and then for *Main Line Magazine*."

"And now you're hard at work on another book," he observed, gazing up at the tree branches overhead.

"Mmm," she said noncommittally. "And how about you, Paul? How did you become a paramedic?"

"Oh, it just happened," he said vaguely.

This time Swann was prepared to press him for an answer. "Did you wake up one day and think, 'Today I'm going to study to be a paramedic,' or what?"

"It seemed to be the easiest thing to do at the time," he said, moving upstream and away from her. He turned his back to her and took a few tentative breaststrokes against the current. The water was too shallow for any real swimming, and he quit, but now he was ten feet or more away from her.

"What kind of education does becoming a paramedic require?"

Watching Paul's aloof reaction to her question, Swann felt as though a glass wall had suddenly sprung up between them. They could see each other, but they were effectively separated.

"Oh, I took a course at a technical college. Say, it's getting late. I need to get home and thaw out those shrimp. I put them in the freezer yesterday when I found out you weren't going to be there for dinner." Paul waded toward the bank, and the wave he created rocked gently against Swann's chest.

Swann reluctantly followed him out of the water, conscious that her T-shirt clung too tightly to her figure. She clasped her arms across her breasts, shivering slightly even though the air was still warm.

But Paul didn't notice. He bent to retrieve the scrapers they had used on the boat and continued on his way. He hadn't looked at her since wading out of the water, and now he was halfway up the slope to the house.

He hurried around the house to his car, and she walked into the cottage where she wrapped herself in a towel. When she heard the slam of the Honda's trunk, she hurried to the front door.

"I'll be back and pick you up in about two hours, okay?" Paul called from where he stood beside his car.

Swann pushed the door open and stepped inside, unwilling to anger him by commenting on the way he had managed to distance himself from her. The undeniable message he was sending was, *Don't try to get too close.*

Still, he wanted to see her tonight. So what all of this probably meant was that he wanted to see her, but he didn't want to discuss certain topics.

Okay, if that was the way it was going to be, so be it. He would, she was sure, communicate more readily once he learned to trust her; in order to trust her, he'd have to believe that she was no threat.

But I am a threat, she thought broodingly as she went to get ready. If she persisted in writing a biography of Paul Thompson, né Child Michael, she would blow his cover.

And that would utterly change the safe and secure life he had built for himself in Reedy Creek.

Chapter Seven

Paul lived in a shingled bungalow set far back from the street in the middle of town. As his car drew to a stop outside, he told her that he rented the house from an owner who lived in Savannah.

The exterior was a cheerful yellow with black shutters flanking the windows; inside, the rooms were painted a soft ivory. The floors were hardwood, and the furniture was a mix of several good pieces, like the beveled-glass curio cabinet in the living room. Books were everywhere, piled on the table in front of the couch, ranged in a massive bookcase along one wall.

"I told you I like to read," he said when he saw her looking at them. "See, here's your book. Why don't you autograph it for me?"

"Oh, but I—"

"Please. I wish you would," he said.

She took the pen he offered and wrote, "For Paul, a special person." She signed it, "Swann." When she handed the book back to him, he looked at what she'd written.

"You didn't sign your last name," he said, sounding disappointed.

"How many Swanns do you know?" she said with a smile, but she took the book back and added her surname.

"That's better," he said, shelving the book in a prominent place.

Now Paul was very much the warm, welcoming host, and not a trace of his standoffishness remained. The whole time she ate the dinner he had prepared, Swann tried to maintain her own objective observation of Paul Thompson, but it was impossible with him sitting across from her, smiling at the things she said and gazing at her with intent interest when she spoke.

After a while he glanced quickly at his watch. "It's seven o'clock—I'm now officially on call," he said.

"I didn't know you'd have to work tonight."

"I'm unexpectedly filling in for a co-worker whose wife is having a baby. If my beeper goes off, I'm afraid I'll have to leave."

"You really like what you do, don't you?" she asked.

"Yes, of course. Oh, I know it's kind of a dead-end job, but it gives me a good feeling to be able to do it. I have to admit, though, that sometimes the work is hard to deal with."

"What do you mean?"

"It can be frustrating when I arrive too late on the scene to help a sick or injured person," he said.

Her head shot up, and she studied his face. She couldn't help thinking, *But why don't you use your healing powers?* Her knowledge of how he had helped Kathy was still unspoken between them, but she was sure that he was thinking of it, too.

He saw that she was watching him. He put his fork down and passed the shrimp. "More?" he said, his expression completely blank.

"Thank you," she said, and then stared at him.

"Here, let me," he offered, and while he spooned out shrimp, she rapidly recovered her equilibrium.

"I should think," she said carefully, "that you'd grow accustomed to losing some patients. Maybe even hardened to it."

"Hardened? Never. I'm a paramedic because I like helping people. As for losing some patients, I know it's inevitable. Our lifesaving methods can't always work. Still, each and every time a patient dies, I feel the loss for days. The last one was especially difficult.''

"Who was it?''

"A few days ago, a man about my age, a truck driver, died in an accident. When we arrived, he was going into deep shock. He said, 'Please don't let me die.' When the breath went out of him, there wasn't a thing I could do about it.''

"I'm sorry,'' Swann said.

"It happens that way sometimes. Like I said, it's never easy. We have our successes, too. A two-year-old kid fell into a pond last week, and we arrived in time to save him. The look on the mother's face when we told her that the boy was going to be all right was worth a month's pay.''

"I'm sure it was,'' she said. Had he used his healing powers on the boy? And if so, what could be his reason for *not* using them on the man who had been in the truck accident?

Paul pushed his chair back from the table. "Let's leave the dishes here and walk down to my friend Bo's house. I've promised to pick up his newspaper for him until he gets home from his vacation.''

He took her hand and led her outside. As they walked, she couldn't stop wondering why some people—like Kathy—were apparently the recipients of Paul's special healing skills and some weren't. She couldn't believe that he would willingly let anyone die. Was he reluctant to practice his powers when onlookers might give his secret away? Somehow she was sure that Paul wouldn't let anyone die for such a petty reason.

The humid air was scented with the heavy, sweet fragrance of jasmine. The night was quiet, with the residents of the street sequestered in their air-conditioned homes. Overhead stars gleamed against a background of deep blue, and a full moon peeped out from behind a wisp of cloud.

Paul swung their clasped hands between them as they walked. Their footsteps made no sound on the sidewalk; they felt isolated from the rest of the world.

"Your friend Bo—I haven't met him, have I?" Swann asked.

"No, he's been away since you got here. Ordinarily he would have been at Linda and Rick's party."

"Is he single or married?"

He grinned down at her. "Why? Are you interested in him?"

"I'm interested in all your friends," she said.

"What did you think of Linda and Rick and that group?"

"I liked them," she said. She hesitated. She saw that he was watching her expectantly as if waiting for further comment. "They seem different from you, though."

"I suppose they are," he said. He went on to tell her how he was a fairly recent member of their group. "Most of the time I think they've accepted me only on sufferance," he said, and he was serious, not joking.

"Really? I don't think that at all. They're fond of you," she replied.

He fell silent. "Sometimes it seems that they expect something more of me. I always figured it was that they wanted me to be more a part of the group. Often I make excuses not to go fishing with the guys or not to go to their parties. It's hard for them to accept that I like a lot of time alone."

Maybe you don't want any of them getting too close to you, either, Swann thought. It was hard not to say the words out loud.

Paul bent and picked up the newspaper from underneath a palmetto tree at the edge of Bo's driveway.

"Let me check the mailbox, too," he said. He ran up the porch stairs and returned in a minute with a handful of envelopes. He tucked those and the paper under his arm and took her hand again.

"It's such a pretty night. Mind if we take the long way home?"

"Not at all," she said.

"I often walk in this neighborhood," he said. "It's so peaceful."

By this time Swann had a pretty good idea what Paul's day-to-day life must be like. He worked his assigned shifts for the local rescue squad, engaged in normal after-work activities, had a circle of friends with whom he didn't feel particularly close, and, as far as she could tell, had no woman in his life at the moment. Altogether it was an unremarkable life, similar to that led by thousands of other people, and yet he had once been famous. She wanted to know what paths had led him to this out-of-the-way village.

The park was a small playground complete with swings, jungle gym and a brick structure sheltering a picnic table. They found a bench beneath a spreading tree where Paul sat down and indicated that she should, too. The ground beneath their feet had been raked clean recently, and the tines of the rake had left a swirling pattern in the sand. Swann traced one of the swirls with the toe of her shoe, using the same foot that Child Michael had healed back at Miracle Farm. She wondered what Paul's reaction would be if she told him that.

"How about you? Do you have lots of friends back home?" he asked.

She smiled. "Gracie Upthegrove is my best friend. I've known her since we both worked together on *Main Line Magazine*. We're part of a circle of women who have been supportive of each others' endeavors for many years."

"No male friends?"

"Oh, of course, but no one special. There hasn't been for a long time."

"I don't know whether to commiserate or cheer," he said with a wry smile.

She laughed. "My friend Gracie is always trying to set me up with someone. It never seems to work out."

"I think I'll cheer," he said, raising her hand to his lips and kissing the back of it gently. The kiss sent shivers down her spine.

"At the moment, I'm glad there isn't anyone else, too," she said softly.

He tipped her face gently toward his. "Let's walk back to the house," he said.

He had left the front door unlocked, and he held it open for her. She ducked beneath his arm to enter, and he tossed the newspaper and letters on a hall table.

The air-conditioned house seemed inordinately cool after the warmth and humidity outside. Swann turned to Paul, planning to comment on the difference in temperature, and without a word he took her in his arms. Her own arms went around him in a gesture so natural that it was as though she had embraced him many times before. His muscles tensed slightly as he pulled her even closer. "I could hold you like this forever," he said. There was an underlying tone of amazement in his voice.

She sighed and lifted her face to receive his kiss. His lips were warm and firm against hers, and she closed her eyes in order to savor the pleasure of it. He took his time about it, deepening the kiss slowly. She loved the smooth softness of his tongue, the way it slid against her teeth, and the teasing elusiveness of it when she wanted more. Her skin was hot inside her clothes.

He stopped kissing her and looked at her in the light filtering into the hall through the door to the kitchen. "I'd like to have a picture of you the way you look right now. You're so lovely, Swann. So beautiful in every way."

She saw their reflection in the hall mirror. She leaned against him until no light showed between their bodies. "We are beautiful," she said. "Together."

"Together," he said, his voice low in his throat. "Is that what you want, Swann? For us to be together tonight?"

Looking at their image in the dim light, she was sure that it was right. She was falling in love with this man, and what it meant, she didn't know. But that was something they could figure out later. Together.

"Yes," she murmured, holding his gaze in the mirror. "Please."

He turned her to face him. His eyes searched hers. "I'm the one who should say please. And I do. Swann, I want you, and I think you want me."

She nodded solemnly, and he kissed her. "Good," he breathed.

He led her into the bedroom. She had a quick impression of ivory walls, a large dresser and a double bed. The room was small but neat.

He was only a shape in the shadows until he turned on a small candlestick lamp. She was glad; she wanted to see him. To see him and touch him and taste him.

He returned to her quickly. His eyes gleamed. "That's better," he said.

"Much," she replied. The word was only a whisper.

Her sundress tied at each shoulder. He bent and kissed her bare skin. She began to unbutton his shirt. She brushed her lips against the taut muscles of his chest and lifted her head to gaze into his shining eyes.

His fingers fumbled at first with the bow at her shoulder, then became more sure. The left side of the sundress slid down to reveal one round breast, bare because the bra was built into the dress.

He touched her reverently, his fingers cool against her warm skin. They cupped the soft swell of her breast and molded it to the shape of his hand. She became lost in sensation, bending her head over his. Her hair slid forward and curtained his face until her own face became hot with his breath.

The other side of her dress fell so that her breasts were illumined in the golden light from the lamp. There was a dreaminess to the scene; she was an active participant but part of her stood away, looking down at the two of them in rapt approval.

He shrugged out of his shirt. His skin was like warm satin beneath the tips of her fingers.

He swung her into his arms and laid her gently on the bed, and just as she was reaching up to pull him down to her, his beeper sounded. The harsh sound shattered their mood entirely.

Paul blinked, then shook his head as if to clear it. "I'll have to phone in," he said.

"It's not good timing, is it?" she said, pulling the sheet over her.

"The worst," he agreed. His gaze lingered on her face as he sat down on the bed and punched a number into the telephone. The conversation was terse and brief, and when it was over he turned to her.

"I'm sorry," he said bleakly. "It's the way my life is, unfortunately. I don't know how long I'll be gone. A tanker truck has overturned outside town, and they don't know yet what kind of load it was hauling or how many people are injured. A friend is coming by to pick me up. You can take my car and drive yourself home if you'd like."

"Would you mind if I wait here?"

"Mind? No, of course not. I'll understand if you'd rather not, though." He kissed her lightly on the cheek, then hurried to the closet and began to put on a uniform.

She sat up on the bed and slowly, with great disappointment, retied the bows at her shoulders as she watched him dress.

"I'll be here when you get back," she told him, following behind him as he rushed toward the front door.

"I'll be back as soon as I can. Sorry about this." He kissed her once on the mouth, a quick kiss, as though his mind was already elsewhere.

She watched as he ran down the driveway and climbed into a car that stopped briefly at the curb. The car disappeared up the street, and she closed the front door.

A glance at the clock on the wall told her that it was only ten o'clock, and there was no telling what time Paul would be back.

She turned on the television set in Paul's room, flipping through the channels and thinking that it was going to be a long, long evening.

THE WRECKED TANKER TRUCK was a big one, and it carried a load of milk. Paul and the rest of the rescue team were thankful that it wasn't gasoline or something else flammable, but the accident site was a mess. Milk flowed across the highway and through the weeds into the encroaching marsh; it floated away insects and twigs and ran in rivulets down the embankment to the ditch.

The driver of the truck was all right, but several occupants of the station wagon that was also involved in the accident were injured.

The rescue team managed to stop the bleeding on a small boy's head wound, and they convinced the boy's mother that she wasn't seriously hurt but merely shaken up. The boy's grandfather had a compound fracture of one of the bones in his lower arm, and that was more complicated. For what must have been the one millionth time, Paul found himself wishing that he could call upon The Power.

Not that he would try if anyone were watching. But during the time that his colleagues were working to load the little boy onto a stretcher and put the stretcher in the waiting ambulance, and while the sobbing mother was being comforted by the ambulance driver and her distraught husband, he could have worked on the grandfather's fracture.

The grandfather was barely conscious. His fracture would take a long time to heal, and under the best of circumstances he might not ever regain full use of his arm. Paul knelt beside him, closed his eyes and concentrated with all his might. All he saw was blackness, not the small pinpoint of light that heralded the inner vibration that he had come to know as The Power.

Where was it? Why couldn't he call on it when he needed it? Where did it go when it faded from his consciousness?

He touched the patient's forehead and tried again. Maybe he hadn't concentrated hard enough, or perhaps he had been distracted by the flashing blue lights of the attending police car, or— well, whatever it was, he had to make an attempt. He forced himself to turn inward, to be at peace inside himself, to find the light, and he waited. And he waited. Nothing happened.

The patient moaned, and the men with the stretcher arrived.

"Paul?"

He had been trying to summon The Power right up until the last minute, hoping that it would come. He opened his eyes and saw the concerned look on the face of his friend Leon, the ambulance driver.

"Paul, are you okay?" Leon sounded worried.

"Yeah" was all he said. He helped to load the grandfather on the stretcher and climbed into the ambulance after him.

The man moaned, and Paul bent over him, trying to make him more comfortable.

"I tried, old boy," he murmured, but the patient didn't hear him and neither did anyone else.

At the hospital there were forms to fill out, and on his way out, one of the nurses wanted to start a conversation, and as he hurried through the emergency room, a bunch of anxious relatives, some of whom he knew slightly, assailed him with worried questions about the victims.

"Want a ride home, pal?" Leon called as he walked out the door.

"Thanks, Leon, I'll walk," Paul replied, setting out from the hospital. His house was only a few blocks away.

The truth was that he wanted to be alone. He was still upset about not being able to find The Power.

This wasn't anything new. The Power had been absent from his life for years ever since it had tapered off at the onset of adolescence. He had given up on its ever coming back.

Then, suddenly, The Power had reappeared. On the night of the party at Linda and Rick's when Kathy had injured herself, he had found it again. Something had made him place his hands on either side of her cut, and all of a sudden it was there as if it had never gone away. This unexpected turn of events had made him wildly hopeful that The Power would return in full force, but now he had put himself to the test both with the injured truck driver a few days ago and the grandfather tonight, and he had failed miserably both times.

It gave him a rotten feeling not to have helped those two people; he had to be doing something wrong. When The Power had been at its height, he hadn't had to call upon it at all. It was, for some unknown reason, there whenever he needed it. Then it started to taper off, and by the time he was fourteen, he could hardly ever summon it. His father had been furious, and— but that was another story. It didn't have any bearing on why he couldn't call upon The Power now.

Since he had stemmed the bleeding from Kathy's wound, he knew that it was still possible to find The Power within himself, and at this point he couldn't help being frustrated. It would be such a boon to others if he could help them. Not that he'd ever want to go back to the way it was before, with hordes of people flocking to see him at Miracle Farm, but if he could quietly use The Power for the good of his patients without drawing attention to himself, he would gladly do so.

He glanced at his watch, holding it up so that he could see its face in the lights from a passing car. It was almost one o'clock in the morning. Swann would probably have taken his advice and driven his car home. He hoped so, anyway. He didn't like to think of her waiting up for him all this time.

What a fiasco this evening had been! He had longed to make love to her, and when it was finally going to happen, they had been rudely interrupted. Now he was exhausted, and he didn't much feel like being with anyone, even Swann. He'd rather go to bed alone.

To his surprise, the lights at his house were still on, spilling out the front windows and across the grass. His car sat in the driveway. Swann was still here, then. His heart lifted momentarily, then sank to the pit of his stomach. She deserved, at the very least, an account of the evening, and she'd probably expect him to resume their lovemaking where they'd been forced to leave off earlier. The thought irked him. She should have gone home. Much as he cared about her, he didn't need company tonight.

"Swann?" he called softly as he closed the front door behind him.

He heard the murmur of the television set in the bedroom, and he looked through the doorway to see her spread out on his bed. She was asleep.

She was lovely as she slept, her hair tumbled across the pillow in deep swirls, her cheeks shadowed by richly fringed lashes. He went into the bathroom and removed his contact lenses, making as little noise as possible. Nevertheless, she opened her eyes when he came out of the bathroom.

"Paul," she said after a moment's confusion, and she sat up.

All he could think of was how tired he was and how disappointed that he hadn't been able to help the old man. She stood up and walked over to him. Her face looked like a beautiful blur—an Impressionist painting—without his glasses. She rested her cheek against his, and he halfheartedly slid an arm around her waist.

"Sorry to be so late," he said.

"I've fixed something to eat. I thought you'd probably be hungry."

He drew away in surprise. He *was* hungry, but he hadn't realized it until she mentioned food.

132   *A Man Worth Loving*

"That sounds good," he said, his astonishment evident in the tone of his voice. He hadn't expected her to do anything like this.

Her smile put him at ease. "I found eggs and sausages in the refrigerator, and I cooked the sausages so that all I'll have to do is heat them up in the microwave oven," she said, and before he realized it he was jamming his glasses on and following her into the kitchen. He was amazed to see that the dinner dishes had been cleared, washed and put away.

"Sit down. I'll do everything," she said, and he sank onto a kitchen chair as she efficiently assembled eggs, a deep bowl and a wire whisk. Despite his surprise that she knew her way around a kitchen, particularly his, he found that he quite liked watching her as she whipped the eggs with a bit of milk and added a few spices from his spice shelf.

"How about the accident—was it bad?" she asked.

"They're all bad, but this one could have been a lot worse. The driver of the tanker sideswiped a station wagon when he lost control on a curve. The driver wasn't hurt, and we managed to patch everyone up at the scene. The grandfather has a pretty bad fracture, and it's going to be giving him problems for a while."

He tried not to dwell on the grandfather, but he kept seeing the man's face in his mind. It was hard to forget someone who had been injured so seriously, especially when he felt he could have done something to help.

"I didn't make coffee, but I could turn on the coffee maker if you'd like. I didn't know if you liked to drink coffee this late, so— Paul, is anything wrong?" She stopped what she was doing and stared at him.

He lifted a hand to the back of his neck and massaged it. "No, only the usual. It was tough not being able to do more for the grandfather."

She shot him a keen look, but her expression softened.

"Here," she said, moving around behind him. "Let me do that."

Her hands were gentle on his neck, and he let his own hand fall away. Her limber fingers stroked and sought out the tight places, and he leaned into her touch. She was really good at this.

When he looked around at her, she said, "Is that enough?"

"I feel much better," he said. "And I'll skip the coffee in favor of iced tea."

While he poured two glasses of tea, she went to the sink, washed her hands, and resumed whipping the bowl of eggs. In a minute or two she had poured them into a pan.

"I like having you here," he said impulsively.

"I like being here," she answered quietly.

They ate their eggs off his familiar plates painted with poppies, and a sense of contentment stole over Paul. He smiled at Swann, and she smiled back.

When they were through, they left the dishes in the sink. He thought about driving her home, and the thought seemed unappealing. He took her hand and led her through the house, flicking off lights as they went.

When they stood in his bedroom, he said, because he'd decided he might as well be truthful, "I'm really very tired. Exhausted, in fact. You could drive my car home, you know."

"I know," she said. She was standing very close, but they weren't touching. "I don't want to go home."

It would be so easy to loosen the bows at her shoulders again, to lift her in his arms again, to lay her on the bed again, but he was so, so tired.

"Swann..." he began, his voice heavy with weariness.

"It's all right," she said softly, and then she took his hand and led him to the bed. She lay down and reached her arms up to him. They looked golden in the pale light.

"Remember you said earlier you could hold me forever? Well, I don't know about forever, but how about for to-night?" She smiled up at him.

He stumbled over a fold of the bedspread and sat down on the bed. She took off his glasses for him and set them on the table. She unbuttoned his shirt, and he sank back against the pillows. His eyelids fluttered closed as her head nestled in the hollow of his shoulder.

"Swann," he said again, letting her name trail away into a whisper, and as he fell asleep he felt her lips brush his cheek once and then twice. He didn't wake up until morning.

Chapter Eight

Swann woke up the next morning and didn't know where she was. She opened her eyes expecting to see Joe-the-Cat's small whiskered face peering into hers. When instead the sight of unfamiliar bedroom furniture filled her eyes, she remembered she had spent the night in Paul Thompson's bed.

She rolled over and discovered that the other side of the bed was empty. The sheets were cool to her touch. Had he gone out on another call? She hadn't heard the beeper.

When she heard the water running in the bathroom sink she sat up. The bathroom door hung slightly ajar.

She let herself fall backward onto the bed where she lay staring contemplatively at the crack between the door and its frame. She wondered if Paul would walk out of the bathroom naked. She imagined how he'd look if he did.

Never mind how he'd look—how did *she* look? She sat up and gazed at her reflection in the mirror hanging over the dresser. She didn't look as tired as she'd thought she would, but her dress was wrinkled. She smoothed her hair nervously. It surprised her that her nose was sunburned from working outside on the boat yesterday.

Her self-scrutiny ended when Paul walked out of the bathroom wearing a pair of shorts.

"Good morning," he said affably. His ears were pink and shiny from his shower, and his towel-dried hair stood out in ringlets, which she thought made him look particularly endearing.

"Hi," she replied. "Are you feeling better this morning?"

"I feel pretty good," he told her. He swooped across the room and planted a kiss on her nose. "In fact, so good that I'd like to pick up exactly where we left off last night before I had to leave."

He wrapped his arms around her, but she pulled away. "I feel so grubby," she told him.

"There's medicine for that." He bowed and gestured toward the bathroom. "Mademoiselle, my shower at your disposal."

"I didn't bring clean clothes. I—"

"You can put on an old T-shirt of mine. If—" and here his eyes twinkled "—you must wear anything at all."

She had stood before him last night, nude to the waist. Yet she felt unaccountably shy with him now. It had been easy to take charge when he was tired and needed nurturing. Now he was clearly in command of the situation, and he wanted to make love to her. As for her, the feeling in her midsection was either love or indigestion. It would, she thought wryly, be a lot easier if it were the latter.

The bathroom was small, with only a shower and no tub. She took off her dress and let it fall to the floor. Her underwear followed. She turned on the shower and adjusted it to the hottest temperature she could stand before she got in.

As the hot water pummeled her skin, her stomach quieted, thus eliminating the indigestion theory. She had to face the fact that soon he would make love to her.

She had carried his little-boy image in her heart all those years like a dear frayed picture, well-worn but well loved. Now, confronted by the man that boy had become, she had fallen in love. At the moment it seemed that all she needed to make her life complete was for Paul Thompson to feel the same way about her.

She wondered if she were doing the right thing. Going to bed with the person who was the subject of her next book would change the way she thought about him. It probably wasn't the wisest move she could have made professionally, but on a personal level she couldn't ignore her feelings for Paul any longer. He was, quite simply, one of the kindest and most *human* human beings she'd ever known.

Swann had no sooner wrapped the towel around her than Paul knocked on the door. She opened it, and he thrust a shirt and a pair of jeans at her. "You can put these on," he said.

She turned her face upward to his. There was strength in the line of his jaw, tenderness in the curve of his lip. In that moment, her whole world became concentrated in him and all her misgivings slipped away.

"I won't be needing clothes—at least not for a while," she murmured, and then she dropped the towel and led him to the bed.

If he'd had any doubt that she was a passionate woman, it soon evaporated. Swann Triplett was the woman Paul had always dreamed about and thought never existed. She was by turns a tiger, a minx and a tease. In the soft yellow beam of sunlight that fell across his bed, her face glowed as though lit from within, and as she slid against his skin, tumbled over and under him, he confused her with the sunshine so that in the end it was like making love with a sunbeam. But light was so elusive—you couldn't touch it. But Swann was real.

Her breasts were high and firm and satin to his touch. Her hips were tight and snug. Her feet were narrow at the heel and wide at the toe, the toes long and slender. If he could have created the perfect woman, she would have been Swann.

She knew what he liked, and this surprised him. Knew deep searching kisses and unabashed exploration; knew where to touch him and for how long. She understood things about making love to him that he had never even realized about himself. The thoughts running through his mind were fragmented and sporadic, that is, when he could think at all. She didn't leave much time for thinking, only for feeling and touching and loving; yes, loving . . . loving.

When it was over he was still stunned by the intensity of it and barely conscious of her draped along the length of his body, replete with satisfaction. He didn't have to ask if it was good for her. He knew.

He lifted his head, dizzy with his newfound knowledge of her. He let his head fall back on the damp pillow, his mind whirling. So this was what it would be like. This was what other people knew when they loved. He had never dreamed it could be so good.

She sighed, her breath stirring the hair on his chest. He stroked her hair thoughtfully. Had she said she loved him? He seemed to recall it. Or had he been dreaming or wishing it?

Birds chirped cheerfully under the eaves of the house, and street sounds penetrated the room. The rest of the world was going about its own business, and his life had changed forever.

Not his life. *Their* lives.

"Paul?"

"Hmm?"

"You're not asleep. I thought you were." She turned her head toward him, her emotions tuned to his to an exquisite degree. How remarkable that love had flowed so easily into her life, taking its form in him! And then she remembered with a guilty heart that he still didn't know why she'd sought him out in the first place.

"I'm not sleepy," he said. He studied her face. She was so beautiful. Her eyes were lovely, glowing golden in their depths under smoky lashes, and they were two of the prettiest eyes he'd ever seen. He kissed her gently on one eyelid, and when he again looked at her, he was surprised to see an emotion he couldn't identify flicker briefly across her face. What was it? Certainly it couldn't be apprehension. Not now. He pulled away from her and sat up, automatically and instinctively putting himself at a remove from her.

He didn't want her to see his own emotions. What was going on here, anyway? They had just made love tenderly and sweetly, and, he'd thought, adoringly. There should be no negatives now, but he knew what he had seen. At the moment when he noticed that vacillation in her eyes, she had not been wholeheartedly part of this mutual experience—she had been entertaining a thought that had nothing to do with their lovemaking. Shaken, he stood up and went into the bathroom.

"Paul?" She sounded startled.

He ran the water in the sink and watched it swirl around the bowl. He filled a glass and drank from it with long, deep swallows. When he put the glass back on the sink, Swann was standing behind him, a blanket wrapped around her.

"I was suddenly thirsty," he explained lamely.

She smiled, and it was as though he had never noticed anything amiss. She slipped her arms around him from the back and he watched her face in the mirror. He saw nothing but her happiness reflected back at him. She rested her chin on his shoulder.

"Come back to bed," she said. "Unless you're hungry as well as thirsty." She pressed her tongue against the warm skin of his neck.

He was an idiot; he had been mistaken. The outline of her body slid lightly against his, and suddenly he had an appetite that would not be satisfied by food. He turned swiftly and swept her into his arms, capturing her lips in a kiss. The blanket fell to the floor, and then so did they. It was a long time before they went back to bed, and then they both slept.

LATER, WHEN PAUL was driving Swann home, they stopped by a marine supply store and bought some caulking compound for the boat.

The morning was cloudless and the air was still. The dew had dried, and the grass tickled their bare feet. Swann fairly danced toward the skiff, her heart buoyant with a new happiness.

Because of the angle of the morning sun, the boat on its sawhorses was still shaded by the trees overhead as they went to work. Paul took off his shirt and bent to the task of caulking.

The caulking material, it turned out, had to be spread between the seams of the wood to keep out leaks. Paul explained that once the boat was put into the water, the wood would swell and it would be watertight.

"Then we'll take her out for a test," he promised, smiling down at her.

Swann thought it was fun to be doing something with Paul, and she was glad that he had insisted on starting this project. She liked working alongside him and letting him instruct her on a topic about which she knew nothing. She especially enjoyed the moments when he guided her hands along the boat's seams or leaned close enough for her to smell the sun-warmed scent of his skin. A few weeks around him, and she was wild about the man. Gracie would never believe it.

Later, Paul had to leave to go to work, and Swann went inside and took out her notebook to write down her impressions of the night before. She stared out across the creek as she contemplated whether or not she had come any closer to getting Paul to tell her who he really was. No, he had revealed nothing about his past that would help her with the biography. But she had found out some important things about him for herself.

He was a thoughtful lover, and she had responded to him as she had to no other man. Thinking about his lovemaking made her want to think of nothing else. She forced herself to banish mental images of the taut sinewy muscles in his neck as he loomed above her in bed, of the way her body had responded to the brush of his hair across the curve of her breast as he sought her nipple with his mouth. Physically they had been as close as two people could be. There was so much to discover about each other and so many ways to express the pent-up passion that they felt.

Now, with her thoughts so full of him, she wrote his name at the top of her notebook paper, entwining it with roses and a great big heart. Seeing his name on paper brought him closer to her, or so it seemed.

She dimly recalled a little trick from her teenage years. You wrote your name and the name of your boyfriend, and then you crossed out all the letters the two names had in common. For instance, the names Paul Thompson and Swann Triplett had the letters *A, L, T, S, P* and *N* in common, so she put a big pencil slash through all of those letters in both names. Then you counted the slashes according to a formula, which went, "Love, hate, friendship, marriage." You were supposed to say that over and over again until you came to the last slash. If the last slash was labeled "marriage," that meant the boy in question was the one you would marry. Likewise, "love" or "hate" meant the corresponding emotions. Once she had cried for a week because one of her boyfriends had registered "hate" on this little game even though he called her twice a day and practically camped out on her doorstep on weekends.

"Love, hate, friendship, marriage, love, hate, friendship," she whispered, counting the slashes in Paul's name. According to the formula, that meant that he thought of her as a friend. Her lips curved in a smile as she counted the slashes through her own name. She supposedly "loved" Paul.

Okay, so she "loved" him. He only felt "friendship" for her. But friendship could grow into love; everyone knew that. And if they happened to end up loving each other, what was the problem?

The notebook slid off Swann's lap and onto the chair unheeded as she realized that there were impediments almost too numerous to count.

For one thing, she had introduced herself to Paul under false pretenses—not a promising way to begin a relationship. For another, she would be going back to Philadelphia. Even if she managed to stretch out her visit to Reedy Creek for months, she would eventually have to go home, and she didn't think that Paul had any intention of leaving Reedy Creek. With his friends, his job, and his attachment to the area, he seemed firmly settled in.

It might turn into "love" for both of them, but for them, that old junior high school formula did not promise marriage.

She was being foolish. She shouldn't be thinking of marriage when neither one of them had mentioned it.

SWANN RAN INTO LINDA, Paul's ex-girlfriend, in the bank later that week. Linda's eyes were knowing, and Swann decided with a certain amount of resignation that the whole town probably knew what was going on between her and Paul.

After the usual greetings, Linda said, "I've been trying to reach Paul for days, but his answering machine hasn't been on. I tried to call you, and the phone company didn't have any record of a number listed in your name. Our group is having an oyster roast on the bluff this weekend, and we hope you and Paul can come."

"Well, I—"

"Oh, feel free to check with Paul before you decide." Linda glanced at her watch. "I had no idea it was so late," she said. "I'd better get back to work. It was good to see you, Swann. 'Bye," and with that Linda was off and running.

"Do you want to go to an oyster roast?" Swann asked Paul that night. Quickly she told him about seeing Linda.

"Do *you* want to go?" he asked.

"That's not fair. I asked you first," she said.

He laughed and pulled her close. "I want to go anywhere you go," he said, his breath stirring her hair.

"Then let's," she said happily. She knew how she would have felt if the situation were reversed and these were her friends instead of his. She would have wanted to parade their relationship in front of all of them so they'd know that the two of them belonged together. If Paul felt that way, she was more than happy to oblige.

PAUL'S FRIEND Jed had hauled a pickup truck loaded with oysters from Savannah on the afternoon of the roast. The oysters waited in bushel baskets in a shed beneath the oak trees on the bluff overlooking the Sudbury River as the guests arrived. Swann watched with interest as Rick and Jed, who had done this many times before, built oak fires in huge metal drums and spread the oysters on grates, which were then lowered over the flames.

Somebody slapped a glove into Swann's hand, and Paul showed her how to grasp the hot shells in her gloved hand and pry them open with an oyster knife.

From time to time one of the cooks would dump a bunch of oysters on one of the long tables in the shed, usually to the accompaniment of enthusiastic cries as the waiting guests dug in. The oysters were steaming hot and, once shelled, ready to be dipped into containers of melted butter or chili sauce laced liberally with horseradish. Butter ran down Swann's chin; Paul laughed and kissed it off.

Swann had a hard time getting the knack of opening oysters, and Rick showed her how to flick her wrist at the crucial moment so that the shells would pop open. Paul was an old hand at this, flipping the shelled oysters onto her plate and his and tossing the empty shells away with a practiced motion.

The women in the group had contributed cornbread and a variety of salads, but few people paid attention to those items. Instead they gorged on oysters, downing bushel after bushel. Swann ate so many that she thought she would burst.

"Come on, Swann, eat up!" Howard exclaimed, dumping several succulent shelled oysters on her plate. Swann ate. Howard applauded and shelled several for Kathy. Swann shot a quick glance at the scar on Kathy's hand, noticing that it hardly showed.

Kathy saw her looking and held up her arm. "It's well healed," she said.

"Well-heeled? Is that so? Jed was telling me it takes a lot of money to keep you in shoes," teased Howard.

"You should see our VISA bill," Jed complained, and everyone laughed, the subject of Kathy's cut on the night of the party at Linda and Rick's forgotten. Swann noticed that the only person not laughing was Paul, whose expression seemed pensive.

Afterward, stuffed to the gills, they all sat around a camp fire, Swann's head resting against Paul's knee, and sang Stephen Foster songs to the accompaniment of Howard's harmonica. Once, after Paul had leaned down and whispered something in her ear, Swann saw Kathy nudge Linda before the two women exchanged a knowing look. Swann understood in that moment that the look meant that she and Paul had been accepted as a couple.

This knowledge brought her a feeling of warmth and happiness that truly surprised her. If she'd thought about it at all before, she probably would have decided that it didn't matter to her what these people thought about her and Paul. Now she realized that it *did* matter; their acceptance of her into their group was like a stamp of approval.

The fire dwindled around midnight, and people started drifting toward their cars, calling sleepy goodbyes to one another.

"We used to come to the bluff a lot when we were kids, remember?" asked Linda, who with Rick planned to stay to clean up the site. She smiled up at him, her face glowing.

"I remember fruit fights. The guys would gather a bunch of rotten fruit from the farmers' market and we'd meet here and divide into two teams. We'd pelt each other for a couple of hours before one side would claim victory and we'd all go swimming in the river to wash off the stink. Boy, those were the good old days!'' He grimaced, and the others laughed.

"I wasn't talking about fruit fights. I was talking about parties. Remember how in high school somebody would bring a portable radio and we'd build a big fire at the edge of the bluff, and we'd all sit on blankets around it like we are now? Later on, the necking would start and—''

"Necking? You mean I was tossing a bunch of rotten fruit around when I could have been necking? I must have passed up something good,'' Rick said with a wink at Paul.

Linda laughed and leaned her head on his shoulder. "Oh, you did. Believe me, you did.''

"Then let's not wait any longer,'' Rick joked. "I say we get this place cleaned up and go home to bed.'' He dislodged his wife's head from his shoulder and stood up. He stretched. "Paul, you want to douse the fire? Linda and I'll bag the garbage.''

"I'll help,'' Swann said, going and getting one of the big green plastic bags from the back of Jed's pickup.

"I get kind of nostalgic sometimes thinking how I miss those old times,'' Linda said to Swann as they stashed bags of garbage in the back of Jed's truck. She turned to Paul, who had finished quenching the fire with water from the river. "I was telling Swann how I enjoy reminiscing,'' she explained.

"It's fun to remember good times,'' Paul said noncommittally.

"Oh, I keep forgetting you weren't here then, Paul. Forgive me. You must get tired of hearing how great everything was in the old days.''

Rick appeared in the darkness. "Come on, Linda, let's get moving. Paul, Swann, see you soon,'' Rick said. He held the car door open for Linda, clearly impatient to leave.

Paul took Swann's elbow and steered her toward his own car. Their feet crunched on dry fallen leaves.

Their farewells echoed out over the river as the cars began to move slowly toward town.

Swann curled up on the passenger seat of the Honda and rested a hand on Paul's shoulder as he drove. She'd enjoyed herself tonight; she hadn't felt ill at ease with the group this time. Maybe they were more interesting now that she knew them better, or maybe she was still basking in the warm feelings of camaraderie generated around the camp fire.

"They all seem so settled, don't they?" she said dreamily, thinking about the passionate looks she had seen exchanged between Linda and Rick before they had left.

"They *are* settled," Paul said.

"They mostly grew up together? That whole group?"

"Mm-hmm. Would you mind massaging my shoulder? Yeah, right there. There's a kink in it from hauling water up the bluff. Mmm, that feels good."

The taillights of Rick's car had disappeared, and now Paul turned onto the creek road. Huge willow oaks vaulted velvet-dark branches over the car, encapsulating them in their own little world. Swann continued to massage Paul's shoulder, drifting her hand upward gradually to his neck. Once he looked over and smiled at her; she felt a familiar tug of yearning for him.

He was beginning to mean so much to her. Did she mean the same to him? She leaned against him, and he curved an arm around her. She had known him only for a matter of weeks, but it seemed like much longer. She could hardly remember what her life had been like without him.

He turned into her driveway, and they got out of the car, walking arm in arm to the house. It was understood between them that Paul would not go home tonight, that they would be together as they had almost every night since the day they had first made love.

Once inside, a feeling of contentment settled over Swann; she hadn't been so happy in a long time. She was with a man she loved, and this evening had been special. Impulsively she pulled Paul down on the couch beside her and nestled close to him. The memory of Linda's eyes when she gazed so lovingly at her husband lingered in Swann's mind; they were truly bonded, those two. Of course, they shared a common background. There seemed to be no secrets between them.

Swann was envious of the well-matched couples she knew. Gracie and Nolan, Linda and Rick; they were free to share the innermost aspects of their lives, which made them grow closer and closer. She longed for that dimension of sharing in her own life.

In that moment, Swann hated having secrets from Paul as she never had before, but she also understood that until he confided in her, she would not feel free to reveal why she was really here in Reedy Creek. She could not have denied Paul anything on this night; could he, would he, deny her? He looked so much at peace, so pleased to be with her, that she didn't think so.

"I was thinking," she said softly, her fingertips brushing the pale hairs on his forearm, "how nice it must be for Rick and Linda. To know all about each other because they've always known each other."

Paul didn't say anything, but she thought she sensed a tensing of his muscles. She decided to continue; she was determined to bring everything out in the open once and for all.

"And," she went on, "I've realized that we really don't know that much about each other's childhoods. I haven't spoken much of mine because it was unhappy. I never got along with my father very well, and after my mother died, our relationship deteriorated. So much money and so little love. It's over and done with, of course, and I can't change the way things were. If I could, maybe I wouldn't even want to. I had to become strong in order to survive. Oh, Paul, do you understand what I'm saying?" She looked up at him for the first time since she began to speak, and he was staring stonily ahead.

"If the past wasn't particularly pleasant, there's no good in talking about it," he said stiffly. His eyes, which usually revealed so much, were opaque and unreadable.

"I wasn't—"

"It's not therapeutic, you know, raking up such things. I know it's the fashion to pour out one's troubles to anyone who will listen, but believe me, Swann, you're better off forgetting the bad things that happened to you and getting on with your life." He stood up and looked down at her, his brows drawn together.

"But I don't pour out my troubles to anyone who will listen," she said indignantly, distressed that he had missed the point. It seemed terribly important to make him understand that when two lives touched in the manner that theirs were touching, self-disclosure became the glue that held them together.

"I shouldn't have said that," he said heavily.

Now she knew that he had not been referring to her but to himself, and she couldn't acknowledge that without letting him know that she knew more about him than he had ever wanted her to know. Well, why not tell him what she knew? Better yet, why not get him to tell her himself?

"If it upsets you, I won't talk about what happened to me. It wasn't me I wanted to talk about anyway. It's you," she said as gently as she could.

He took one step backward, putting distance between them. She sprang to her feet as soon as she realized what he was doing.

"Do you realize that every time I bring up your childhood, you change the subject? That I don't know anything about you before you arrived in Reedy Creek?" she said on a rising note of annoyance.

"Swann, there's nothing to tell. Nothing."

She shook her head, assailed by a wave of despair. He was going to stick to that story even now. Suddenly she was sickened at her audacity. Clearly he wasn't ready for this, and she had mishandled the situation. Her love for him knotted tightly in her stomach.

"I want to know all about you, Paul, because I'm beginning to care about you very much. And how can we discuss our future when we haven't even discussed the past?"

This time he let her rest her hand on his shoulder, and he closed his eyes for a moment. He swayed slightly, and she increased her grip, sliding her arm around his neck and leaning her cheek against his.

"Oh, Paul, I'm sorry. It's just that we have so much together now that I can't help wanting *more*." She felt perilously near tears.

He sighed and rested his hands on her hips. "I'd better leave," he said.

"But—"

"I'll call you," he said, twisting away from her, but he didn't say when. He was out the door before she even understood what had happened, leaving her staring after him with tears pouring down her face.

I've really botched it, she thought hopelessly, and all because, under the influence of moonlight and a loving look between a husband and wife, she'd developed a false sense of security about their relationship.

There was nothing to do now but to wait for him. And wait. And wait.

Chapter Nine

All next week Paul didn't call. Swann missed his quiet laughter and the way he squinted when his contact lenses felt uncomfortable; she missed his low voice and his habit of clearing his throat when he was about to say something important. She missed sleeping with him.

She imagined that the people in the Little Bit, the town hangout, knew about the rift between them after she took Angelyn and the kids there for a special treat later that week. LaRue, the waitress, seemed to be studying Swann under lowered lashes. Did LaRue know that she and Paul were no longer seeing each other? Heaven forbid, was LaRue someone in whom Paul would be interested? Swann was abashed when she finally noticed the wedding ring on LaRue's finger. Her imagination was overreacting to everything these days.

During the week following their argument, Swann couldn't help wondering if Paul was as skittish with all the women with whom he'd been involved, but she reflected that, other than Linda, now safely married to Rick, she didn't know of any other women he'd dated. That, too, might be a symptom of his fear of intimacy. What was he so afraid of? If someone were to find out that he was Child Michael would that be the end of the world?

Swann had always wondered if Linda had been privy to the secret. One day when she saw Linda walking along the street, she stopped her car and waved.

"Hi, Swann," Linda said enthusiastically as she came over to the curb and leaned over to talk through the car window. "It's hot today, isn't it?"

"Very," Swann said. "I was just going into the Little Bit. Want to join me for a Coke?"

"Oh, I— well, sure. I'm off work this afternoon because they're painting the office, and the paint gives me a headache, so I have time to visit for a while."

Swann parked the car and joined Linda in a booth at the back of the tiny restaurant.

"How's Paul?" was Linda's first question. Swann could have kicked herself for not seizing the initiative and directing the conversation to Paul in a more roundabout way, but she quickly saw that there was no point in avoiding the inevitable. Linda probably knew that Paul hadn't been anywhere near her for a week and was merely trying to glean more information.

Swann shrugged lightly. "I don't know. We had an argument and haven't seen each other since then."

Maybe Linda didn't know after all; her look of dismay was certainly genuine. "I'm sorry, Swann, I hadn't heard. Paul's funny, you know. He doesn't talk much about himself."

"I've noticed," Swann said, trying to inject a note of wryness into her tone. She must have succeeded because Linda smiled. Then she became more serious, leaning forward over the tiny table to speak confidentially so that the waitress wouldn't hear.

"You've been good for Paul, Swann. You're more like him than the rest of us are. You're more—oh, I don't know. Worldly? Perhaps that's not the word I want."

"We're both from someplace else. Maybe that's what you mean," Swann suggested.

"Maybe. Paul's always been different from the men around here. He's more interested in the world around him, and at the same time he tends to withdraw into himself. It's paradoxical, I know. I never understood him, which I guess is why we broke up. Paul needs someone like you, Swann. I hope you'll patch things up."

"So do I," Swann said, trying not to sound as forlorn as she felt.

"When are you going back to Pennsylvania?"

"I'm not sure," Swann said.

"Paul would miss you if you left."

"He hasn't missed me enough to call me for the past week," she said.

"I could put in a good word for you, but I doubt that it would help. Why don't you call him?"

"Maybe I will," Swann said with obvious reluctance.

Linda smiled and reached swiftly across the table to squeeze Swann's hand. "Go ahead, call him, you've got nothing to lose," she said, but Swann was not so sure. She had spent a lifetime pursuing a better relationship with her father, and it was only in recent times that she'd recognized the futility of it. If she chose to pursue Paul, she'd be setting herself up for a similar cycle of pursuit and rejection, and what if she only frightened Paul away again?

Or was she only being stubborn? After all, Swann *did* know that she was good for him; she'd known it even before Linda had remarked on it. Paul ought to know it, too. The idea that he didn't appreciate her made her angry. Why, he didn't deserve her!

He didn't value her highly enough. If he had, he never would have walked out.

No. That wasn't it. It was something else.

The problem was the way Paul Thompson felt about himself, not the way he felt about her.

Of course that would be it, she thought in a flash of intuition. His childhood, to some extent, was known to have been abusive, and Swann understood from writing about

Winky Tapps that a child in an abusive situation often felt worthless.

No, she wasn't the one that Paul didn't value highly enough; the person that he didn't value was himself.

Did he realize that? Or was he so caught up in burying his past that he didn't understand what he was doing to himself?

One thing that seemed clear was that Linda apparently had no idea that Paul was Child Michael. Surely she would have given some clue, and thinking back over the conversation, Swann could find none. It was entirely possible that Paul had guarded his secret so well that no one in the small town of Reedy Creek knew or cared about his childhood.

Should I call him? she asked herself after she said goodbye to Linda in front of the restaurant. When she didn't know the answer, she decided to wait. It would be better if he'd call her.

PAUL WAS NOT ACCUSTOMED to women who knew how to be aggressive.

The women whom he'd dated during the past couple of years tended to be passive in relationships, waiting to take their lead from the man. They could be plenty aggressive at work or in social situations, but they'd always looked to him to guide the relationship. That was why, he thought unhappily, the relationships had all come to nothing. His idea of manipulating a romance was to merely skim the surface of the emotions, never probing too deeply. If anyone ever got too close, he'd run.

Which is what he'd done with Swann. He'd panicked. He didn't like to remember things; he'd cut himself so completely free of his past that he was able to forget for days at a time what it had been like to be Child Michael. Correction: He *used* to be able to forget. Lately it had grown more difficult, what with the return of The Power and Swann's presence in his life.

Not that she had done any uncomfortable prodding of his wounds until the night of the oyster roast. She'd always kept things entirely within the limits that he had set out—limits that he'd never outlined to anyone. Still, he knew that those carefully built walls made him incomprehensible to some women, Linda for instance.

Linda was a classic case of the woman getting too close. That was why he'd carefully extricated himself by making her think that they were calling a mutual time-out from each other. She'd gone on to fall in love with Rick, which caused her to break off the relationship with him. This left Paul free and clear. He felt guilty about the way he'd maneuvered her out of his life, but the plain truth was that he'd had to get away. The bright spot in the whole affair was that Linda and Rick were happy.

Now here was Swann, and he loved her. With Swann, he felt complete and part of a whole. He'd never realized how alone he was until she came along and changed the way he looked at things.

She was somebody to call late at night when he'd come in from an emergency and was too wound up to go to sleep. She was someone to talk with over the dinner table, someone whose opinions were interesting and shed new light on the way he looked at things. She was someone to wake up to on misty mornings and someone to pull close when it wasn't yet time to get out of bed. She was someone to love.

The trouble was that Swann's idea of love made him uncomfortable. In his view, love was something to pick up at this point in his life and carry forward like a banner. Swann's view seemed to be that love was something you picked up and put in a basket along with all the other emotional burdens you'd lived with in the course of your life. He saw love as separate; she saw it as a part of the whole.

Some things should never be told. And he knew he would never tell them.

If she couldn't accept him as he was now, today, then she couldn't have him at all. It was that simple.

The only trouble was that he missed her.

BY THE SECOND WEEK of her estrangement from Paul,
Swann found that she couldn't concentrate. Justin called
one afternoon, as he often had, finally working the conversation around to her progress on the book. Swann was extremely evasive, and she knew that he was worried. In her
present state of lethargy, it didn't matter. Nothing did, not
even Joe-the-Cat, who did his best to amuse her with his
antics.

She was slipping slowly and inexorably into the dol-
drums of depression, and she was at a loss to know what to
do. She hated feeling the way she did, but nothing seemed
to help. The cottage, where she had grown so comfortable
and which she had in fact learned to love, was only a source
of painful memories now. Everything about it reminded her
of him, calling to mind the way Paul looked sprawled on the
floor in front of the television set, concentrating on the
screen . . . loping on long legs across the grass to where the
boat stood on its two sawhorses . . . bending over her while
she lay in readiness on top of rumpled sheets. She thought
of those days through a haze of love and longing. She ached
for everything to be the way it had been then.

She had tried working, but that was no good; she had
tried getting more sleep, but she could only lie awake and
wish that Paul would stir beside her and throw a careless
arm across her stomach so that she would wake up and learn
that what happened between them wasn't real but a terrible
nightmare.

Swann didn't eat much, having lost her appetite, but
eventually her food supplies became low enough that she
had to go to the store. It was with a noticeable lack of enthusiasm that she dressed and went out into one of the hottest afternoons of the summer.

On the road heading toward town, heat waves shim-
mered up from the hot asphalt, distorting the images of the
few cars she met coming toward her. Out here on the creek

road, one didn't see many cars and even fewer pedestrians. It was with some surprise, then, that she slowed the car as she approached a lone pedestrian trudging through the dusty sun-scorched weeds at the side of the road. She gave the woman a second glance because it was unusual to see someone walking so far from town. Why she should have been surprised that it was Angelyn, she didn't know—Angelyn didn't own a car—unless it was the fact that for once Angelyn's children weren't with her.

Swann stopped the car immediately and leaned over to open the door on the passenger's side.

"Hi, Angelyn," she called as the hot rush of moist air hit her in the face. "It's too hot to be out walking today. Climb in and I'll give you a ride."

"Thanks," Angelyn said as she slid into the seat. She pushed damp strands of hair out of her face and offered a shy smile.

"You're going into town?" Swann asked as she edged back onto the road.

"Yes, Rhonda's hay fever is so bad that I want to get some medicine from the drugstore. I thought I'd stop at the grocery store, too."

"Do you always walk?"

"Mrs. Dawson, our social worker, usually gives me a ride, but her husband is sick today," Angelyn said. Her blue cotton dress was limp with the heat.

"I'm stopping at the store, too, so we can go together. That way I'll be able to give you a ride home."

"That's wonderful. I don't like to leave Mott in charge of the other kids for very long."

"He's taking care of Carlie and Rhonda?"

"I didn't want to take them out in this heat, especially with Rhonda's hay fever so bad. Mott keeps care of them sometimes 'cause there isn't anyone else. Anyway, both Rhonda and Carlie are taking naps. They'll sleep till I get back."

"Next time, call me when you have to go somewhere. The kids can come over," Swann said. It had never occurred to her to offer to help with child care before.

"Oh, Mott's used taking care of them. The kids mind him, mostly. And he's mighty good with Rhonda."

"Mott's awfully young for such a responsibility, isn't he?"

"He's had to grow up fast," Angelyn said. "He seems like a right smart boy—at least that's what his teachers tell me. I hope he'll be able to go to college. He'll have to get there on his own, though. That's the thing that worries me. I won't be able to send him."

"He can get a scholarship, Angelyn, and there are loans for people who can't afford tuition," Swann said gently.

Angelyn sighed. "I know. Maybe once he gets through college, he can help the other two kids. Maybe I'll even have a job then."

"Angelyn, haven't you ever worked?"

"I got married so young, you know. All I did after that was have babies, and then my husband left. I don't know how to *do* nothing."

Swann glanced at Angelyn out of the corners of her eyes. Her neighbor was twisting the strap of her pocketbook and staring straight ahead. Swann sensed that this admission had cost Angelyn something; she was a proud woman.

Swann was saved from having to answer by their arrival at the supermarket.

"I'll just run into the drugstore and meet you in the grocery afterward," Angelyn said, and she was out of the car before Swann could reply.

Swann went into the grocery store and was wheeling her cart down one of the narrow aisles when she was joined by Angelyn.

"We can share a cart," she told Angelyn. "I'm not going to buy much." Indeed, she didn't need to keep a lot of food around now that Paul was no longer there.

"Oh, I don't need but a few things, either," Angelyn told her, and while Swann proceeded to select items like frozen dinners and canned pâté de foie gras, Angelyn chose basics like dried beans and rice.

After the clerk had added up their bills, Angelyn pulled a carefully folded stack of food stamps out of her battered wallet and paid for her food with them. Swann tipped the bag boy before they got in the car.

She noticed on the way home that Angelyn had taken the bottle of decongestant out of the drugstore bag on the way home and was studying the directions intently, her face screwed up in concentration. Swann thought nothing of this. She kept talking of the weather, the potholes in the road, a lot of things as she drove up outside Angelyn's house.

"Thank you so much, Swann," Angelyn said, but she made no move to get out of the car. Thinking that she would help her with the heavy bags, Swann started to open her door, but she was restrained by Angelyn's urgent touch on her arm.

"Please," Angelyn said hesitantly, her cheeks flooding with color. "There's one more thing I need you to do for me."

"Why, Angelyn, is something wrong?"

"It's just—just—"

Swann was stunned to see the tears welling in Angelyn's eyes. Tears of pain? Tears of anger? No, Swann attributed them to something else.

"I can't read too good, Swann. I'm not sure I know how to give Rhonda her medicine." Angelyn blinked back the tears and looked down at her lap in sheer mortification.

"Well, of course I'll read the directions to you," Swann said automatically, embarrassed for her, but at the same time she was thinking with a certain amount of horror, *Angelyn has trouble with reading? Can't she read?* Yet she knew that Angelyn, as proud as she was, would never divulge this confidence unless it were true.

Swann took the bottle from Angelyn and read it carefully. "It says you're to give her one teaspoonful every four hours, and that it might make her sleepy," she told Angelyn.

Angelyn nodded gravely. "Every four hours. Well, that's good. She's been right uncomfortable lately with her stuffy nose. Thanks, Swann. I mean, you're such a good friend to do all this for me."

"But I've hardly done anything," Swann objected.

"Oh, but you have." Angelyn brushed the tears from her cheeks before she got out of the car and prepared to lift the grocery bags out of the back seat.

"Here, I'll help you with those," Swann told her. She carried the largest bag while Angelyn carried the smaller two. They were greeted ecstatically at the door by Mott carrying Rhonda, with Carlie, rosy-cheeked from her nap, close behind. Stropstripe roused herself from her place on the couch and trotted over to rub against Swann's ankles as she deposited her bag of groceries on the kitchen table.

Unbidden, the two older kids quietly began to put away the food, and Angelyn lifted the baby into her arms and solicitously wiped her nose with a tissue.

"Angelyn," Swann began as she stood with her hand on the front doorknob. She didn't want to offend her friend, but suddenly she knew how she could help this family.

"Would you like to stay for a glass of iced tea?" Angelyn offered quickly.

"I can't this time," Swann said. "I would like to come back tomorrow, though. Angelyn, I could help you with your reading. If you'd like me to, I mean."

Angelyn's face lit up with a radiant smile. "Would you? Oh, Swann, that would be wonderful. Why, I never learned properly in school. The teachers always seemed to pay attention to the kids who knew how to read well. And I dropped out of school so early that no one ever found out that I could barely read. Maybe if I spent some time with somebody who wouldn't make fun of me, I could get better.''

"I'm sure you could. Tomorrow perhaps we could begin your lessons at a quiet time, maybe when the kids are asleep.''

"Early in the morning would be best. *Real* early, like the time we went to see the otters together.''

It would mean giving up her morning walk along the edge of the creek, but Swann didn't mind.

"I'll see you early then, before it's really light," she told Angelyn. Angelyn was still smiling through the screen door when Swann got into her car.

Finally, Swann thought to herself, *I've found something I can do for that family.*

Best of all, in helping them she saw her own salvation. If she could concentrate on Angelyn, she wouldn't have so much time to think about herself. And that would ease the pain of Paul's defection—at least a little.

THE READING LESSONS went well from the very beginning. Angelyn was an eager pupil, and, when Swann showed her how to sound out words phonetically, she began to make rapid progress. Swann and Angelyn met in Angelyn's kitchen every morning before the children were awake, and Angelyn soon progressed from reading the kids' Dr. Seuss books to a few lines in the weekly *Reedy Creek Gazette.*

By the time a few weeks had passed, Swann realized that if it weren't for Angelyn and her children, there would be no real reason for her to stay in Reedy Creek. She had alienated Paul; it seemed unrealistic to believe that she would write his biography now. She packed up some of her books in a cardboard box, and she called the airlines to inquire about departing flights for Philadelphia. However, she always stopped short of making a reservation. That step seemed all too final.

One day after coming home from a long round of errands in Reedy Creek, Swann stepped out on the porch, where her eyes were immediately drawn to a twig bearing a tiny bird's nest balanced carefully on the table that held her word processor. *A hummingbird's nest,* she thought. Entranced, she picked it up and turned it this way and that in the light. It was a gem of architecture, woven of bits of fluff from fern stalks and crisscrossed with cobwebs. She knew that it was a gift from Angelyn, who had so little to give but loved to share beauty with others and knew that Swann would appreciate such a gift. This was the second such present that Swann had received; last week it had been a symmetrical stone from the creek polished to a high gloss, left after she mentioned that her papers kept blowing off the table on the porch.

Swann set out for Angelyn's house to thank her. As she made her way through the woods, she wondered where Paul was on this somnolent summer afternoon. At work? At home taking a nap? A sudden longing to see him wrenched her heart.

Swann found Angelyn, Mott, Carlie and Rhonda sitting on a faded old blanket by the creek. Sunlight pierced the tree branches overhead and wove sharp patterns of sun and shade on the faces of the children. Angelyn, totally in shade and looking cool despite temperature and humidity both in the high nineties, was reading aloud from a book in her lap. Her voice was confident, and although she stumbled over a couple of the words, the children paid rapt attention. Swann's heart warmed to the little family group.

Swann waited in the cool shadows by the creek until Angelyn finished, then stepped forward to thank Angelyn for the gift.

"I didn't see you walk up," Angelyn said as the children flocked around Swann and begged her to sit down with them to listen to the stories. Angelyn was clearly flustered at the thought of being observed.

"Go ahead," Swann urged. "Read another one. I'd like to hear you." She smiled encouragingly at the reluctant Angelyn.

Angelyn picked up another book. They were easy books that they had picked up at the library, and Angelyn had shown amazing progress in learning to sound out the letters.

Swann was beaming with quiet pride by the time Angelyn closed the book and sent Mott and Carlie to the house to get their fishing gear.

"That was wonderful, Angelyn," she said warmly.

Angelyn patted the cover of one of the books. "I never thought I'd be able to read to my kids. I'm going to read more and more all the time."

Swann held the weekly newspaper out to her. "Why don't you read some of the stories in the paper tonight and we'll talk about them tomorrow?" she said. She had discovered that Angelyn was like a blotter, soaking up information as fast as it was presented to her.

"Okay. I was thinking that I might try to get my high school diploma. It would take a few years, but maybe I could do it."

"Of course you could," Swann replied, delighted that Angelyn was thinking about it.

Mott and Carlie arrived with fishing poles and dangled the hooks in the water. "I'm going to catch the first fish," Carlie announced.

"You are not!" Mott said.

"Am so!"

"Are not!"

"Kids, hush," Angelyn said, leaning back against the tree.

Rhonda stretched out full-length on her stomach on the blanket, sucking her thumb, and in a few minutes she was asleep. Bees buzzed around the showy red flowers of a scarlet locust nearby.

"Swann, I thought I saw Paul Thompson over at your house this morning. His car, anyway. I knew you had gone into town, so I guess you missed him," Angelyn said.

Swann sat up straighter. "Oh?" she said. "I didn't see him. I wish I had."

Angelyn looked sympathetic. "I thought about walking over and speaking to him, but the bottom of my skirt was wet from bending over in the creek shallows gathering 'cress, and I'd left the kids playing here on the blanket. I didn't feel right about letting them out of my sight for more than a few minutes."

"It's all right. I wonder what he wanted." Swann knew that Paul hadn't left a note for her; she would have found it if he had.

"Maybe he was working on the boat."

"The boat? Well, maybe," Swann said, her mind turning over that and other possibilities.

If Paul had been at her house, he must have planned to see her. After all, he wouldn't have known that she was out. He would have expected her to be sitting on the porch working as she usually was in the morning.

She hummed to herself as she hurried home. The first thing she did when she reached the cottage was to walk down to the boat and find out if Paul had been working on it. Yes, he had; the old tube of caulking compound lay underneath it in the tall grass, and she saw signs that he had filled in some more of the seams. A shirt of his was tossed over a nearby tree limb. It looked as though he had run out of caulking compound and perhaps had gone to buy more.

If he had resumed work on the boat, didn't that mean that he expected to see her again? Surely Paul wouldn't put more time and effort into a boat that he never expected to use. Thoughtfully she walked back to the cottage.

The branch that always caught in the hinges of the back door was now being chewed off by the edge of it. Swann brushed it aside and tried to tie it back with a length of string, but it was too feisty to stay where she put it. It fell forward and slapped her in the face with its wide waxy leaves.

The week before, Swann had found, under a lamp in the living room, a key that might fit the utility room's lock. She went inside to get it and then marched to the utility closet on the porch. *Good,* she thought, *the key fits.* She wrenched open the door, brushing away cobwebs to rummage in the closet's dark innards trying to find scissors or a hedge trimmer or clippers—anything to cut the recalcitrant branch.

Finally she found a rusty pair of clippers that might do the job, and she went outside and attacked the offending plant with a vengeance. Not only did she lop off the hated branch, but she cut the rest of the shrub almost to the ground. When she had finished, she regarded the heap of debris with loathing and realized that she wasn't finished. Now she wouldn't be able to get in and out of the back door.

Muttering to herself, she gathered some of the branches in her arms and toted them to the edge of the woods, where she dumped them in a pile. She rubbed absently at her left arm, which was starting to itch. As she walked back to the house, she looked down at the skin and saw that it was beginning to raise up in red welts. So was the skin on her right arm. As she watched in amazement, the welts became bright scarlet weals, and the itching intensified until it became so painful that it brought tears to her eyes.

She fought panic as she broke into a run toward the house; what was happening to her? It must be some kind of allergy to the sap in the plant she had just cut down. Whatever it was, the itching was becoming unbearable.

Inside the house, she recalled, was a book that had been there when she arrived, some kind of medical book. Swann leaned against the bookcase, trying to catch her breath as she scanned the titles on the shelves. *Obedience Training Your Dog At Home*—no, that wasn't it; *Reader's Digest Condensed Books.* Well, that certainly wouldn't do. She remembered that the one she was looking for was a short fat green volume, but where was it? Ah, there it was, high on a shelf. She'd have to stand on a chair to reach it.

The welts now covered her hands and arms almost to the shoulder. She could never have imagined anything so painful, and she had no idea how to treat them. Her breath came in short gasps as she dragged a chair over to the bookcase, climbed up and teetered to and fro trying to pull the book from the shelf. Finally it fell forward onto the floor, and after clambering down, she hung dizzily onto the back of the chair for a moment before she could pick it up.

Swann sank onto the couch and leafed through the book. She found the section on allergies and read the paragraphs about hives.

"Apply a baking soda solution or calamine lotion," she read.

She knew there was baking soda in the kitchen, and she forced herself to rise to her feet and walk the few steps into the kitchen. She took the little yellow box of baking soda out of the cupboard. She'd have to mix it with water to make a paste, and she looked around for a pan. The box fell to the floor and broke open, spilling its contents across the kitchen floor. Joe-the-Cat appeared and blinked at the mess while Swann collapsed into a kitchen chair and began to sob.

It was at that moment that she heard the sound of Paul's Honda in the driveway. Paul...Paul. He would know what to do.

He was carrying a fresh tube of caulking compound and had headed around the house toward the boat when she stepped out the back door. As soon as he saw her face, he knew something was wrong.

"Swann?" he said, stopping in his tracks. Then he saw the scarlet welts on her arms. "What happened?" he asked sharply.

"The bush—I cut it down," she said, gesturing with her head toward the stump of it. "Then this happened."

He dropped the tube of caulking compound, raced across the grass, took one close look at the raised weals and bundled her inside the house. He made her lie down on the couch while he examined her arms more closely. The severe shortness of breath, the hives—it pointed to anaphylactic shock.

He recalled that she'd once told him that she'd contracted a rash from plants when she was a baby. This could be more of the same; she could be hypersensitive to that plant she had cut down. There was no doubt in his mind that her reaction was serious.

"I'd better call the rescue squad," he said tersely. He picked up the phone.

Swann couldn't breathe. She inhaled ragged breaths and twisted her head from side to side, trying to open her airways. She began to panic as she realized that she might lose consciousness.

Paul stopped in middial. He looked down at her contorted face and heaving chest and realized that he didn't have time to wait for the rescue squad. It was her difficulty in breathing that alarmed him most. He'd never seen such an acute case of urticaria, and if he'd had adrenaline with him, he'd have administered an intramuscular injection immediately.

He touched the skin on her arms and she moaned. If only he could call on The Power...if only The Power would be there for him now. He tried to feel it, tried to call it forth from that place in his soul where he knew, he *knew* it was. At first he didn't feel it, couldn't find it, but he made himself concentrate, searching desperately for the pinprick of light deep within himself, trying to make it appear.

And then he saw it in the blackness, nothing more than a tiny seed, and the seed grew and blossomed and he knew that he could do it. He gripped Swann's hands in his and let the light flow through him to her, let it surge into the hurt places, let it make her well. His hands tingled and a humming sound filled his ears, and he wanted to laugh with the joy of it because The Power was there for him and for Swann.

Chapter Ten

Swann should have realized what he was doing when he gripped her hands so tightly, but she was almost fainting and it simply didn't register. It wasn't until she felt the sensation of intense but not painful heat at the point where his hands touched hers that she understood.

It was almost as though her body were weightless in those moments when the healing was working; she felt light and bright and pure. A vibration worked through her hands into her arms, and it filled her ears with its sound. She opened her eyes to look into Paul's face, his beautiful face, and it was as though she were looking once more into the smiling countenance of that curly-haired six year old who had long ago straightened her foot, but then that face faded and was replaced with Paul's own dear face only inches from hers.

"Paul?"

"It's all right," he said soothingly, but his voice shook.

"You—?"

"You're going to be fine," he said.

She knew he had spoken the truth when she looked down at her arms and saw that the welts were fading rapidly.

She sat up, at a loss for words. All this time she had wanted to confront him with her knowledge of who he really was, and now he had performed one of his miracles on her. He must have known that he would give himself away, and yet he had done it anyway. She had no idea what to say.

"I'll get you a glass of water," he said. He had to get away from her for a moment and retain control of himself. Now he had found The Power twice in recent months, and the knowledge that he could find it when he needed it shook him to his core. He went into the kitchen and steadied himself for a moment before filling a glass with water and taking it in to Swann.

By this time she was sitting upright on the couch. Her eyes were wide, and she watched him with an enhanced awareness. She knew about him now; there would be no denying it the way he had that time after he'd helped Kathy at Linda and Rick's party. He steeled himself for the explanations that must surely follow.

But she surprised him. She only took the glass from his hands and sipped from it.

He noticed the first-aid book on the floor and picked it up. "I guess you know you probably have an allergy to whatever kind of plant that was," he said finally.

She nodded.

"I meant to cut the shrubbery back earlier," he said.

"I didn't expect you to," she replied. Her tone was so normal that he could almost believe that she didn't know what he'd done.

The silence that followed felt awkward. He waited to see what she'd say next.

But she didn't say anything. She was determined that he would be the one to make explanations; she would not drag them out of him piece by piece. Any talk of what had just happened here should be initiated by him. After all, she had tried once before to elicit information, and the results had been disastrous. She didn't see how he could avoid discussing the method by which he had made her hives disappear almost instantaneously.

He leaned forward, elbows on knees, and studied her. "How are you feeling?" he asked cautiously.

"Fine, now," she answered.

"That's good." He looked around the room, trying to figure out what to say. The odd thing was that now that he knew she wasn't going to pounce on him and demand to know what exactly it was that he had done to relieve her of her hives, his mind seemed to snag on what had happened in this room the night he'd walked out. He'd suffered miserably over his action, and he'd decided that he had to put things right between them. That was why he had resumed work on the boat.

He swung his head up when she set the glass down on the table with a sharp *clink!* She moved as if to get up from the couch but he touched his hand to her knee and said, "Wait."

She thought, *This is it. He's going to tell me.* She waited expectantly.

When she cast a wary look in his direction, Paul realized that Swann was as uneasy as he was. He had never been comfortable revealing anything of himself, but now it was necessary. She sank back amid the cushions, looking at him with those enormous golden eyes and making him lose track of how he meant to start out.

"I, uh, I'm sorry I walked out the night of the oyster roast," he said uncomfortably. "I shouldn't have done that." He watched her steadily for her reaction.

She stared at him, and she seemed to be taken aback. He could read her more easily now than he'd been able to in the early days, and what he saw in her expression was disappointment. He knew there was more to be said, but he'd get to that later. At the moment the important thing was to let her know that he wanted to put things right between them.

She compressed her lips for a moment, thinking. "It hurt my feelings," she said at last.

He flushed slightly. If she meant to make him uncomfortable, she had. He hated the idea of hurting anyone in any way; wasn't he dedicated to helping, not hurting?

"What can I do to convince you that I'm sorry?" he asked, his voice low.

"You know," she said, "I believe you're sorry. So it's not that. I'm just—" She stopped, looked out the window, then back at him. She managed a weak smile. "I'm confused. Maybe the less said about that night, the better."

The words he wanted to say lumped at the bottom of his stomach. He wished he had the ability to heal torn emotions as easily as he'd healed torn flesh. Maybe what had happened that night couldn't be fixed. Perhaps there was no point in even talking about it. He'd be much better off if he left a lot of things unsaid, especially an explanation of The Power and how it had ended and the aimlessness of his life ever since.

He stood up and walked over to the door that opened onto the porch. He supposed it was too late now to start working on the boat. He wished he had never decided to begin the project anew. No, wait, that wasn't right. If he hadn't been here when Swann had the attack of hives, she would have been in serious trouble.

"I'd better go get that new tube of caulking compound in case it rains tonight. I wouldn't want it out," he said. He was aware of her close behind him. He shot a look over his shoulder and was surprised by the tenacity in the set of her chin.

So she wasn't going to let him get away with it so easily. Paul's heart began to pound, and he felt suddenly claustrophobic. It was all too much, too hard to explain. He'd been a fool to think that he'd be able to tell her about himself and The Power. Of course she knew about it after what he had done, first with Kathy and now with her, but putting it into words was too difficult. He would feel demeaned if Swann were to find out how useless he felt when he tried for The Power and couldn't find it. Oh, it was one thing to feel that way, and quite another to say the words, to hear them as she would hear them. It would only make the worthlessness that he'd felt all along official.

He had to get away, had to pull free of her! He broke into a cold sweat and bolted out the door and across the grass.

Swann perceived that Paul had slipped into his avoidance mode; she couldn't believe his sheer folly in thinking that she would let him get away with this. She cared about him. She loved him, and she didn't care how he perceived himself, he was worth fighting for. He was a man worth loving. She'd given him his chance to bring up the subject of his healings on his own, and now she was ready to confront him even if he didn't like it. The time for subtlety had clearly passed. At the moment, as far as she was concerned, they really didn't have a relationship, and she had nothing to lose by having it out with him.

Paul was no sooner out the door than she was running after him, her hair and clothes flying. She caught up with Paul halfway to the creek and seized his arm with surprising ferocity. At her touch he spun around, shaking her off. Her hair whipped wildly around her face, but she wouldn't let him go. She gripped both of his arms and shook him with a strength she hadn't known she possessed.

"Paul! I know who you are! You're Child Michael!" she blurted, and at the sound of the words he had never thought to hear, never *wanted* to hear, all the fire went out of him. All he felt was the sadness that she had finally found out.

Through the haze that covered his eyes, he heard Swann say more calmly, "I know who you are, and it doesn't matter. To me you're still Paul Thompson. You're still the man I love."

The haze slowly melted away, leaving the world—cottage, creek, trees, sky and most of all, this woman—clearly delineated. He closed his eyes and swallowed. His mouth felt unaccountably dry. She had said she loved him.

He opened his eyes and stared down at her. She was gazing at him with an expression both loving and compassionate. In that moment he felt a reeling in of his connection to her, as though it had never been broken. And in fact, it hadn't. It had only been stretched to the limit.

He saw there was no point in denying who he was. After all, today he had given her proof. He discovered in that instant that he didn't want to deny it, that, contrary to what he had thought he would feel if the time ever came to reveal his identity, it felt right. His love for her in that moment was so overwhelming that he accepted the fact that she knew, and he accepted her.

"Swann, oh, Swann," he said brokenly, burying his face in her hair.

When he held her in his arms again, it was as though they had never been apart. He thankfully inhaled the fragrance of her hair, kissed her soft cheek, listened to their hearts beating in unison.

"I've missed you," she said, her breath warm against his ear.

"I've missed you, too," he told her.

She laughed a little then, and he sensed that she was perilously near tears.

"We need to talk," he said.

"About us?"

"Eventually. But right now I want to talk about me."

"That's unusual," she said.

"I know." He smiled down at her. "Do you mind?"

She shook her head solemnly. "I'm glad you don't mind my knowing."

"Can we sit by the creek? It'll be cool there, and I've got a lot to tell you."

She took his hand and they found a grassy spot on the bank where Swann could lean up against a big rock. Paul sprawled on the ground at her feet. He looked up at her, a self-conscious smile on his face.

"I never thought I'd be telling this to anyone," he said. "Can it remain a secret between you and me? I'm not ready to go public yet."

There was only a moment of hesitation on her part. "I'll keep the secret," she said evenly. "Just tell me."

And so he did.

PAUL COULDN'T REMEMBER his mother at all, but his father had always been there.

Paul's earliest memories were of the rickety travel trailer where he, his father, and his father's girlfriend Brenda lived as they traveled the United States. It was Brenda who had provided the warmth and nurturing that a small, motherless boy required; it was Brenda who spent the most time with him.

His father was a carnival huckster who was employed by a small, down-at-the-heels carnival that had seen better days. Mac Thompson had rescued Brenda from the carnival's dancing girl show, and he never let her forget it. Many were the nights that Mac came in drunk and slapped Brenda around; many were the nights that Paul listened to her cry herself to sleep.

It was when Paul was barely four years old that he first found The Power within him. A playmate, the daughter of the carnival's business manager, had tumbled down the skimpy set of stairs leading to the door of the trailer and skinned her knee. Paul crouched beside her in the dust to offer what comfort he could, and he couldn't help staring at her knee.

It was quite interesting the way the top layer of skin had peeled away, and, like most little boys, he had a most avid curiosity. Millie was still crying when he poked an experimental finger at the skinned spot. Then something happened; his hand began to tingle and feel unnaturally warm. This was odd, and he wanted to know why. It had never happened before; why was it happening now? It must have something to do with Millie's scraped knee.

If Brenda came outside, she'd take Millie back into the trailer to wash off the wound and put medicine on it, so if he were to find out what the heat in his hand had to do with Millie's injury, it was imperative that Millie stay where she was.

"Shh, Millie, don't cry," Paul whispered. He touched her knee again, and, wonder of wonders, she did stop crying to watch him. For the first time he sensed that when he touched her, she felt something, too.

"You know, your knee's not bleeding now," Paul said. He positioned himself closer. For some reason he put one hand above the skinned place, the other below it. He felt a strange vibration welling up inside him, kind of like the time they had stayed in a motel on vacation at Weeki Wachee Springs in Florida. That night Brenda had given him a quarter to put in a slot next to the bed, and the whole mattress had shaken. He had said "Ahhh" in a long, drawn-out way, and Brenda had laughed at the way the sound came out, all broken and growly. This was like that, only he didn't say "Ah."

He asked Millie, "Does it hurt?"

Millie wiped her tears away. "It feels good," she said cautiously. "Like sunshine." Only it was a cloudy day; the sun had been hiding behind clouds since lunchtime.

Paul took his hands away from her knee. The vibration stopped, and the heat did, too.

"My knee feels *real* good," Millie said in an awestruck voice.

"I guess I made it well," Paul said.

"Well, anyway, it's not bleeding anymore. I can go home now." And she'd stood up and skipped away, apparently feeling no pain at all. The next day, they could hardly detect the place where the skin had been scraped.

That was the first time. There were other times, too, that Paul was able to help children, and even, one time, a dog with a mangled ear. All this went unnoticed by adults until Millie bumped her head on a cabinet drawer, and as the bruise was swelling on the back of her head, she tearfully demanded that her parents take her to Paul, "so he can fix it."

Her perplexed parents confronted Paul's father, who narrowed his eyes and dragged Paul away from his TinkerToys to ask, "What the hell are they talking about?" Paul held his hands to Millie's bruise, it diminished considerably, and from that moment on, Paul's life changed dramatically.

Mac Thompson set Paul up in a tent a stone's throw away from the dancing girls and devoted his considerable talents as a barker to drawing in the customers. At a dollar a shot, they could have Child Michael, the stage name Mac had chosen for his son, place his chubby little hands on their broken arms, mysterious rashes and arthritic fingers. Afterward they'd go away cured, or at least they'd think they were cured. Despite his own skepticism, Mac Thompson noticed that more people were flocking to Child Michael than were interested in the hoochy-koochy girls. Paul's reputation spread so far, in fact, that people began lining up outside the tent as soon as the carnival grounds opened wherever they went.

This got Mac Thompson to thinking that a dollar wasn't much money to pay for being cured. After all, look at doctors. They charged considerably more and, he liked to brag to his friends, Child Michael probably had a higher success rate.

The carnival owner tolerated Child Michael because he was a new novelty act and much better than the man who billed himself as The Human Lizard or the aging fire-eater who half the time refused to eat fire. But when Mac raised the price of a cure to five dollars, the owner demanded a cut of the proceeds. Mac quickly nixed that suggestion and set out on his own.

Brenda was bitterly opposed to Paul's working so hard. She said that sitting in a dusty, drafty tent until all hours of the night was no life for a kid and that Mac was probably violating child labor laws. For that observation, Mac swatted Brenda a few times, and not gently, either, so that was the end of that. In Biloxi, Mississippi, Brenda disappeared one day. Just up and left. When Mac offered no explanation for her absence and Paul had the temerity to ask what had happened to her, Mac said, "Guess she got a job in a honky-tonk somewheres.'' They never heard from Brenda again.

From their early days, attracting customers to Child Michael was no problem. Mac would send an advance man ahead to put up a few posters in the towns along their route, and by the time they got there, people were waiting in droves. People in wheelchairs, people on crutches, people of all ages.

Small-town newspapers began to pick up on the story, and before long the national media did, too. Paul remembered nights when huge stacks of money were lined up on the beds of the motels where they stayed by this time; the Thompsons were moving up in the world. Before long, Mac declared his intention to find a place where the world could come to Child Michael's doorstep. He bought a tract of land in rural Pennsylvania and dubbed it Miracle Farm.

Child Michael and Miracle Farm were a huge success. Hordes of people flocked to see him. Mac started a thriving mail-order business so that people could buy Child Michael key chains, Child Michael coffee mugs, Child Michael pen sets. People sent money to Child Michael so that he could continue his good works. Soon Mac built a huge consultation center with an adjoining hotel; he and Paul and their retinue moved into an enormous house on the grounds.

Paul owned every kind of toy imaginable, and tutors came to see to his education, and the press adopted him as a kind of mascot. A Los Angeles newspaper columnist gushingly referred to him as ''a male Shirley Temple—sweet Child Michael and his good works uplift us as much as that little girl who came along and saved us from feeling so miserable during the Great Depression.''

Mac Thompson was on a roll. Things had never been so good. The former carnival huckster had hit a gold mine.

Nothing could stop him. Nothing except Child Michael himself.

"IT WAS IN ALL THE PAPERS when you left Miracle Farm," Swann said when Paul fell silent.

"Everything I did was in all the papers by that time," he said.

"What happened?"

"I was fourteen years old and beginning to feel conflicts with parental control as most normal teenagers do. I wanted to throw away all those cute little suits my father made me wear. I was beginning to feel not so much dressed as upholstered in them. And there were lots of other things I'd have liked to change. It was the worst possible time to lose The Power."

"But how did you lose it, Paul?"

He stared off into the distance. "After I reached puberty, The Power was no longer reliable. When I wanted to call forth The Power, I'd try to enter myself like I'd always done, looking for the speck of light deep inside me and seeking to bring it out into my hands, but it wasn't there. And I didn't know how to get it back."

"Where did it go?"

"I don't know. I never knew where it came from in the first place, so I couldn't very well know where it went. Some people thought it came from God, but I really can't say that with any authority. The Power was just this ability that I had, and then I didn't have it anymore. It was as simple as that."

"Your father must have been upset."

"Upset? That doesn't begin to describe the way he was. He was livid, furious, accusatory. 'You had it before, you can get it again,' he'd say, and then he'd curse me and spend half the night screaming at me."

Swann felt a sharp pull of sympathy. She knew the pain of having a parent who ranted and raved at the slightest opportunity. Paul must have felt under terrible pressure to perform.

"When I told Dad that I couldn't do the Help Meetings anymore, he really flew off the handle. He yelled and said I had to do them, that I didn't have any choice. He said that it didn't matter whether I had The Power or not, that I could perform at the Help Meetings without it.''

''Then what happened?''

''I said that I didn't think it was right to pretend that I was healing people when I knew I didn't have The Power. That's when he grabbed me and yanked me up close to his face and told me that he'd made me what I was, and he could un-make me, too. I told him that he wouldn't do that because then he wouldn't have anything. I knew very well where all our money came from. He lit into me with his fists, and one of his assistants had to drag him off me. It was a terrible scene.''

''Paul, how awful! It hurts me even to think of it,'' Swann said in a low tone. She was remembering his look of under-standing when he'd seen her father slap her all those years ago. Now she understood the young Child Michael's com-passion for her; they had both been subjected to the same type of discipline.

Paul reached for her hand and held it for a moment be-tween both of his. ''Dad threw me into my room and didn't speak to me for days. Then he dragged me out to a Help Meeting. I looked out through the curtain at all those peo-ple waiting for me, and I felt sick. I knew I couldn't help them, so I refused to go out there. Dad could hardly hit me backstage with so many people around, so he had his assis-tants haul me back to the house.''

''What did he tell the people?''

''Oh, he went onstage and made some hokey speech about how Child Michael had been working so hard that he was exhausted, and it ended with everyone praying for my recovery. What an irony!'' Paul smiled bitterly.

''I'll say,'' Swann said.

''So this went on for a while, with me balking and Dad ordering me to perform. It got to the point where I was a virtual prisoner in my room. I was terrified because I didn't understand where The Power had gone. I'd never been without it as long as I could remember. It was like losing some other capability that you've learned to rely on—for instance, being able to read music if you're a musician or being able to type if you're a secretary. And then there was Dad. I had no idea what he was going to do next. He seemed totally irrational."

"So you left," Swann said softly.

"I was well guarded, but I managed to escape one night. I walked to the police station in the town of Montberry and announced to the desk sergeant that I was Child Michael and that I needed help. After that it was curtains for Miracle Farm. All the attention made the Internal Revenue Service take a close look at the finances, and my father was arrested for income tax evasion."

"What happened to you after he was arrested?"

"I was put in foster care, and after my father went to jail, I ended up in a group home for boys in Ohio. Both places were better than where I'd come from, and I never wanted to be Child Michael again. I couldn't anyway. The Power was gone, and I couldn't get it back."

He sighed deeply and squeezed her hand. "There you have it, Swann. The Child Michael story. Sometimes I can hardly believe that it really happened to me."

Swann was deeply moved. She lifted his hand and rested her cheek against its palm. "The Power obviously returned," she said after a time.

"It came back that night when Kathy cut her arm, and it was totally unexpected. For some reason, I knew that if I tried to heal her, I would. I don't know why The Power came back, just like I don't know where it went."

"How wonderful it would be to have it from now on," she said thoughtfully.

"I can't count on it, though. I never know when it'll be there for me. That's why I became a paramedic—I knew I'd be able to help people with medical problems even without The Power. The medical help I give now is more reliable."

Paul glanced at his watch. "Do you realize what time it is? It's past six o'clock! I'm on duty from seven until eleven tonight." He stood up.

"I wish you didn't have to go," Swann said.

"I'll come back later after my shift. That is, if you'll let me."

She went willingly into his arms and lifted up her face to kiss him.

"I'll be waiting for you," she said.

She watched him leave, striding across the grass. There was a bounce in his footsteps, and she thought he looked as though a huge weight had been lifted from his shoulders.

SWANN HAD A SANDWICH ready for Paul when he came in from work. Even though it was almost midnight, both of them were ready to talk. They wanted to share news of what had happened in their lives during the past weeks.

They took their snacks outside and sat in lawn chairs beside a small wrought-iron table that Swann had found in the utility closet. Swann told Paul about teaching Angelyn to read.

"And Paul, I think Angelyn's off to a very good start. She can read on a rudimentary level now—maybe third grade or so," Swann told him.

"It's hard to believe that Angelyn went through so many grades of school without learning to read any better than that."

"It's sad, isn't it? She says she was always in the lowest reading group, and that no one seemed to care that she was lagging far behind. She was very shy as a child, and she didn't ask questions."

"If you spend so much time working with Angelyn, won't your work on your book begin to lag behind schedule?"

Swann's spirits took a nosedive. After Paul had revealed the secret about his past, she felt even more guilty about hiding her real reason for coming to Reedy Creek. Her mind groped for a way to be honest, but she knew that his revelation was still too new for her to suggest writing his biography. It was a situation that had to be handled delicately. Oh, she was so tired of her subterfuge! She wished it was over and done with. She wished—

"Well, won't it?"

She looked away, unable to meet his eyes. "I suppose so," she said. She set the rest of her sandwich on the edge of her plate; she couldn't eat anymore.

"Want to walk down by the creek for a while? There aren't many mosquitoes out yet." He stood up and pulled her up with him; he slid his arm around her shoulders as they walked together down the slope. Swann had never felt so guilty.

And if she were to say, "Paul, I want to write your biography," right now, this very minute, what would be his likely response?

He had said before he told her about his life as Child Michael, "Can it remain a secret between you and me?" And she had agreed.

He had said, "I'm not ready to go public yet." And she had said nothing to give herself away.

She couldn't reveal herself now. She wanted him back in her life. Not just for now, but for always. To tell him that she had come here under false pretenses would drive him away from her forever.

A new moon hung over the treetops. A soft breeze brushed the tops of the reeds in the shallows of the creek, and the leaves overhead rustled and danced on their branches. Because of the wind, the mosquitoes weren't out in full force.

"Linda asked about you tonight. I saw her at the hospital when she and Rick stopped by to visit a sick friend," Paul said.

"Oh? And what did you tell her?" Swann tried hard to maintain an even tone of voice.

"That we're back together and getting along just fine," he said, turning her toward him and trailing his lips across her forehead. "We are, aren't we?" he said, holding her away from him so that he could look into her eyes.

"Oh yes," she said faintly as his hands drifted upward to cup her breasts.

"Thank goodness," he said. "I couldn't stand being apart from you, Swann."

"I couldn't, either," she said, succumbing to the sensations that rose from somewhere below her breastbone.

He rubbed the flat of his palms over her nipples. "I thought I could wait," he said, the words soft against her ear. "I didn't mean for this to happen here." A chill rippled over her, and it wasn't from the wind.

"Let it happen," was all she said, and she took off her jacket and spread it on the damp ground.

With trembling fingers he undressed her until she stood before him wearing only her pearl earrings and the gossamer-pale light from the moon. She helped him undress, and they stood for a moment drinking in the sight of each other. His fingers caressed her shoulders and threaded upward through her hair, urging her head toward his. Swann quivered at his touch; she had missed him so much. Had longed for his lips upon hers, and ached for his skin against hers, and wanted—oh, all of him.

His kiss at first was reverent, soon becoming more insistent. His body was hard and hot as it pressed against hers, and Swann felt her knees begin to buckle. In a single graceful movement he caught her and eased her to the ground where they tumbled upon their clothes in their eagerness. They wound around each other, the world obliterated. Their desire sent shock waves through them both. He was magnificent, and together they were extraordinary. She lost herself in the hot delirium of body upon body, body lost in body and finally in the mindless flowing one into the other. When it was over, he gasped in her arms. She clung tightly to him as the world ebbed back into her consciousness.

When she could speak, she said, "We should go in the house."

He lifted himself above her and rolled over, pulling her along with him. Her hair fell like a cloak across his chest. Her mouth was soft against his skin.

"We should," he said, but they didn't leave until the breeze stilled and mosquitoes descended, driving them inside to bed.

Chapter Eleven

The next morning, Swann slid out of bed while it was still dark. Paul slept beside her, breathing softly. She silenced Joe-the-Cat's inquisitive mew and carried him into the kitchen where he wouldn't wake Paul.

She left Paul a note and propped it on the bathroom sink so that he'd find it if he woke up while she was gone. Then she slipped out into the predawn light.

Angelyn, her slight figure framed by her back door, waited with a finger pressed to her lips. She led the way into the kitchen where they closed the door so that the children wouldn't hear their voices.

They started with a spelling test and ended the lesson with Angelyn reading two short stories from a book that Swann had found at the local library. Angelyn's skill continued to grow, much to Swann's satisfaction.

Swann declined Angelyn's invitation to stay for coffee and hurried home through the pale lemony light sweeping upward from the eastern horizon. Paul was barely awake when she slipped back into bed beside him.

"Where've you been?" he asked sleepily.

"To Angelyn's house for her reading lesson," she murmured against his shoulder. "I told you about it."

"So you did," he said as he wound his arms around her. "You smell salty like the mist. Taste like it, too." He nuzzled her hair.

She turned in his arms, thinking how good it was to come home to him in her bed. "Are you ready to get up?"

"Almost." He sat up and rubbed his eyes.

"I'll put on the coffeepot while you shower," she said. He kissed her before she pulled on her robe and padded into the kitchen.

"That can't be ordinary coffee—it smells so good," he said when he appeared later. She told him about the fresh Colombian coffee beans that she liked so much. "I could get used to this coffee," he said reflectively.

Could you get used to me? she thought involuntarily, and then she turned away to drop the toast into the toaster. They hadn't talked about the future yet. Maybe they never would. She'd better stop thinking about it.

They sat down across the tiny table from each other, smiling in the bar of buttery sunlight that now peeped through the curtain.

"I'm glad you've adopted Angelyn and her kids as a project," Paul said. "They needed someone to take an interest in them."

Swann's expression grew somber for a moment. "It's not a project, Paul. Angelyn is my friend." Swann thought of the many times that she'd seen Carlie's trusting hand held firmly in Mott's grubby one. "Not only that, I admire what Angelyn is doing. She's held that family together, Paul, perhaps through sheer willpower. The Soameses may be poor but they have one another."

"I've seen Angelyn in town, leading those kids around. She's a spunky woman despite her frail looks."

"I know. I'm thinking, Paul, that there must be more I could do for them. A scholarship fund for the children, perhaps, or— oh, I don't know."

Paul glanced at his watch and pushed his chair back from the table. "Look, I'm really sorry, but I've got to run. The squad's shorthanded this week because of summer vacations, so I'm working a lot of split shifts. I'll call you later."

He kissed her lingeringly at the door and hurried out to his car.

Swann barely had time to catch her breath before the phone rang. It was Justin.

"Well, Swann, how's it going down there? I haven't heard from you in a long time," he said.

Swann sank down on a nearby chair. The last person she wanted to talk to was Justin.

"Swann?"

"It's just that I've been busy," she said.

"Are you making any headway?"

Swann realized that she was caught in a bind. Paul had asked her not to tell anyone that he was Child Michael; surely the assurance she had given him last night was not meant to cover people who already knew.

"Swann, have I called at a bad time? Is something wrong?"

Justin had known her all her life, and she might as well level with him. "Justin, I don't know what to say. Last night Paul Thompson told me that he is Child Michael, and I promised not to tell anyone. Now I'm torn in two directions. I wouldn't even feel comfortable discussing him with you, to tell you the truth," she said.

Silence on the other end of the line while Justin digested this. Finally he said, "I see. What's going on, Swann?"

"I feel an obligation to protect his interests, that's all. I'm aware that my loyalty should be to you and the book I want to write, but it's not working out that way."

"What in the world—! Swann, what are you trying to say?"

"I think I'm trying to tell you that I'm in love with him," Swann said in a very small voice.

Justin was speechless.

"I know what you're going to say," Swann said. "You're going to tell me that I don't know what I'm talking about, that I haven't known him long enough to decide if it's love, that I'd better think this over very carefully. I've told my-self the same things. I love him anyway.''

"Why don't you come to New York for a few days and we'll discuss the whole project?" Justin suggested. She detected a note of exasperation in his voice.

"I don't want to come to New York. I'm going to stay right here with Paul."

"Does he know that you want to write a biography of him?"

"Obviously not, since he swore me to secrecy," Swann retorted testily.

"Okay, okay, I see your problem."

"I have reams of notes, Justin, and I think his life story would make a terrific book. If anything, I want to write about him more now than I did when I first arrived. I wasn't too sure, as you recall, that it was a project I wanted to tackle. Now I know that if anyone is to write the Child Michael story, I'm that person."

"My advice is to tell him that's what you want to do. Get his cooperation. If the guy's in love with you, this is the time to get him to agree to it."

"I wouldn't dream of using his emotions that way," Swann said indignantly.

"Wouldn't you? Then you're not thinking straight." Justin sounded miffed.

"Justin, I *love* the man!"

"All right, all right, whatever you say. Don't be a fool for love, Swann. Don't give up a bestseller."

They hung up on that note. Swann was relieved that the conversation was over. If only she could get it out of her mind; Justin's cautionary words, "Don't be a fool for love" played themselves over and over in her mind.

Was she being a fool for love? Was it ridiculous to think that somehow she and Paul might stay together? She couldn't think; the thought paramount in her mind at the moment was that she was so happy that they had resolved their difficulties. All she wanted was to enjoy that happiness and to live in it for a while before other problems brought pressure to bear on their relationship.

Later, because the hours until Paul could call seemed to stretch endlessly in front of her, Swann walked over to Angelyn's and brought all three children back to her house for an early lunch. "That way you'll have time to practice reading," she told Angelyn, who seemed grateful for the time off from her busy child-care duties.

Just how busy a mother could be was what Swann found out as she chased after Rhonda, stashed breakable objects out of the nimble reach of the curious Carlie and supervised Mott's play on the porch. Rhonda was like quicksilver, slipping out of her grasp and running all over the place. Nothing was safe from Carlie, especially Swann's word processor, which seemed to hold a special fascination for her. Mott was calmer, but Swann had to make sure that he didn't make paper airplanes out of the notes for her book. By the time she delivered the children to their mother, Swann's respect for Angelyn had grown tenfold.

"I hope they behaved," Angelyn said.

"They were good, but they have a lot of energy, don't they?"

"It must agree with you, Swann. You look right happy today."

"Oh, I am. Paul and I got back together last night."

"I'm so glad for you! Want to tell me about it?" Angelyn's face shone with interest.

They sat down on the lopsided back porch while the children played nearby.

"Angelyn, I love him. I've never felt this way before about anyone, and I think he feels the same way about me," Swann said.

"But, Swann," Angelyn began before gazing off into the distance.

"What is it?"

"Are you sure you know each other well enough? I mean, Bobby and me, when we fell in love we hardly knew each other at all. That's what the problem was. And we were too young, of course." She focused troubled eyes on Swann.

"Paul and I have become very close," Swann said slowly. She would have liked to tell Angelyn the Child Michael story, but she couldn't. She had promised Paul.

"But love," Angelyn said. "What is it, Swann? I don't even think I know anymore. I thought I loved Bobby, you know, and now I'm not so sure I ever did."

Swann focused on her feelings for Paul. They encompassed so many emotions: happiness, acceptance, sexual pleasure. There was one thing missing, however, and it was what troubled her the most.

"What worries me," she said slowly, "is that Paul hasn't said anything about commitment, and I don't know how to handle it."

"I'm not one to advise anybody," Angelyn said ruefully. "Look at me, after all. I'm still trying to put my life back together. One thing I know from being married to Bobby. Unless your partner is mighty committed to the relationship, it's not love yet. Besides, what good would it do for you to be committed to the relationship if he's not?"

"I see your point."

"Anyway, maybe that's not what you want."

"I'd like to be with Paul for the rest of my life. The only thing is that it's hard trying to figure out if that's what he wants, too."

Their conversation was interrupted when Mott and Carlie begged to be allowed to play under the house where it was cool. Angelyn turned them away with a firm "no," and Swann was again amazed to see how easily she controlled her children with only a change in her tone of voice. She had never witnessed any hitting in the Soames household.

After Swann left Angelyn, she went home and, from force of habit, took out her notebook. She proceeded to fill in a lot of the blanks about Paul's background. She bent over her notes, writing rapidly and becoming totally absorbed in her work until Paul arrived. Then she carefully hid her notebook away and tried to forget that it existed.

That night they ate dinner at the Little Bit, rented a video of a Stones concert and went to bed early. Before they drifted off to sleep in each others' arms, Swann thought about asking him if he'd ever thought of a book as a way to set his side of the story before the public.

But then he shifted position so that his leg slid between hers, and she adjusted her head so that her cheek rested against his hair. Lost in a haze of contentment, she fell asleep, and by the next morning, asking that particular question didn't seem like such a good idea.

"I ONCE HATED MY FATHER for making a public spectacle of me," Paul said a few days later as they were waxing his car under an oak tree at the bluff one afternoon.

"Perhaps he meant well," Swann ventured.

Paul considered this. The wide river rippled beyond him, and a cool breeze ruffled his forelock. He spread on more wax with wide circular strokes.

"I don't know if he did or not," Paul said finally. "He was doing all he knew to make a living, I guess. When fate handed him a surefire draw, he knew how to bring the people in."

"You're still bitter, aren't you?" Swann asked.

"Only at times. I've forgiven him."

"Where is he now, Paul?"

"He died a few years ago. My one regret is that I never made my peace with him when I could have. He died thinking that I hated him. We'd lost touch after he went to prison."

"Oh, Paul," Swann said. "I'm sorry."

"I am, too. I should have—but why worry about it now? That's what I keep telling myself, at any rate. I wish I didn't think about it so much."

"How did you know where he was?"

"I learned through a mutual acquaintance that he was in the hospital and not expected to live. I didn't think I wanted to see him. By the time I changed my mind, it was too late." Paul stopped spreading wax and studied Swann curiously. "Why are you so interested?"

Swann looked away. "Only because I'm interested in anything about you," she said quietly.

He capped the can of wax and walked around the car. He put his arms around her and pulled her close in an impulsive hug. "I like that," he said. He kissed her on the nose.

"Now," he said, breaking away, "if you don't help me polish this car, we're not going to be through in time for our picnic, and then there are going to be some disappointed youngsters."

"I wonder if we should pick up some Popsicles for dessert," Swann said, picking up a rag and joining in the work.

"Good idea. I get dibs on the red ones."

She laughed and flipped the end of her rag at him. "Mott will lay claim to the red ones, if I'm not mistaken. By the way, Angelyn is looking forward to this picnic even more than the kids are. She's bringing a salad."

"We didn't expect her to do that," Paul said with a frown. The picnic on Swann's back lawn had been conceived as a treat for the Soames family.

"I know, but she insisted."

"Have you told her about the money you decided to put in trust for the kids?"

"Not yet."

"You will tell her, won't you?"

"Sure," she answered.

"My father put money in trust for me. It wasn't much, but it's the only money the IRS couldn't touch when he was convicted of tax evasion. I probably wouldn't have gone to college without it. After earning my bachelor's degree, I got scholarships to medical school, or I wouldn't have gone at all."

Swann stopped in midpolish. "You went to med school?"

"Sure, for a while. In fact, I was about a year short of finishing."

"Why in the world didn't you graduate?"

"Some of the guys got wind of the fact that I was Child Michael. I couldn't stand being identified that way again."

"But so much time had gone by! I should think you wouldn't have minded," Swann said.

"I was embarrassed and ashamed of my father," he said slowly.

"Surely you see now that you're an adult that you were to blame for none of his problems with the Internal Revenue Service. You didn't commit any crimes. He used you, Paul," Swann said firmly.

"I see that now, but I hadn't reached that point then. Being Child Michael was something that I regarded as a stigma, and I'd tried so desperately to be free of it ever since I left Miracle Farm. Anyway, I dropped out of med school in Chicago and left that part of the country. Then I came to Georgia and enrolled in a tech college to become a paramedic."

"Oh, Paul," Swann said despairingly.

"What do you mean, 'Oh, Paul'? In retrospect I see that it may have been a dumb decision, but it seemed right at the time."

"Haven't you ever thought of finishing medical school? Of becoming a doctor after all? You'd be such a wonderful doctor, Paul."

"I've thought about it, but I don't have the money. I'd have to get a scholarship."

"If you got a scholarship before, maybe you could get one again. Why don't you try?"

Paul shrugged. "Discouraged, I guess."

"I think you should."

"Yeah, I always thought that becoming a doctor would allow me to help people in a more acceptable way than being a hands-on healer." He paused. "Do you really think I'd be a good doctor?"

"Absolutely," she said.

"Of course there's nothing wrong with being a paramedic, either," he said, watching her.

She ducked around to the opposite side of the car and went to work. "Of course not," she said, hiding her face.

But she was struck with the thought that an emergency paramedic's work with patients was fleeting, giving no opportunity to develop a relationship with his patients. In other words, it was another area of his life in which Paul did not have to involve himself with anyone. Not even the people he helped.

THE PICNIC FOR ANGELYN and the children was a rousing success. Swann and Paul bought fried chicken, and Angelyn brought potato salad.

Angelyn was full of excitement over her plans to start taking adult education classes in the fall.

"There's a school-subsidized nursery where I can leave the kids. Mrs. Dawson told me about it," she said, her eyes shining.

Swann told Angelyn about the trust fund she wanted to start for the children's education.

"But I can't let you do that," Angelyn said, her eyes wide.

"Of course you can. Anyway, I've already started the paperwork on it."

"But, Swann—"

"Consider me a kind of honorary godmother to Mott and Carlie and Rhonda," Swann said. "I don't have any children of my own."

Tears filled Angelyn's eyes. "I can't tell you how much this means to me," she whispered.

Swann patted her hand. "The best thing you can do to pay me back is to finish your education," Swann told her.

"I'll do it," Angelyn said with feeling. "I'll graduate from high school. You wait and see."

The children had worn their swimsuits under their clothes, and later Swann set out a sprinkler that she'd found in the utility room. The sprinkler had long arms that flipped water around in watery arcs, and the rays of the setting sun made rainbows in the spray. Mott and Carlie ran past the sprinkler, laughing hysterically. Their round bodies in their swimsuits were sleekened by water; they reminded Swann of the otters in their play. Swann brought towels from the house so that she and Angelyn could dry the children, and after the sprinkler had been turned off, a drowsy and docile Carlie crept into Paul's lap.

Angelyn went to find Mott after he had stayed too long in the house, and Paul smiled at Swann and said, "This is nice, Swann. These kids are nice. *You're* nice."

"Nice is nice," she mimicked. He laughed, and the laugh put a twinkle in his eyes.

"I'd like to have kids someday," he said. He looked far out over the creek, and Swann held her breath.

He had not said he'd like to have them with her. But maybe that's what he meant.

Angelyn came back, and Mott played with Joe-the-Cat until fireflies wreathed the bushes. When Mott began yawning every couple of minutes, Paul drove the Soames family home, and then he came back to Swann.

As she lay in his arms that night, she thought about what it would be like to raise a family with Paul. He'd be a good father. Her heart had warmed to him as he'd solemnly inquired about Mott's most recent fishing expedition, and he'd been tender with Carlie when she'd climbed into his lap.

Swann fell asleep and dreamed of plump healthy babies, hers and Paul's, with blond curly hair and blue eyes and a handsome father who doted on them.

ONE DAY during the following week, Paul declared the boat to be seaworthy and suggested that they take it out on the creek.

"Only if I don't have to row," Swann said. "I've never been any good at it."

Paul laughed. "I'll do all the rowing," he told her.

The creek was beautiful in the hot bright light of August, meandering slowly and gracefully past majestic cypress trees festooned in Spanish moss. Here and there the skiff's passage was shaded by masses of lush shrubbery. Turtles sunning on the banks splashed into the water at their approach. Swann sat in the bow of the boat while Paul, true to his word, did the work.

"I've been thinking," Paul said as he rested the oars for a moment, "about what you said about going back to medical school."

Swann whipped her head around to gauge his expression. It was sincere. "Do you want to?" she asked.

"Maybe. It would depend on what kind of scholarships I can get. You know, there are several pretty good med schools in Philadelphia."

Swann caught her breath. She hadn't expected this. "Are you interested in it?" she said, barely daring to hope.

"I'd say so," he replied.

Swann hadn't expected a serious discussion to take place in the middle of the creek. She was unprepared to deal with it. She could only stare at him.

Paul rested on his oars, watching her, a gentle half smile curving his lips. "Does that please you, Swann?" he asked quietly.

"Oh, yes," she said, her eyes shining. She was afraid to say too much.

"I was thinking," he said carefully, "that if I went to school there, we could be together. I mean, at least we'd be closer to each other."

She could have thrown her arms around him, but she didn't dare risk overturning the boat. All she could do was smile. "I think it's a wonderful idea, Paul. *Wonderful*," and her smile grew so wide that she feared her face would split in two.

Paul gazed at her, pleased at her enthusiasm. He bent over the oars and kissed her.

"We could be part of each other's lives then," he said thoughtfully and more seriously, taking up the oars and beginning to row again.

Sunlight glistened on the froth curling away from the bow, and the oars in the oarlocks seemed to creak in rhythm with the beat of Swann's heart. Everything seemed light and bright and happy; today she couldn't think of a thing to worry about.

Paul hadn't said anything about commitment or marriage, but wasn't "being together" a prelude to it?

Life was wonderful; she and Paul were going to be together. Maybe for always.

PAUL TELEPHONED the Medical College of Pennsylvania in Philadelphia and received application forms in the mail. He sat down and filled them out immediately. Swann began to think of his enrollment as a sure thing. Perhaps it was premature to anticipate it so strongly, but she longed for Paul to be accepted and to begin his course of study there. She did not think she could bear to be apart from him now.

She ignored Justin's phone calls and began to live in a state of total bliss. She and Paul were happy together; he had practically moved into the cottage with her. Other than Angelyn and the children, they saw no one. They needed no one. Progress on the book had ground to a standstill, and Swann never ever worked on her notes anymore.

"When are you going to send me an outline?" Justin asked her impatiently one day when he called, but Swann only told him that she was bogged down in the middle of it. After she hung up, she thought she should have told him that the project was off. She didn't feel like writing the book anymore. She had lost her sense of perspective after falling in love with her subject. Now she was as eager to protect his privacy as he was.

Without planning to, she had drifted into a decision not to write the book. It was true that a biography of Child Michael would probably make the important bestseller lists, and Justin would be disappointed that she wasn't going to write it. But Justin always had so many projects in the works that she was sure he wouldn't sulk for long. Eventually he would rejoice with her that, through him, Swann had found the man she loved. The hardest part was going to be telling Justin that she wanted out.

She wrote him a long letter one day, stamped and sealed it, and then, after a great deal of soul-searching, she didn't mail it after all. *I'll tell him in person after I go back home,* she told herself. Perhaps Justin wouldn't take the news so hard when he saw how happy she was.

Life was unadulterated bliss. She continued to float along through the days, her feet barely touching the ground. For Swann it was a vacation of sorts. It was wonderful not to have deadlines, not to be dealing with the problems of living in the city. She thought she might inquire into buying the cottage from its absentee owner. It would be a good place to visit on vacations after she and Paul were married.

ONE NIGHT AFTER DINNER, she and Paul sat reading together on the couch. Paul sprawled out with his stockinged feet propped on the coffee table and Swann sat with her bare feet in his lap. The silence between them was comfortable. They often spent the evenings like this, sitting together and saying very little.

After about an hour, Paul snapped his book closed. He tickled the soles of Swann's feet and she pulled them away, laughing. She dug a big toe into his ribs in retaliation, and he deftly rolled out of the way, landing on his feet.

He bent over and kissed her, and she smiled up at him. "I think I'll get some ice cream. Want some?" he asked.

"Sure, if you're getting up anyway," she said. "Have you finished your book?"

"Yes, and remind me not to read any more by that particular author. I kept waiting for the action to start but it never did."

"Give him another chance. He's one of Justin's favorite protégés."

"Well, he ought to stick to writing something besides adventure yarns. Do you want chocolate-raspberry swirl or lime sherbet?"

"Lime, please, and I have another book you might like better. It's got excitement from the word go. It's about this escaped convict who holes up in an abandoned paper mill, and—"

"Swann, don't tell me the plot. If you do, I won't want to read it," he complained. He returned from the kitchen and handed her a dish of lime sherbet. "Where is it?"

"The book? Oh, it's out on the table on the porch. Justin sent it to me a couple of weeks ago and asked for my opinion. I told him I loved it."

Paul set his own dish of ice cream down on the coffee table and ambled out onto the porch. He switched on a light, and Swann returned her attention to her own book, which was just getting interesting. It was about a homeless woman with amnesia who got lost in a Wyoming snowstorm and ended up on a llama ranch with a handsome rancher...

If she had been paying attention, she would have realized that Paul had lingered on the porch for an exceedingly long time. When she heard the wooden floorboards under the living room carpet creaking with Paul's weight, she looked up inquiringly and saw him standing in front of her, his face ashen.

"Didn't you find it?" she asked.

He held out several three-by-five-inch file cards. Her heart clenched convulsively when she realized what they were.

"I looked behind the table and found—these," he said. His words sounded strangled.

In her panic Swann half rose, then fell back onto the couch. Her mind whirled in circles; how much did he know?

He advanced to stand before her. "Why did you write down all these things about me?" he demanded.

"I—" She bit down so hard on her lip that she tasted blood. She couldn't meet his eyes.

"It's not a diary. Not a journal. These are notes, almost scientific observations. They're even cross-referenced, aren't they?" His face was twisted in anger; she had never seen him like this.

He didn't wait for her to answer. Instead, as she cringed, he read, "'Paul—laying on of hands at Linda and Rick's house (see card filed under Kathy).'" He lifted his eyes, damning her with his glance, and shuffled the cards. "Here's another. 'Child Michael was exhibited by his father in carnivals—became part of freak show.' Is that how you think of me, Swann? As some kind of freak?"

"No, Paul, it's not like that," she cried.

"Oh? Then maybe you could explain to me why you have such an interest," he said. He narrowed his eyes at her. "That book you're writing, Swann—who is it really about?"

She tried to gather her defense around her, but it felt like a tattered curtain. "Paul, sit down for a minute and we'll talk about it" was all she could manage.

She thought Paul had been angry before, but now he erupted. He crumpled the file cards in his hand and slammed them down on the floor.

"We're talking about a massive invasion of my privacy, and all you want to do is talk about it?" he raged, storming out onto the porch. Swann leaped up from the couch and followed him.

"It wasn't—"

"How many more of my secrets do you have hidden here? Secrets I poured out to you in utter confidence?" He wrenched drawers out of the file cabinets and gathered papers up in his hands, sifting them onto the rug. He snatched a magazine article out of the pile and stared at it in disbelief.

It was an article that Justin had sent Swann. The article had been published in a slick women's magazine that had been popular in the sixties. Child Michael had been featured on their cover, and the article about him showed him leading his supposedly normal life in the big house at Miracle Farm. Paul's childhood face smiled sweetly from the cover, and in the article, he was pictured eating breakfast with his father and playing with a friend.

"I haven't seen this in a long time," Paul said in a choked voice. The article slipped out of his hands, but he attacked her filing cabinet with renewed vigor. He pulled another drawer out and found her all-important loose-leaf notebook. In a frenzy, he ripped it open and rummaged through the pages, reading passages here and there.

"Paul, please, I can explain," Swann said, feeling as though she were suffocating. She could not have imagined such a horrifying and disorganized scene such as this; they stood ankle-deep in papers. She didn't care about her notes, but she did care about Paul. He was furious.

Without a word Paul pulled pages from her notebook and pitched them in a flurry at her feet.

"I doubt if you can explain anything," he said. His face was shrunken in its anger.

In her terror, she tried to scoop up some of the papers into her arms, but he was beside her in two strides and yanked her upright. His face only inches from hers, he said, "Your book is about me, isn't it?"

She could only stare at him dumbly, unable to speak.

He pinned her to the wall and held her so tightly that if he had released his grip she would have fallen.

"It is, isn't it? You were never writing a book about your father. It was Child Michael all along, wasn't it?"

A long pause while he waited for her answer. There seemed to be no point in denying it. Holding his eyes with her own, she nodded.

He stared at her for a moment before his face registered a grimace of pain. Slowly he released her as the tension drained out of his muscles.

"I trusted you. I never thought you would betray me like this," he said heavily, as though the air had been crushed from him.

"It wasn't a betrayal," she insisted, her voice low. Now maybe she could reason with him, make him listen to her side of the story.

"You lied to me, you said the book was about your father. All along you *lied,* Swann."

She lifted her chin. "Is that any less honest than what you did, Paul? You've *lived* a lie, you know. You've acted as though Child Michael never existed!"

"If you were me, maybe you'd understand why I did that. I had to survive, and that seemed like the only way to do it. Anyway, we're not talking about me here. *You* are the one we're talking about. You came to Reedy Creek for the express purpose of weaseling your way into my confidence so I'd talk about my life as Child Michael, didn't you? Tell me this, Swann. Was it always part of your plan to make me fall in love with you?"

"No! I only wanted to find out if I could do a good job writing the book!"

"Of all the rotten self-serving schemes! I never should have let you get closer to me than anyone ever has. I should have done what I always did before—I should have run away when you started getting too intense."

"When I started out, I wanted information for a book, sure, but then I began to love you," she said. With his look of incredulous disbelief, the room tilted ominously, and she reached blindly for the edge of the table for support.

"Don't talk about love," he said. "There isn't any such thing." Coldly and without hesitation, he turned and walked out of the house.

In the quiet aftermath, all she heard was the rush of blood in her ears. A wave of despair washed over her. She had tried to explain but he wouldn't listen, and all the progress of the past weeks, when he had learned to open up to another human being, was lost. He had finally, in the heat of their argument, admitted that he'd fallen in love with her. Now he would never trust anyone again.

Swann slumped into a chair and covered her eyes with her hands. It was over. She would never hear him say those words she had longed to hear from him—the words ''I love you.'' This time Paul was gone for good, leaving her with nothing but ruptured hopes and shattered dreams.

Chapter Twelve

"Here, Angelyn, you might as well take this food home with you. Otherwise I'll only have to throw it out," Swann said. She was cleaning the cottage's refrigerator preparatory to leaving in the morning, and Angelyn was watching her mournfully from her perch on the edge of the kitchen table.

"I wish you wouldn't go," Angelyn said.

"There's no point in staying now. Actually, the sooner I get back to my town house in Philadelphia, the better. I can't forget about Paul here."

"Are you sure you want to?"

Swann ignored Angelyn's searching look as she tossed sticks of butter and small cans of fruit juice into a bag.

"Of course I want to," she said stoically. "It's over, and I have to get on with my life."

"Oh, Swann, I'm afraid I'll never see you again," Angelyn said.

Swann paused in midtask. She smiled at Angelyn encouragingly. "Don't be silly, Angelyn, I'll be back for your high school graduation ceremony." She knew, though, that she would miss Angelyn, too.

Swann folded over the top of the bag and handed it to Angelyn, who surreptitiously brushed a tear away before going to the door and calling to the children. "Mott! Carlie! Come say your goodbyes!"

Swann picked up Joe-the Cat and caressed his soft fur one last time. In the absence of anyone else who wanted him, Angelyn had agreed that he should be reunited with Stropstripe. She and the children were going to take him home with them today.

Mott finished the somersault he was turning and raced over to Swann to wrap his arms around her waist. Carlie, with Rhonda toddling along beside her, lagged behind. She stood with a finger in her mouth and tears in her eyes until it was her turn to be hugged.

Swann tried to swallow the lump in her throat as she pressed her cheek against Carlie's sweet round face. She would miss these kids; perhaps one day she would have children of her own, but now, with Paul out of her life, that day seemed very far in the future.

Carlie's soft gulping sobs were punctuated by little hiccups. Angelyn embraced Swann, and tears shone in her eyes, too.

"I'll never forget you, Swann," she said.

"You'd better not," Swann answered, trying to smile.

"I'm going to hold you to your promise to come to my high school graduation," Angelyn said.

"I'll be there," Swann assured her. She handed Joe-the-Cat over to Mott. "Take good care of him," she said. She felt sadder than she'd thought she'd feel about leaving the kitten behind.

"Well, goodbye then," Angelyn said. She hoisted the baby in her arms and briefly brushed the thin, fine hair from Carlie's face. Then Carlie slipped her small hand into her mother's and, locked together, the little group headed for the path toward home.

Swann knew that Angelyn and her family had affected her life as much as she had influenced theirs. For the first time she had been privileged to be part of a family unit that was all a family was meant to be—supportive, loving, kind and caring. These were the strengths that Swann hoped she would bring to her own family someday when she was at last lucky enough to have one.

The next morning Swann went for a walk along the creek for the last time. The water glinted coolly in the shallows, purling away to the river. Many memories assailed her; the time she and Paul had gone swimming fully clothed, the night they had made love in the grass after he had admitted to her that he was indeed Child Michael, the afternoon when they had first taken the boat out and he had told her that he was thinking of applying to medical school. She wondered what had become of his application. Probably he would not pursue a career as a doctor. He'd be content to live the life that he had made for himself here in Reedy Creek.

Swann drove away from the cottage before eight o'clock, resolutely refusing to look back. All that was left to her now was to look forward to the future, no matter what it held.

IT WAS A WEEK LATER that she caught a morning flight from Philadelphia to New York and surprised Justin in his office.

"Why, Swann," he said, looking up when she appeared in her doorway. "I thought you were still in Reedy Creek."

Swann drew herself up to her full height and pretended that this was easy. She was looking her most exquisite in a curry-colored suit with padded shoulders and a nipped-in waist. She swept into his office, accepted the chair he offered and sat down, mustering her thoughts and her confidence.

"I've been back for a week," she said. She forced a smile.

Justin walked ponderously around his big desk and sat down. He arched an eyebrow. "Where's the outline of the book?" he asked.

Swann drew a deep breath. "There isn't going to be any outline. I'm not going to write it."

Justin, without bothering to conceal his astonishment, leaned back and studied her. "I can't believe it," he said.

"I'm sorry, Justin. I meant to write a letter to you—in fact, I did write one, but I never mailed it. I thought I'd feel better about it if I told you face-to-face."

His expression was unreadable. "This is a momentous decision. I take it you're going to marry the guy?"

Swann's false bravado dissolved in an instant. So many times she had dreamed of announcing to Justin that she and Paul were going to be married. She had pictured it in her mind, and it would have gone exactly like this. She would have worn her newest dress and her highest heels and come sailing into Justin's office to make her grand announcement, and Paul would have been waiting in the reception area to be introduced at the appropriate moment. Now she was living that scene, but it was vastly different from what she'd planned.

"Oh, Justin," she said, her face crumpling into misery. She groped in her purse for the handkerchief she had put there, but she couldn't find it. Tears streamed down her cheeks.

Justin handed her a clean handkerchief. "Here," he said gently.

It was several minutes before she could stop crying, during which time Justin rang his secretary and instructed her to hold his calls. When at last Swann looked up, he was sitting on the edge of his desk and gazing down at her with kindness.

"I take it that this means that you're *not* going to marry him," he said in a dry tone.

"You've got that right," she said, trying to match his tone but failing miserably. New tears sprang to her eyes, and she blotted them ineffectually.

"There, there," Justin said, patting awkwardly at her shoulder. Suddenly Swann realized that he had absolutely no idea now to cope with her untimely display of emotion. The thought helped her to pull herself together.

"I'm sorry about the book," she said.

"Well, next time I want a book about a handsome young man, I'll know better than to send a beautiful young woman out to write it," he consoled her with false jocularity.

"I'd like to tell you all about Paul and me," she said.

"You're on. Think you can handle lunch at Nouvelles? But you can't cry in my soup, you know. They put entirely too much salt in their food as it is."

Swann blew her nose, tucked his handkerchief away in her pocket and slipped her hand through Justin's arm.

At lunch she told him the whole story. It felt good to get it off her chest.

She also ordered two gin and tonics, but they didn't even begin to dull the pain.

PUTTING HER LIFE BACK together was going to take some doing, Swann reflected. Her town house with its moiré draperies and deep-piled Chinese silk rugs, its well-chosen collection of English porcelain and antique furniture, seemed larger than she recalled. Gracie, back from the beach, was wrapped up in Nolan and therefore not much company. Swann invited Margarita, the housekeeper, to her place for tea one Wednesday afternoon, which she knew was Margarita's day off.

Margarita arrived amid a bustle of stiff petticoats and revealed that Evan Triplett, for once in his life, did not have a current girlfriend. After Swann's departure for Reedy Creek, Margarita said, Evan had moped around the house for days. He'd even asked her a few times if she'd heard from Swann.

"I always told him, no, why didn't he call you in Georgia? And he'd say he didn't have your phone number. I'd tell him he could get it from your friend Gracie, and he'd go 'Harrumph,' and he'd look like he wanted to but didn't know how to humble himself."

"He called Gracie," Swann said. "She wasn't in, and when her houseguest answered the phone, he didn't know my Reedy Creek phone number. What's going on, Margarita? I can't believe my father would actually care where I was."

"Oh, he is a lonely man," Margarita said more seriously.

"But his girlfriends," Swann objected. "They've always kept him from being lonely."

"Have they?" Margarita asked pointedly.

"Well, they seemed to," Swann answered, remembering the endless stream of women he had paraded in and out of the house since Mimi had died.

"Your father is getting on in years, Swann. Why, I believe he's tired of these bim—bim—"

"Bimbettes," Swann supplied.

"I asked him, 'Mr. Triplett, you are home for dinner so much more often these days. Is something wrong?' and listen, Swann, you won't believe it. He laughed! Your father! Why, he never laughs! And he said, 'Margarita, maybe something is right with me!' He went down into the basement and puttered around there. He has bought a power saw! And something called a drill press! And he makes things, working in the basement until all hours of the day and night!"

"What kind of things?" Swann asked skeptically.

"Oh, birdhouses. He made lots of houses for the birds. You know how you say something is for the birds when you don't like it much? Well, his first birdhouses were very much for the birds! Crooked. Kind of hammered together every which way. After he got tired of birdhouses, he made me a stool for the kitchen. I needed it to reach the top shelf in the pantry. Now he is making something big. A cabinet maybe."

"My father has a hobby," Swann said, wondering at this.

"He is different, Swann. I think he misses you."

"Oh, Margarita," Swann said in instant dismissal.

"No, I mean it," Margarita insisted.

Margarita left after another hour of gossip, but Swann couldn't help wondering what was going on with Evan Triplett. She found herself thinking about Paul and his regret that he had never reconciled with his father. Cautiously she began to think that maybe she should drive out to the estate over the long Labor Day weekend and see the change in Evan for herself.

When Swann called Margarita to tell her that she was coming on the Friday night before Labor Day, the house-keeper was delighted. "I'll fix your favorite dinner. Do you still like chicken and dumplings?" she asked wistfully. It had been Swann's favorite dish when she was a child.

"Of course I do," Swann told her, smiling.

Swann had finished putting together the photo album during her happier days at the cottage with Paul, but, re-calling how their discussion about family photographs had sparked their last disagreement, she was reluctant to take the album to show to her father. At the last minute, she tucked it into the trunk of her car anyway, thinking that she would share it with Margarita.

When Swann arrived at the family home, Margarita told her that Evan was working in the basement. Usually when she came to visit her father, Swann was ushered into the drawing room where her father would mix her a drink, but this time the drawing room was empty.

"Mr. Triplett knows you are coming for dinner. He said to send you down to the basement as soon as you arrived," Margarita said.

Shaking her head at this new order, Swann tiptoed down the basement stairs. The last time she could recall her fa-ther's descending into the vast, dark cellar was when the furnace had broken, and that must have been fifteen years ago.

"Dad?"

"Swann," he said, and she turned a corner into a pool of light emanating from the old storeroom.

The dingy cubicle had been transformed. Now it was paneled in a light wood, and bright fluorescent fixtures were recessed into a drop ceiling. Every manner of woodworking machine stood about, ranging from jigsaws to lathes to sanders. Swann actually gawked.

"This is my new shop," her father said expansively. "Do you like it?"

"It's lovely," Swann said, disconcerted by the array of gadgets.

"My doctor told me I needed a hobby. I remembered that I used to be pretty good at wood shop when I was in high school, so I thought I'd give it a try," he said.

As he spoke he clamped two pieces of wood in a vise. Swann edged closer to see what they were.

"Some molding in my closet fell off. I'm gluing it," he said. He led her over to a shelf at the far end of the room.

"Here's a birdhouse I hammered together when I first started working down here. It needs painting, but I haven't been able to get around to that yet. Did Margarita show you the stool I made for the kitchen?" He seemed boyishly eager to show off his accomplishments.

Swann shook her head. "Not yet," she replied.

"You can look at it later," he said.

Margarita's voice echoed down the stairs. "Dinner is served," she called.

Bemused, Swann preceded her father upstairs. They sat at the long dinner table in the dining room with its carved walnut wainscoting. Only the two of them. As usual, the tablecloth was lace and the room was lit by long tapers in crystal candle holders. Margarita dished out the chicken and dumplings with pride, moving back and forth from kitchen to dining room with heavy footsteps. The atmosphere was weighty and ponderous.

This was the time, thought Swann, for a father to inquire about her work, to mention, perhaps, her new project. Instead he ignored her, occasionally asking her to pass something with an air of bored condescension.

This was the way it had always been, but now, particularly now, it wasn't enough. Swann chewed and swallowed methodically until the tension was almost unbearable. She knew she would have to be the one to break it and so, hiding her uneasiness, she asked him what he was making in his shop.

He looked at her down his long nose, and she realized that she had overstepped an invisible boundary between them. The silence lengthened, and she began to think that he wasn't going to answer.

Then, when she'd already decided that he was going to quash her interest with one of his disparaging remarks, he said quite calmly, "I'm building a corner cabinet," and went on to describe it.

This led into several neutral topics of conversation. *At least he's being civil; he's even being nice,* she thought to herself. As they finished eating, and with the evening looming before them, Swann wondered how best to say goodbye. She and her father had managed to make it this far without an outburst, and she didn't wish to press her luck.

Evan surprised her again by making it easy. "Well," he said when Margarita had begun to clear away their coffee cups, "I guess I'll get back to my shop." He stood up.

Swann had expected a few critical comments, at least, about her clothes or her hair or *something*.

"Thanks for having me over," she managed to say.

Evan pinched his mouth together, and Swann thought, *Uh-oh*. But he was apparently in a hurry to get back to his woodworking. He only nodded his head curtly and disappeared in the direction of the door to the basement.

Later, when she and Margarita were sitting in the kitchen poring over the photo album together, they heard Evan's footsteps tramping up the wooden stairs from the basement. Swann and Margarita exchanged meaningful looks, silently debating whether it would be worth the trouble to disappear into the dining room and wait for the coast to clear before they resumed their perusal of the album. Then the basement door burst open and Evan walked through, looking surprised to see them there.

"Thought you'd gone," he said gruffly to Swann.

"I was showing Margarita the family album I put together while I was in Georgia," she said.

"That so?"

"Maybe you would like to see it also," Margarita suggested, much to Swann's astonishment.

"Well, maybe," Evan said, hesitating. He bent over the table and peered at the pictures on the page.

"Hey, that looks like me," he said in surprise.

"It is. We were in Nassau for a regatta."

"I don't recall wearing that silly hat," Evan said doubtfully.

"You did, though. Mother bought it for you in the native straw market and made you put it on because the sun was so hot. She was afraid you'd get sunstroke."

Evan pulled out a chair and sat down. "I took that one," he said, pointing to a photo of Swann and her mother waving from a dock.

"I remember," Swann replied. She glanced over at him. He seemed to be enjoying this.

Margarita yawned a bit too earnestly. "I think I will go to my room. I have had a hard day." She stood up and, with elaborate casualness, arranged a set of canisters to be more centered on the counter before shooting Swann a look that was meant to be encouraging. Swann raised her eyebrows, but Margarita ignored her and plodded heavily off toward her room.

"This glue isn't strong enough," Evan said huffily when one of the photo hinges came off in his hand. His mouth turned downward in disapproval. "I have some glue that we can use to fix it," he said. "It's in my shop. Remind me before you leave."

Swann shifted uneasily on her chair, but she said nothing. If glue was the only thing he complained about on this evening, she would consider herself lucky.

When they were through looking at the album, Evan disappeared into the basement and reappeared with a tube of glue.

"Best on the market," he told her. "Try it."

Even though his tone was peremptory, for once the atmosphere between them was not highly charged with tension. Swann was afraid that Evan would not be so accepting the next time she saw him; she was afraid to let this chance go by.

"Dad," she said when they stood in the large foyer so brilliantly lit by the huge chandelier. "I—I want to apologize for last time I was here. I said some things that I've regretted, and I hope you know I'm sorry." Her piece spoken, she inhaled a deep breath and started to turn away.

"I, uh," he said, clearly taken aback by her admission.

"I'll be back soon," she said, hoping to make a quick exit.

"Swann, you didn't have to say that. I mean, I know you were upset about those photos I threw away. I honestly saw no point in keeping them at the time." Her father looked uncomfortable, and she understood what an effort it must have been for him to come so close to admitting that he had been in the wrong. She forced a smile and opened the door.

"Maybe, uh, maybe sometime when I'm in town, we could go out to dinner together," Evan said to her back, and when she turned around, her surprise showing on her face, he said, "Really. I mean it. You used to like to go to Figaro's for spaghetti when you were a kid. Do you still like spaghetti?" His expression was pleading and somehow pathetic.

Now she really smiled. "I love spaghetti," she said.

"I'll call you sometime," he said, and when she looked doubtful, he said, "No, I mean it."

In the privacy of her car driving back to town, Swann thought over the events of the evening. This upsurge in feeling between her father and her was unprecedented, but maybe it was a beginning. Perhaps it was exactly what she needed after the grim ending of her relationship with Paul.

As SHE OFTEN DID after she walked into the house, Swann switched on a television news network. The chatter of the announcer's voice made her feel less lonely.

She was so emotionally burned-out from her visit home that she only wanted to relax; she strewed her clothes from one end of the bedroom to the other, put on her nightgown and slipped into bed. She regarded the television as background noise until she glanced at the screen and saw that the weatherman was standing in front of a large multicolored map of the southeastern United States.

"Hurricane Jamal is presently hunkering off the coast of north Florida where it's packing winds clocked at one hundred and thirty-five miles per hour," he said, wielding his pointer. "It's expected to make landfall somewhere south of Savannah, Georgia, before dawn."

Swann sat up straighter and pushed the button on the remote control to increase the volume. The projected path of the storm showed it passing over the town of Reedy Creek.

She had paid this particular hurricane scant attention over the past week or so as it raked the Leeward Islands east of Puerto Rico and meandered lazily toward the mainland United States. Jamal hadn't seemed like a particularly dangerous storm, and it had claimed no lives in the Caribbean. Now the weatherman said that the hurricane had intensified and built up strength during its slow progress across the Atlantic.

"Jamal is a Class Four hurricane and considered very dangerous. The Atlantic coastline from Jacksonville, Florida, to Cape Hatteras, North Carolina, is presently under a hurricane warning. Residents are advised to evacuate low-lying areas and to take all due precautions," the weatherman announced.

Swann sank back against the pillows. If Reedy Creek was in danger, then Paul was, too. And Angelyn and her children in that creaky little house—would they be safe under the onslaught of such high winds?

She glanced at the clock. It was so late. She didn't want to phone Angelyn, who always put her children to bed early. She didn't feel that she knew Linda and Rick well enough to disturb them when they probably had enough to do to secure their house before the storm hit. And she certainly couldn't call Paul.

Swann arranged her pillows more comfortably and lay back to keep an uneasy vigil with her television set on.

She dozed until about two o'clock in the morning when the shrill ring of her telephone woke her. She groped for it on her bedside table, her eyes bleary with sleep. On the television screen a somber announcer was intoning the latest hurricane advisory.

"Hello?" Swann said. All she could hear on the other end of the line was a buzz of static.

"Hello?" she said again.

"Swann? Is this Swann Triplett?"

Swann recognized Angelyn's voice immediately.

"Angelyn? Is that you?"

"Yes...yes, it's me. Oh, Swann, I'm so worried. When I heard that the hurricane was coming, I stayed at our house, and now the creek is rising, and the wind is blowing harder and harder all the time, and—" A child wailed in the background. Was it the baby? Or Carlie? Angelyn spoke softly to the child and the crying stopped.

"Anyway, Swann, I can't think of what to do. I have no way to get into town, and I want to take the kids to an emergency shelter. I called Bobby's uncle. He lives across town. There was no answer at his house. Swann, what should I do?" Angelyn's sentence ended on a sob.

Swann sat up in bed and tried to think. Angelyn should have gone to the emergency shelter long ago; she couldn't imagine why she had thought she could weather the storm in her own flimsy house. There was no sense in pointing this out, however. Angelyn needed advice, and Swann knew that, as proud as she was, it had probably cost Angelyn some of her hard-earned self-respect to ask for it. The trouble was that she, Swann, was hundreds of miles away. There wasn't much she could do to help.

"Don't you know anyone you could depend on? Someone who might come and get you?"

There was no answer for such a long time that Swann feared that the connection had been broken.

"Angelyn?"

"Maybe Mrs. Dawson from Family Services. She's always been real nice to us and she likes the kids." Angelyn sounded doubtful.

"Can you telephone her right now and see if she or someone she knows can send a car out to pick you up?"

"I guess so," Angelyn said, but she sounded less than enthusiastic.

"Phone her right now and call me back after you find out if she can come and get you," Swann said.

"Okay," Angelyn said, and she hung up abruptly.

Swann swung her feet over the side of the bed and went quickly to the box of books she'd brought back from Reedy Creek. In there somewhere was a Reedy Creek telephone book.

Her attention was diverted when the weatherman on TV switched to a new, more detailed map. He said that Hurricane Jamal was expected to smash into the Georgia coast earlier than was originally expected.

Angelyn didn't have much time.

Swann chewed on her fingernails, a habit she pursued only when she was nervous. It took Angelyn over half an hour before she called back, and she sounded as though she had been crying.

"Swann, I keep calling Mrs. Dawson, but she doesn't answer her phone. I guess a lot of people got worried and have gone to stay with relatives inland. Oh, Swann, what am I going to do? I can't—"

The connection was broken in midsentence.

Swann hung up immediately and tried to call Angelyn's phone number. All she got was the infuriating message: "Your call cannot be completed at this time—"

Swann slammed down the receiver and pressed her hands to her eyelids, trying to think.

She would call Emergency Services. That's where Paul worked, but she knew that he would make sure that someone got through to Angelyn and took her and her family to a shelter.

At first, she got the same message over and over: "Your call cannot be completed at this time." She kept trying. Circuits were no doubt overloaded because of people calling their friends and relatives in the Savannah area, but eventually, if she kept trying, she would get through—unless high winds had already toppled telephone lines.

Finally, when her index finger had gone numb from repeatedly pressing the Redial button on her telephone, someone at the Emergency Services office in Reedy Creek picked up the phone.

"Is Paul Thompson there, please?" she asked.

"No, he's out on a call. How may I help you?" The female voice was warm and caring, and Swann poured out her concerns about Angelyn and the children.

"I can try to send some of the National Guardsmen out to get them, but the winds are getting bad right now," the woman said.

"Please, I'm afraid for them. Mrs. Soames has no car, no way to get to town. You've got to send someone."

"We'll try," was the promise, and Swann hung up and dialed Angelyn's number.

Her call could not be completed at this time.

Swann's attention was captured by a television report from the waterfront in Savannah. The reporter was holding onto his hat in a gale, rain dashing in his face as he tried to give viewers an accurate picture of the storm's progress. His voice was almost drowned out by the wind's roar. In the background, almost out of range of the camera crew's lights, she saw that the wind had bent a stop sign nearly in half.

It was ten minutes past four; it wouldn't be long now until dawn.

She tried Angelyn's telephone number again. This time she received nothing but a busy signal that beeped faster than normal. She worried that Angelyn might be talking on her telephone, trying to find help and more desperate than ever.

More than anything, Swann wanted assurance that her friends were going to be all right, but there was no one to whom she could turn for that. Instead she settled back into her pillows, determined to catch a bit of sleep before she tried calling Angelyn again.

And Paul—where was he on this terrible night?

Chapter Thirteen

Everyone knew that Hunter Epling was eccentric, but no one expected him to ride out the hurricane in that shack of his at Bell Bow, a bend in the river three miles outside the town of Reedy Creek. The place was nothing more than a swamp.

And then Hunter had to go out in the middle of the storm because he heard a dog barking and thought it might be in trouble.

"Didn't Hunter think that *he* might be in trouble if he left his house?" Paul asked incredulously after Mary Epling called Emergency Services. Winds were blowing at an estimated sixty miles an hour and rising fast.

Leon, his partner on the rescue squad, shrugged. "All I know is we've got problems, Paul. Hunter's wife says he hasn't come back, and he has a history of heart trouble."

Paul and Leon exchanged looks of resignation. Paul stood up and said, "Let's go," and they both silently put on their raincoats. It was going to be a long night.

Outside, the wind howled through the streets. Store signs careened madly to and fro, and debris of all kinds slammed into anything in its path. Rain pelted the windows of the ambulance so hard that the windshield wipers were ineffective against the deluge, and Leon strained forward in his seat trying to see.

"Too bad we can't put it on automatic pilot," Paul said as one particularly violent gust rocked the vehicle on its springs.

They met no other cars; people knew better than to go out in the storm. Many had boarded up their windows in anticipation of Jamal's fury, and despite the flickering streetlights, the town was strangely dark. As they were leaving the town behind, the streetlights gave one last gasp and died.

The ambulance headlights were insufficient to illuminate the highway in front of them, and they had to creep ahead slowly on the rain-drenched roads.

"I can't imagine old Hunter going out in this," Leon said anxiously as they turned into the narrow track leading to Bell Bow.

"He should have had more sense," Paul said, but he knew Hunter and he realized that the old man would never ignore a call for help from man or beast.

A tumbling tree branch slammed into the side of the van, bringing them to a shuddering halt.

"Wow, that scared me," Leon told Paul, his voice shaking. The wind lifted the offending branch and bore it away into the darkness.

They had to leave the road once to get around a large tree that had been uprooted; visibility now was virtually nil. Leon worried that he might not be able to find the road again, but Paul had a large flashlight, and he trained its beam ahead of the ambulance.

"We're lucky the ground here isn't swampy," Leon said through clenched teeth.

"Stop!" Paul yelled as they reached a dip in the road. Leon braked hard, and the ambulance engine stalled.

A surge of water swept across the road in front of them bearing branches, pebbles, old beer cans and a child's plastic bucket in front of it.

"The bridge has washed out," Leon said. "This looks like the end of the road for us." He had to shout to be heard over the roar of the wind.

"We can't leave Hunter out in the storm," Paul argued.

"We can't go any farther with the bridge out," Leon said, peering out at the wildly waving branches of the large trees on either side of them. They both knew that at any minute one of those trees could come crashing down on the ambulance, crushing them both.

"Wait," Paul said. He rolled his window down and rainwater drenched the inside of the ambulance.

"Stop it, Paul! I want to get this rig turned around before the river rises any higher!"

"I hear someone," Paul said feverishly.

"You're not going out in the storm!"

"I am, and I hope you'll come with me. Someone out there is in trouble, and it's probably Hunter Epling." Paul fastened the front of his raincoat and produced a length of rope from beneath the seat.

"You're as crazy as he is, you know that?" Leon said, but he grabbed a first-aid kit and slung the strap over his shoulder. The two men stared at each other grimly.

"Ready?" Leon said finally.

"Ready," Paul replied, and they stepped out into the tempest.

As they paused to tie themselves together with the rope as a precaution, lightning erupted overhead, flashing eerie blue light over the raging river. Paul tried to get his bearings. He thought he heard another cry for help, so he aimed the flashlight in the direction from which it came.

The Sudbury River had overflowed its banks and had torn the narrow bridge from its moorings, upended several palmetto trees, and now hid the road from view. To their right they saw an obstruction of tangled logs, branches, palmetto fronds and wide boards that Paul recognized as having been part of the bridge.

It was hard to see with rain pelting into his face, and the sound of the thunder crashing overhead was terrifying. Instinctively he hunched over and headed for the obstruction.

"Help! Help me!"

Paul's head jerked up as he tried to see exactly where the sound was originating. Leon grabbed his arm and pointed toward the immense log jam.

"Over there," he yelled.

Water swirled around their ankles as they fought their way closer to the faint cries. Paul clung to a palmetto tree and focused the flashlight's beam on a bushy tree that was part of the log jam. The tree was nearly stripped of its leaves, and its branches whipped frantically in the wind. Paul could barely make out what looked like a heap of old clothes clinging to the lower branches.

A flash of lightning confirmed what he suspected—this was not a heap of old clothes but a human being suspended over the raging river.

As they drew closer, Paul could see that Hunter was wedged between two large branches and that the rising water had almost reached him.

He tried shouting to Hunter to hold on, that he would be there soon, but he wasn't sure if his voice carried that far.

Leon grabbed his arm. "Paul, we can't go any farther," he shouted.

The dark water churned around their knees, threatening to sweep them off their feet. In the wavering circle of illumination from the flashlight, they saw that Hunter was clinging with terror to the branches of the tree; his eyes were wild with fright.

"We can't let him die," Paul said.

"It's no use," Leon said. "We'll never reach him in time."

Paul thought about the light in Mary Epling's eyes when she looked at her husband. She and Hunter were a devoted couple.

He took in the seething floodwater and the raging winds; the sound of thunder echoed in his ears. He knew what he had to do.

"I'm going after him," he said, and before Leon could object, he plunged into the rapids.

His last thought was of Swann. Maybe things always worked out for the best. If he had gone to Philadelphia with her, who would have been here to rescue Hunter Epling from his folly?

THE JANGLING PHONE aroused Swann from a fitful sleep. She reached out and grabbed it on the first ring.

"Swann?"

"Justin! What time is it?"

"Seven o'clock. Have you heard from any of your friends in Reedy Creek?"

"Only Angelyn, my neighbor. She called around 2:00 a.m. She was trying to get to an emergency shelter, but I don't know if she was successful."

"Have you been watching the news on TV?"

"I fell asleep around four."

"The hurricane hit farther south of Savannah than they predicted, so Reedy Creek probably took the brunt of it. Turn on your TV."

"It is on, but I need to adjust the volume," she said. She angled herself to a sitting position and focused scratchy eyes on the screen.

"Well, I only wanted to know if your friends were safe," Justin said. "Let me know if you hear anything."

Swann thanked him for his concern and turned her full concentration to the television reports.

The hurricane had slammed into the coastline, devastating several small barrier islands. The calm eye of the storm had now passed inland, but since Jamal was such a huge weather system, winds continued to slash at the coastal communities. Pictures of the damage were not available yet.

Despite her lack of sleep, Swann knew she couldn't stay in bed. She telephoned Angelyn, only to get that strange, too-fast busy signal again. She even called Linda and Rick's number with the same results, and then she phoned the sheriff's department to find out if anyone had filed a report indicating whether Angelyn and her family had reached an emergency shelter. It was impossible to get through; apparently, phones in that area were still inoperative.

She showered and dressed, picking up last night's hastily doffed clothes as she went along. She had no idea what to do with herself; most of her friends were away for the Labor Day weekend, and she didn't want to go to the estate. She was glad when the phone rang and Gracie invited her to come to brunch with her and Nolan.

Swann wasted no time in driving to Gracie's nearby apartment.

"I thought you probably wouldn't want to be alone," Gracie said.

"You're right. It's frightening not knowing anything," she said.

"We'll keep you busy," Gracie promised, and she led Swann into the kitchen where Nolan was whipping up a batch of hollandaise sauce.

Swann and Gracie took over the cooking of poached eggs, Canadian bacon and toast, and soon they sat down in Gracie's breakfast nook overlooking the Delaware River. Gracie switched on her television set so that they could watch for reports of the hurricane.

It was ten-thirty in the morning, and by this time the cable news station was beginning to broadcast scenes of the devastation in Savannah. The historic waterfront area had been flooded by the storm surge, and a boat sat in the middle of River Street near the place where Swann and Paul had shared their first kiss. Many shop windows had been blown out, and all trees had either lost some limbs or been blown over. The only mention of Reedy Creek was when the reporter said that the roads to Reedy Creek and other outlying communities were blocked by debris.

"That doesn't tell me much," Swann said, her fears for her friends mounting. She telephoned Angelyn from Gracie's phone, but she only received the same busy signal she'd heard so many times before.

Nolan had cleared the table by the time Swann returned to the kitchen.

"Let me load the dishwasher," Swann said. "At least that will give me something to do."

The three of them stayed glued to Gracie's television set, trying to absorb the amount of damage. Even communities far inland had sustained a great deal of devastation, and the governor of Georgia had flown over the area in a helicopter and stated that there must be three billion dollars' worth of damage. He was asking the federal government to declare Georgia a disaster area.

Swann's imagination worked double time as the scenes on the television screen kept unfolding. Everywhere, huge trees had been uprooted and buildings had lost their roofs. Movie marquees had disappeared; cars were destroyed. Swann tried to imagine the town of Reedy Creek without its beautiful trees arching over the streets, without the steeple on the First Baptist Church. She simply couldn't.

"Didn't you tell me that Paul was in some kind of emergency work?" Gracie asked.

"He's a paramedic," Swann answered.

"He's probably been busy since the storm hit," observed Nolan.

If I only knew he was safe, Swann thought unhappily. Even though she and Paul were not together and never would be, she still loved him; maybe she would always love him. She couldn't bear the thought of his coming to harm.

Swann didn't go home until shortly before midnight, and even then she had to turn down Gracie's offer of a bed in the guest room.

"Let's get together tomorrow," Gracie suggested. "I know you don't want to be by yourself."

"I'm okay," she told Gracie, but after listening to news reports all day, her fear for the Soames family, for Paul and for Linda and Rick and all the other people who had been hit by Hurricane Jamal, had only escalated.

Stories had been broadcast of people who had gone to emergency shelters, such as school gymnasiums, only to find themselves captive without an escape route when the water unexpectedly began rising there; they had held their children on their shoulders to keep them from drowning. Others told of staying in their homes because they felt they would be safe, only to have a tree crash through the ceiling during the height of the storm. Early in the morning, a child had drowned in a car that was swept away by floodwaters. His parents had escaped but had been unable to rescue him.

Swann's heart was heavy with the suffering of these people, and she knew that those were only a few of the stories that would surface in the aftermath of Hurricane Jamal. Other stories had not yet been told, and some of them had surely taken place in Reedy Creek.

Even though Swann felt tense and upset, she was exhausted, and once in her bed she fell asleep quickly.

The next morning, as planned, Swann met Gracie and Nolan for a walk through Independence Park.

"Any luck in calling anyone in Reedy Creek yet?" Gracie asked as they strolled along a path dodging bike riders and skateboarders.

Swann shook her head. "No. I still have no idea if they're okay. I left my phone answering machine on in case anyone calls."

"This morning Nolan was contacted by a Quaker group that has been attempting donations of food, clothes and medical items for hurricane victims. They asked him to pilot a plane to some air-force base near Savannah," Gracie said.

"That base is near Reedy Creek!" Swann said in surprise.

"I'll have some free time once I'm there. If you'd like, I'll see if I can find the people you're worried about," Nolan volunteered.

"Oh, would you? When will you be leaving?"

"Tomorrow morning. They'll load the plane tonight, we leave in the morning, they'll unload the plane and I'll fly back the next day."

"Do you think I could send some things to Angelyn? Food, clothes, money?"

Nolan smiled at her. "I'll deliver them personally, I promise."

"You may have trouble finding her. I'm not sure if she's at a shelter or at home. If there are a lot of trees down, you might not be able to drive out the creek road."

"If I can, I'll do it."

Gracie slipped her arm through Nolan's. "He's real responsible, Swann. You can count on him," she said.

Swann smiled in relief. "I can't tell you how much better you've made me feel," she said. "I'll go home and put together a package. And maybe if you can't deliver it to Angelyn's house, you could leave it at the Family Services agency. Angelyn knows the social worker there, and Mrs. Dawson would make sure that the Soameses got it."

She bade Gracie and Nolan goodbye at the corner. On the way home, she stopped at a grocery store to buy canned goods, stocking up on chicken-and-rice soup because she knew that Carlie loved it, and buying a large supply of canned milk. When she arrived at home, the red light signifying that a message had been left on her telephone answering machine was blinking.

The first message was from Justin, who was inquiring as to whether Swann knew anything about the conditions in Reedy Creek yet. The second was from Angelyn.

"Swann, it's me, Angelyn. We—we got out of our house okay. Some men came and got us. But Carlie—" and here her voice broke "—Carlie is hurt. She's in the hospital here in Reedy Creek. Oh, Swann, she's hurt so bad! The phones at the hospital are working now, but they keep going out of order. I'll call you later if I can. 'Bye."

Swann reached out and switched off the machine. Carlie hurt? It was unthinkable.

Angelyn had given her no clue as to the nature of Carlie's injuries, but Swann knew that Angelyn wouldn't have said it was serious unless it was very serious indeed. Swann's hand shook as she looked up the telephone number of the tiny Reedy Creek Hospital and tapped out the numbers on her phone. She waited apprehensively for the phone to ring.

She only got a busy signal. Well, communications in the Savannah area were clearly haphazard, and with what Swann could tell from news reports, they could be expected to stay that way for quite some time.

Swann knew that she had to keep busy or she'd go out of her mind with worry. She dumped her books out of the cardboard box and packed it tightly with the food she'd bought. She counted all her cash on hand and came up with over two hundred dollars, which she sealed in a white envelope for Nolan to take to Angelyn. She realized that she had no idea whether the Soames's house was still standing, but from what she had heard and seen on television, she thought there was a good chance that it was a casualty of the storm. After a moment's thought, she found a comforter and two blankets to send as well as some clothes that might fit Angelyn.

When she had finished packing, she took the boxes over to Gracie's apartment. Gracie answered the door and ushered Swann inside.

"Swann, you look as pale as a ghost. Is everything all right?" Gracie asked.

Tears welled in Swann's eyes. She shook her head, unable to speak.

"Swann! Here, sit down," Gracie said, clucking like a mother hen. Nolan appeared in the doorway, his forehead knit with concern.

"Have you had bad news, Swann?" he asked.

"It's—it's Angelyn's daughter, Carlie. She's only five years old, and she's hurt, and Angelyn left this message on my answering machine, but she didn't say what happened, and—'' She couldn't go on. She wiped away the tear that was trickling down her cheek.

"Swann's been under so much pressure lately," Gracie said to Nolan. "First breaking up with Paul, and then the hurricane and not knowing how her friends are, and now this."

"It's just—just..." Swann began, wanting to explain how Angelyn's family was so perfect, despite their lack of money, and how their small family circle had seemed protection against so many things, and that if the circle were broken by Carlie's death, she didn't know how Angelyn could keep going. Angelyn seemed to derive so much of her strength from her children.

Gracie's cool hand soothed her brow. "It's okay to cry, Swann," she said gently.

"Anyway, I have news that might help," Nolan said.

Swann blew her nose on a tissue thoughtfully provided by Gracie. "Like what?" she asked.

"I'm flying down there tomorrow on a plane chartered by that Quakers' group. It was supposed to be me, a copilot and twelve members of their relief committee to help distribute the supplies once we get there. My friend who contacted me about flying this job called a little while ago and happened to mention that one of the committee members who was planning to go was going to drop out because of a family emergency. How would you like me to see if I can get you on the plane in his place?"

Swann stared at him. "Could you? Really?"

Nolan stood up. "I don't know," he said. "I certainly can try." He patted Swann's shoulder and strode away to the telephone. They heard him talking convincingly to the other party, and when he reappeared he was beaming.

"Consider it done," he said expansively. "Be ready to leave tomorrow morning at seven."

Swann flew from the chair and enveloped him in a hug. Then she hugged Gracie, and the three of them hugged each other.

"Hey," she said to Gracie. "You know, I like this guy."

"Me, too," said Gracie, smiling up at Nolan. "I think I might just keep him."

SWANN PRESSED HER FACE to the window of the plane. Below, as they descended for a landing, she saw mobile homes that seemed to have burst apart at the seams. A once-proud forest was now devastated, the trees thrown every which way like a child's game of jackstraws. She saw houses with no roofs and cars flipped upside down. She pulled back from the window, sick at heart.

A rental car waited for them at the air-force base. After Nolan had checked in with the proper authorities, he and Swann were free to leave. Today the wind was calm and the sun shone brightly, giving no clue that a monster storm had ever passed that way.

"How are things in Reedy Creek?" Swann asked the guard who waved them out the base gate.

"Pretty bad," he replied. "Only a few places have electricity, and authorities have cautioned everyone to boil their drinking water. If they have any, that is. The generators for the pumps at the water plant have failed, and there are no backups."

With Nolan driving, they headed toward Reedy Creek. They passed a gas station where Swann had once bought gas, and it lay in ruins. Its sign had blown nearly a mile down the road, where they spotted it lying in a ditch.

Everywhere, crews of volunteers with noisy chain saws were working to clear fallen trees from the roads, and the pungent scent of pine sap filled the air. Most of the side streets in town were still impassable. Since the road past the hospital had been one of the first to be cleared, they had no trouble reaching it.

Swann was relieved to see that the church steeple still stood, but the portico in front of the hospital had blown away, leaving only crumbling ruins of the brick columns that had supported it. Down the street, the Little Bit's window had been shattered; two men were boarding up the space with a sheet of plywood. A magnificent oak tree had smashed into the real-estate office, and several people were working to remove it.

In the hospital lobby, grim-faced people milled about, looking as if they were numb with shock and hardly able to fathom the disaster. Nolan waited near the door while Swann threaded her way through the crowd in order to inquire about Carlie at the reception desk. When Swann came back, her face was white and a curl of dread had begun to uncoil in the pit of her stomach.

"The receptionist knows Angelyn. She says Carlie is in a coma," she said.

"Do you want me to go with you to see her?"

Swann shook her head. "There's no need," she told him.

"I think I'll go volunteer my services to some of the work crews who are trying to clear the streets," Nolan said. "I'll check with you later." He hurried away.

When Swann asked where she could find Angelyn, the receptionist directed her to a waiting room through two swinging doors to the rear of the lobby. Once through the doors, Swann hurried down a hallway with an arrow pointing to the intensive care unit.

Swann hesitated at the door of the small waiting room. A band of sunlight fell across Angelyn's bowed head; she sat in a straight chair with her hands clasped. Every line of her body expressed extreme anguish.

"Angelyn?"

Angelyn's head shot up, and she leaped from her chair. "Swann! Oh, Swann, I'm so glad to see you!" She ran to embrace her friend.

"How's Carlie?" Swann asked after she had explained how she happened to be there.

They sat down side by side on a plastic-covered couch. The print hanging on the wall opposite was of a happy family walking on the beach. Swann couldn't help thinking that a landscape would have been a better choice for this room.

"We don't know yet if Carlie's going to come out of the coma or not. The doctor isn't real hopeful," Angelyn said, dabbing at her eyes. Her face was ravaged with grief.

Little Carlie with her round cornflower-blue eyes and pudgy baby face; Swann's heart ached to think of those eyes forever closed.

"What happened, Angelyn?" she asked gently.

Angelyn sighed. "Well, the men from the National Guard came to the house and picked us up after you called the Emergency Services number. They evacuated a lot of people out on the creek road, I guess. They drove us directly to the old armory, which had been set up as an emergency shelter. The wind was roaring mighty hard by that time, and the kids and I, we were all scared. I was carrying Rhonda, and one of the men was carrying Mott. The other one had Carlie by the hand. We were running toward the doorway of the shelter when something—I think it was a shutter torn off of a house—hit Carlie in the head. She's been unconscious ever since," Angelyn said, twisting a handkerchief around her fingers.

"Then you had almost made it to safety," Swann murmured.

"Almost. After it happened, they brought Carlie and me to the hospital right away. A nice lady we met at the shelter is taking care of Mott and Rhonda."

Swann felt a sudden fierce anger toward the uncontrollable force of nature that had brought so much suffering and grief to the people who lived here. Her anger disappeared almost immediately, leaving a sense of helplessness, which was even harder to accept.

There was one question she wanted to ask, but probably Angelyn wouldn't know the answer. Perhaps she might as well ask it anyway.

"Angelyn, have you seen Paul since the storm?"

Angelyn's eyes brimmed with sympathy. "Why, no, Swann, I haven't. I haven't thought of nothing but Carlie since she was hurt."

Swann swallowed and tried not to think about Paul. She had come to help Angelyn. She was suddenly struck with how exhausted Angelyn looked.

"Have you had anything to eat today?" Swann asked.

"I've not been hungry," Angelyn said.

"You'd better eat something," Swann told her. Angelyn would need all her strength for whatever ordeal lay ahead.

"I don't feel like it," Angelyn told her. "Anyway, the food supply is running low. No trucks have been able to come to town since the storm hit, and fallen trees block the highway to the interstate. The hospital is full. I've heard that they're trying to conserve food for the patients."

"I've brought a small box of canned goods for you and the kids, but we should save it for when you return home. Let me see if I can find you something to eat," Swann said.

Angelyn smiled tremulously. "Okay. After I eat, maybe they'll let you see Carlie."

Swann went downstairs and explained to the receptionist at the front desk that she needed to find some food for her friend who was here with her sick child. The receptionist was sympathetic, but she said that the hospital snack shop had closed. There were, however, Red Cross volunteers who had brought coffee and sandwiches for the work crews who were still clearing the hospital parking lot of debris. Perhaps they could help.

Swann walked outside. The sound of power chain saws drew her to the far edge of the parking lot, and she went to ask if anyone knew where she could find the Red Cross workers. She was surprised to see Nolan standing there and talking to a man who was leaning against a car and eating a sandwich.

"Nolan!" she called.

He turned around. "Swann! They're bringing another chain saw, and I'm going to help these guys."

"Have you seen anybody from the Red Cross?" she asked, eyeing the man's sandwich.

The man pointed toward the back of the hospital. "They've got a truck over there," he said, waving in the general direction of a pile of fresh-cut logs.

From what Swann could tell, the Red Cross truck must be located near the hospital's emergency entrance.

"Thanks," she said, starting to walk away.

"Wait, I'll come with you," Nolan said, falling into step behind her. "I figure I might as well eat something before they put me to work." He slung his jacket across one shoulder and whistled as he walked.

"Good," Swann said as they rounded the log pile. "I see the truck. Let's—"

But she never finished the sentence, because there, waiting beside the truck for a coffee refill, stood Paul Thompson.

Chapter Fourteen

His uniform was rumpled and his shoes were muddy. His face was lined with fatigue, and his eyes were rimmed with red. But her heart leaped when she saw him, and she didn't know what to say. She could not have spoken if her life depended on it.

His eyes caught hers and their gaze locked. She didn't want to be the one to look away first. She wanted to feast on the sight of him, to feel the impact of his presence, to let her heart bathe in the joy of his instant recognition.

He drew himself up, pulled himself away. He did it without moving a muscle; he was, had always been, superb at distancing himself. His glasses were a shiny barrier, effectively screening the expression in his eyes.

She wanted to say, *Paul, it's me, I'm back and I love you,* but of course she couldn't. And it was clearly not what he wanted to hear. He wheeled around and walked away, tossing his cup in a trash can as he went.

"Do you want turkey or ham?" the woman in the truck asked.

"Um, turkey," Swann murmured.

"What's that?"

"Turkey," she repeated more loudly. Nolan gave her a puzzled glance. She recovered long enough to say, "Two sandwiches, please."

The woman handed her the sandwiches and two disposable cups of coffee in a small cardboard tray.

"Swann, are you okay?" Nolan said, studying her even more carefully.

"Sure, I'm fine. I'll see you later, Nolan. I need to get back to Angelyn." She tripped off toward the hospital, walking blindly, leaving Nolan staring after her with a worried frown. A huge rushing sound filled her ears, and she felt absolutely numb.

At least Paul was all right, she thought as she hurried unseeing through the lobby. At least he was all right. Only now was she able to admit her extreme anxiety, her fear that he had been hurt or killed in the storm.

He was all right. But he had made it plain that he was no longer hers.

PAUL STOOD IN FRONT of his locker, trying to quell his agitation. Swann was here; he had seen her with his own eyes. Not that he had believed it at first. When he'd seen her walking toward him, he thought that she was a figment of his imagination. He had thought about her so much and for so long that he wouldn't have been surprised if, in his exhausted state, he had conjured her image out of thin air.

But, and this had been the tip-off, if he were going to create Swann, he would have made sure that he imagined her alone and eager to see him. The guy walking alongside her and whistling that irritating tune would not have been part of the picture.

Why should he be surprised that Swann had already found somebody else? A guy could fall head over heels in love with her at the drop of a hat; witness how easily he himself had accomplished it. What surprised him was that she had brought her new boyfriend to Reedy Creek, and now, of all times. A pall of melancholy settled over him.

"Hey, Thompson! I'm on duty. How about you?"

He turned at the sound of Leon's voice and forced himself to adopt the same bantering tone.

"Nah, I just got off. Had a bad accident over on Oglethorpe Street—a guy cut himself with a chain saw. We
couldn't get the ambulance through."

"Yeah? How's the guy?"

"Oh, he'll be all right," Paul said.

"You heading home?"

"For the first time in twenty-two hours," Paul said,
glancing at his watch. It was a few minutes after noon.

"Have they cleared your street yet?"

"A few of my neighbors are working on it. It's a good
thing I can walk home from here."

Leon clapped him on the shoulder. "I've got to get to
work. See you tomorrow, buddy."

Paul closed his locker and headed out of the locker room.
Fatigue had made him punchy. And seeing Swann and the
look on her face; she hadn't expected to see him standing
near the Red Cross truck any more than he had expected to
see her. For a moment he was so surprised that he'd almost
forgotten the pain he still felt at her betrayal.

And yet, the flip side of his feelings for her was still ad-
miration. After all, he had received from her something that
no one else had been able to give him. Her love had contributed to his self-image. If Swann Triplett loved him, he must
be okay. All the cruel things his father had done to him, all
the mean things his father had said—they had been
superseded by Swann's love. For the first time since he was
a kid, he'd liked himself.

He realized now that he had not only been a dropout from
medical school, but a dropout from life. It was time to get
on with what he was meant to do. It was time to move out
and move up. The sad thing was that he was going to have
to do it in a way that had been unimaginable a month ago.
He was going to have to do it without Swann.

Someday maybe he'd have the chance to tell her how important she'd been to his life. But it wouldn't be soon, he
was sure of that.

AROUND FIVE O'CLOCK in the afternoon, a nurse preceded Swann and Angelyn down a long pale green hall and paused in front of a window. In the room beyond was Carlie.

"I'm sorry, but you can't go in to see her," the nurse told Swann who had not been permitted inside the intensive care unit until now.

At the sight of Carlie, Swann tried to catch her breath. She felt as though the air around her was too heavy to pull into her lungs; she gripped Angelyn's hand.

Carlie lay in a high bed surrounded by monitors and machinery with a vaguely sinister look about them. Her head was swathed in bandages, and her tiny face was distorted by tubes. Swann's eyes filled with tears at the sight of her.

"I—I didn't know it would be this bad," Swann whispered.

"I'm so worried," Angelyn said, her face pale. "So worried."

"That's enough for now," the nurse said with a gentle touch on Angelyn's shoulder.

Swann and Angelyn retreated down the long hall and resumed their places in the waiting room, Angelyn looking more wan than ever. She had been sleeping at the hospital on the couch in the waiting room ever since Carlie's accident, catching catnaps so that she'd be awake if Carlie needed her or if the doctor wanted to speak with her.

"If there were only something we could do," Swann murmured.

"All we can do is wait."

A plan began to form in Swann's mind.

"Where are you going?" Angelyn asked when Swann stood up.

"I'm going out for a while," Swann said. "I have to try something."

"Swann—"

"I'll be back, Angelyn. Soon, I hope."

Swann left the hospital at a run, her determination fueled by her memory of Carlie's tiny face so gray against the pillow.

She had to try it—for Carlie.

ON THE STREET where Paul lived, wet, fallen leaves layered the ground to a depth of six inches or so. An immense oak tree lay across the street, and two cars had been crushed by it. Another oak tree had smashed into a small frame house, and had almost obliterated it. Swann shuddered and wondered how Paul's house had fared.

As she approached, she saw with relief that the small yellow bungalow seemed to be in good repair. The surrounding trees, although almost denuded of leaves, still stood. One listed heavily to the east. Other than a bit of metal rain gutter lying on the front porch, the house looked nearly the same as usual.

Swann marched up to the front door and knocked.

"It's open. Come in, I'm in the bedroom," Paul said.

Her heart began to pound at the sound of his voice, and she thought in that moment that she would rather do anything than ask him for a favor, even so important a favor as this. She paused for a moment, steeling herself to brave the next few minutes. At last she turned the doorknob and walked in.

It was clear when Paul saw her that he had expected anyone but her. He stood in the bathroom doorway, one half of his face covered with shaving soap, a razor in his hand. He wore a towel twisted around his hips and that was all.

The part of his face that was free of shaving soap turned pale. "I was expecting Bo," he said.

"Well, I'm not Bo," she said heavily. She felt beyond everything now, even pride.

They stared at each other for a moment. Paul turned toward the bathroom mirror and recommenced shaving. She thought she detected that his hand was shaking. Taking heart from this, she went to stand in the doorway behind him and watched his reflection in the mirror. She had been right; his hand *was* shaking.

"Paul," she said quietly, "I've come to ask for something."

"You left your tan sandals here," he said evenly. "They're in the closet."

"I don't want my sandals. I—"

He cut himself with the razor, cursed, and reached for a tissue. She watched as he blotted the cut.

She drew a deep breath. "Paul, Carlie Soames has been hurt. Severely hurt. She needs your help."

Paul finished scraping the shaving cream from his face and held the razor blade under running water.

"Take her to a doctor," he said. He rinsed his face, dried it with a towel and brushed past her into the bedroom. He scooped up her sandals from the floor of his closet and tossed them on the bed. "Here," he said.

Swann picked up the sandals. "You're not supposed to put shoes on the bed. It's bad luck. Angelyn said so."

Paul snorted derisively. "It seems to me that Angelyn has had more than her share of bad luck, so I guess she would know," he said.

Swann dropped the shoes on the floor, where they landed with a solid thud. Paul was flipping through the clothes in his closet, and he removed a pair of blue pants and a white polo shirt.

"I can't believe that you can be so heartless. Especially when it's a child. Carlie's in the hospital in a coma, Paul. The doctor has given Angelyn almost no hope that she'll recover."

Paul's face showed absolutely no expression. He reached for a pair of socks from his dresser drawer.

He yanked the towel from around his hips and tossed it into the bathroom, then pulled on a pair of briefs. He acted as though she wasn't even there, Swann thought in despair. The sight of his nude body should have brought back all kinds of memories, but she was beyond being titillated. All she wanted was his cooperation, and she'd never ask him for anything again. She'd never *see* him again.

He pulled the polo shirt on over his head, then stepped into the pants and zipped them.

"I think I left my belt at your house," he said absently.

It infuriated her that he wasn't taking her seriously. Carlie lay near death in a hospital bed, tubes and machines connected to her body, and Paul didn't even care!

She clenched her hands into fists and followed him into the living room.

"Listen, Paul Thompson, I can't believe that you can be so callous about Carlie! Remember the picnic we had at my house when you told me that you would like to have a little girl just like her someday? Remember how she climbed into your lap and rested her head against your shoulder when she got sleepy? Remember—"

He wheeled around, his eyes blazing. "I remember a lot of things, Swann, so just skip it! What is it you want me to do, anyway?"

She stared him down, her chest heaving. When she could speak, she said, "I want you to try The Power."

A hush fell over them, a deep silence punctuated only by their own breathing.

"I can't, Swann. It doesn't always work. You know that." Paul's expression was pained. For the first time she noticed that he still looked tired; blue circles of fatigue underscored his lower eyelids. There was a bruise in the middle of his forehead.

"I know. I'm only asking you to try," she whispered.

He made a gesture of dismissal and headed toward the door. "I'm going down to Bo's. Don't lock the door when you leave."

She flew at him, pulled him away from the door. "I'm not asking for my sake, you idiot! Can't you get that through your thick head? It's for *Carlie,* Paul!"

Stung by her fury, Paul shook his head. "Swann—"

"Don't give me any more excuses! Please, Paul, please, I'm begging you. Come to the hospital and *try!*"

"Try! All I've done is *try!* And when I get results, it's a fluke, nothing more! Maybe I never had The Power in the first place. Perhaps it was an idea planted in my impressionable young mind by a father who knew all about persuasion! Maybe we were all his patsies—me, the people who thought they had been cured, the newspapers, everybody!" His eyes blazed at her in anger, the eyes she had remembered all those years since she was a small child. Blue, so blue, and she knew how they could be kind and caring and sympathetic.

"Oh, you cured people all right," she said, matching his fervor with her own. "You cured me."

Once she had spoken the words, his expression changed to uncertainty.

"Yes, Paul, you did. I was a little girl not much older than Carlie, and my foot had been broken in a fall. I didn't get the medical care I needed because my parents were away, and the bones healed the wrong way so that my foot was crooked. I walked with a limp. My parents brought me to Miracle Farm one cold winter's night, and you healed my foot."

"You, Swann?" he said in disbelief.

"I didn't have to have the operation the doctor said I needed. My foot grew straight and strong. So don't give me the excuse that you never had The Power! You had it, all right. I'm the proof."

"I—" he began, but he couldn't go on. Swann wouldn't say it if it weren't true. And deep in his heart he knew she was right. He *had* helped people. He had been devastated when The Power had left him, but not knowing where it came from in the first place, he could hardly know how to get it back. He should be grateful that it was now sometimes with him.

He looked at Swann, really looked at her. Did he remember her from those days so long ago? He would have been so young, and there were so many people who came to see him. He couldn't say that he recalled her face, although it was hard to believe that he could have forgotten someone so beautiful. God help him, he still loved her. He couldn't let her down.

"Paul?" she said shakily. He realized that she was clinging to his arm.

Slowly he slid his hand over both of hers.

"All right," he said. "All right. I'll try."

She released her grip, and her hands fell to her sides.

"Thank you," she whispered.

EVEN PAUL, WHO WAS USED to such things, was shocked to see Carlie hooked up to so many machines. She would have been unrecognizable if he hadn't known who she was.

At first he was told that due to hospital regulations, it was impossible for him to go into the intensive care unit where Carlie lay, but a well-placed phone call to a doctor friend who was on the hospital board solved that problem.

Paul left Swann in the lobby and hurried through the swinging doors to ICU. He stood outside Carlie's room summoning his strength. If he hadn't promised Swann he'd try, he wouldn't even be here. He'd be over at Bo's sipping a beer by this time. But he *had* promised, although perhaps it had been foolish. He had no idea whether he would be successful at this.

He walked softly to Carlie's bedside and studied her for a long moment. Such a sweet little face, and she looked so helpless. He remembered how she had felt nestled in his arms; that seemed like a long time ago. Well, there was nothing to do but to try. He sat down on a chair near the head of the bed.

Back in the old days, The Power had often waned when he was exhausted. He took a deep breath and closed his eyes, trying to center himself. He concentrated on the darkness behind his eyelids, willing the light to come through. The light would be there for Carlie, just as it had been for

Kathy on the night of the party and Swann when she had the attack of hives, and he would—

But it wasn't there. All he found inside himself was a deep black void, cold and dark.

He opened his eyes and focused on Carlie. She was breathing with the aid of a machine. Such a tiny child, such a big machine.

All right, he'd make another attempt. He closed his eyes and blotted out the room, its occupant, and everything else. He was looking for the light, looking . . .

"As far as I'm concerned, Paul Thompson ought to get some kind of medal or something," Rick said. "He rescued Hunter Epling from a tree in the middle of the Sudbury River, and then he even located the dog that Hunter went out in the storm to find."

"I didn't know that," Swann said in a small voice.

"A lot of people don't. He's one of the unsung heroes of this storm. Well, Swann, I've got to get home. I only stopped by to see you because one of the nurses is a friend of Linda's and she said you were here."

"Did you have any storm damage?"

"Our new swimming pool sustained major damage, and a few shingles flew off our roof. We're a lot better off than some people, though, because we're both okay."

She said goodbye to Rick, who had found her in the hospital lobby, and went in search of Angelyn. She should be back from visiting Mott and Rhonda at the shelter any minute now.

There she was, her shoulders sagging as she hurried up the front steps. Swann met her at the door.

"How are the kids?" she asked as she and Angelyn hurried back to ICU.

"Upset. Rhonda keeps crying for Carlie. I tried to prepare them for the worst," Angelyn said. She looked gaunt and hollow-eyed.

"Maybe—" Swann began, wanting to keep Angelyn's spirits up.

"No, Swann," Angelyn said wearily. "Don't give me any false hope."

After that, Swann could think of no words of comfort. She had heard nothing from Paul since he left her in the lobby almost an hour ago.

PAUL LEANED HIS ELBOWS on his knees. He took off his glasses and rested his head in his hands, massaging his eyelids. This hurt the bruise on his forehead, which he tended to forget until he looked in a mirror. He straightened and stretched, glancing at the small figure in the bed.

Other than the hiss of the respirator and the bleep of a monitor, there was no sound in the room. He should have been able to concentrate better than usual, but it wasn't working that way.

If he helped Carlie... But what was the use of thinking that he might help her when he couldn't summon The Power?

He shouldn't have paid any attention to Swann. He should have ordered her from his house when she appeared. She had no right to demand from him what he couldn't give.

Only when it was a child, the situation was even more poignant than if it had been an adult. And if he had risked his very life for Hunter Epling, could he risk less for Carlie Soames?

Soon the nurse might come in and ask him to leave. She had already walked by twice, and she looked as if she were trying to figure out what to do about him.

He inhaled a deep breath and closed his eyes. His hands were clasped lightly in front of him, and he felt relaxed and calm. He banished all thought of Swann from his consciousness and let himself drift into the darkness. He was looking for the light.

This time, perhaps, he would find it.

AN HOUR LATER, Swann looked up to see Paul walking toward them from the direction of Carlie's room. Angelyn, who had been dozing on the couch, opened her eyes. She looked startled to see him there.

Paul shook his head imperceptibly. Swann bolted from her chair and ran after him as he headed for the swinging doors to the lobby.

"Did you—?" she asked, her eyes searching his face.

"I tried," he said. "And failed." He kept walking.

"So there's no change?"

"No change." He stopped in front of the doors. "I don't know why it didn't work," he said. "I thought I'd found The Power. It was all there—the heat in my hands, everything. But Carlie didn't wake up. I'm sorry, Swann." He looked beaten, crestfallen.

"I'm glad you tried."

He managed a weak shrug. He seemed eager to be gone, to put distance between the two of them.

She attempted a smile, perhaps to provoke an answering smile from him, but he was already through the doors. They swung after him for a few seconds, then stopped.

So much for miracles, Swann thought as she walked slowly back to join Angelyn in the waiting room.

SWANN WAS AWAKENED from her doze by the sound of pounding feet in the corridor outside the waiting room. She glanced at the clock; it was almost ten o'clock in the evening. Three hours had elapsed since Paul had left.

Angelyn, who had been sitting and staring out the dark window, lost in one of those agonizing reveries that seemed to insulate her from the routine happenings on the floor, jumped up. So did Swann, her heart in her mouth. They rushed to the door of the waiting room.

At the other end of the hall, two nurses disappeared into Carlie's room, and a doctor followed swiftly on their heels.

"What's happening?" Swann asked a nurse's aide who was rushing past.

"The little girl woke up," she answered.

Swann and Angelyn ran to the door of Carlie's room. The nurses, a doctor, and the nurse's aide were gathered around her bed. Swann and Angelyn couldn't see Carlie; there were too many people.

Slowly Angelyn walked into the room. The group parted and made room for her beside the bed.

The tubes had been removed from Carlie's nose and mouth. Her cheeks were pink, and her eyes were open.

"Hi, Ma," she said, and she held out her arms.

IT WAS AFTER ELEVEN o'clock before Swann walked to Paul's house. Electricity on this block had finally been restored, and the sides of the street were piled high with tree limbs and other debris. From one of the houses echoed the sound of laughter. The storm was over, and it was time to start living again.

Her footsteps echoed on the wooden steps of Paul's front porch. He wasn't expecting her, and she hesitated before knocking. His house was dark, but his car was in the driveway, so he was probably at home. He wouldn't be happy to see her, especially if he were already asleep, but she had to let him know that The Power had worked. She would be leaving in the morning.

He didn't answer her knock right away, and for one dreadful moment she thought that he might not be alone. When he opened the door, he was wearing his glasses. She knew how he would have had to grope around for them on the table beside the bed before he got up.

"Paul, I had to see you," she said urgently.

"Come in," he said, opening the door wide.

"It's Carlie. She's all right. She woke up."

He was deathly still. For a long time he didn't speak. Then he managed to ask, "How did it happen?"

"The nurse walked past her room about nine-thirty and thought she heard a noise. It was Carlie, and she was trying to get the tubes out of her nose. The first thing she said to the nurse was, 'I want my Ma.'"

Paul looked amazed. "I can hardly believe it. There was no change when I left her."

"I know you were responsible for her recovery, Paul," she said. "I *know* it!"

"I'm not so sure," he replied, massaging the back of his neck for a moment. All his senses had been thrown into chaos by this information.

"I just wanted you to know," Swann said. She turned to go.

"Wait!" he said. His voice rang out too sharply. Tempering his tone, he said, "I can't possibly go back to sleep. Won't you—won't you stay for a while?"

She stared at him. The light from the street lamp fell across his face. He looked awkward and confused.

"I should go back to the hospital," she said. "Angelyn wants to return to her house tonight. The people who cleared the creek road said that her place had some water damage, but basically it's all right, and the creek road is passable now. Oh, and the cottage is okay, too," she added as an afterthought.

"Do you have to take Angelyn? I mean, isn't there some other way for her to get there?"

"Mrs. Dawson said she'd drive us. I don't have a car."

Paul thought about the man he'd seen her with at the hospital. Where did he enter into any of this?

"This calls for a celebration," he said. "I have a bottle of champagne in the refrigerator." He turned on the lamp on a nearby table.

The tension that had kept Swann going throughout Carlie's ordeal had settled in her shoulders and neck; a glass of champagne might be exactly what she needed.

"I'd better call Angelyn and tell her to go on without me," she said.

"I'll drive you to her house later," he said.

She paused for a beat, quickly assessing the flicker behind his eyes. She turned away to use the phone, and he went into the kitchen. She heard the pop of the champagne cork before he returned with the bottle and two glasses.

He sat down on the couch and set the bottle and glasses on the low table in front of him. After a moment's hesitation, she sat down on the couch, too. He poured the champagne.

"To Carlie's recovery," he said, and they clinked glasses. The champagne was a good one. She savored it thoroughly before swallowing and almost immediately she felt the tension draining out of her body.

Swann realized that she had no earthly idea what to say to Paul. It had been a mistake to stay; she should have left when she had the chance. She took another sip of champagne. She would leave when she had finished the glass.

Paul seemed as ill at ease as she was. He looked out the window, at his glass, at the floor—everywhere but at her. For her part, she pretended to be infatuated with the wood grain of the table. She should bring up some topic, any topic, so that they wouldn't be sitting here in uncomfortable silence.

"I heard about your rescue of Hunter Epling," she said. "That was a brave thing to do."

Paul shrugged. "It was nothing," he said dismissively.

"Oh, you're wrong, Paul," she answered.

"Well, it wouldn't be the first time," he muttered under his breath.

She wasn't sure she had heard him correctly. "What?" she asked.

He lifted his eyes to her face. They lingered on her chin, her lips, her nose and finally her eyes. Neither of them moved, and then he saw the tremor of her chin and the tears in her eyes.

"I said," he said clearly and distinctly, "that I have been wrong before." He stopped and took a deep breath. "For instance," he said, "I've been thinking about what you said.

About how I had been living a lie by never letting anyone know who I really was. You were right, you know. Although I didn't think it would hurt anyone."

"It didn't, Paul," Swann said.

"Oh, but it did. It hurt you. And ultimately it hurt me. It kept me from facing the things I needed to think about, and it contributed to losing you."

"You have a right to be angry with me," she said in a low tone. "I shouldn't have kept the biography a secret. I didn't want to lose you, Paul, which is what I thought would happen if you found out. Then my deception snowballed so that there was no way I could tell you. And yet I felt so close to you from the very beginning all those years ago when my parents and I went to Miracle Farm and you healed my foot. I felt drawn to you in some inexplicable way. Your eyes, the way you looked at me so compassionately that night at Miracle Farm when my father slapped me—"

"He hit you?"

"Oh, plenty of times, but never before had anyone except my mother seemed to care. I was only a little kid, but you seemed so kind, and I always remembered you. When Justin asked me to write the book, I had to try to find out what you were like and if I could write about you. The more I learned, the more intrigued I was."

He looked away. He couldn't bear to look at her at that moment. Her expression was too intense, her love for him so obvious. She was the one person who had refused to let him devalue himself, ever. When he saw himself reflected in her eyes, he thought he could do anything she believed he could do. He could move mountains, go to med school, find The Power—anything at all.

He knew now without a doubt that there *was* such a thing as love. It was the ache in his heart that wouldn't go away, and it was the sweet memory of her that was always hovering on the edge of his consciousness, and it was a lot of other things that made him wish that their relationship could be the way it was before.

"What—what happened to your application to med school?" she asked.

"I've been accepted at the Medical College of Pennsylvania."

"Are you going?"

"Yes." He drained his champagne glass and poured another. Hers was still almost full.

"I'm glad," she said quietly. "I was afraid that you'd change your mind."

"My mind has been made up ever since we talked it over," he said. He hesitated. He'd been wanting to ask her about the man in her life ever since he had seen them together.

"And what about you, Swann? Your relationship—is it serious?"

"My relationship?"

"I saw you with a man outside the hospital emergency entrance," he reminded her. He tried to keep the accusatory tone out of his voice with limited success.

She stared, and color suffused her cheeks. "That's Nolan. He's Gracie's boyfriend. He's a charter pilot, remember? He flew a planeload of supplies down here, and I came along for the ride," she said.

He was flooded with a relief so immense that he couldn't speak.

"I thought—" he said helplessly.

"You thought wrong," she answered.

"Then there's no one?"

She shook her head. Maybe she should have made someone up, a perfect lover who would make Paul regret what he had so foolishly given up, but she didn't have the heart for it. She had told too many lies already.

She tried to breathe regularly, but it wasn't easy. This scene didn't seem real to her. Only a week ago she couldn't have imagined herself sitting so close to him, within touching distance.

He thought how beautiful she was and how peaceful it had been when they were together. The little cottage by the creek had seemed imbued with a kind of magic in those days, and no matter how he tried to push the memories to the back of his mind, they kept popping out at inconvenient times, threatening to overwhelm him with their poignancy. He missed her in his life. He wanted her back.

He closed the space between them in one easy motion, enfolding her in his arms before she had time to object. She seemed inclined to resist for a brief moment, then went limp in his embrace. And then she was kissing him, covering his face with kisses, and he was smiling against her hair, and she was saying his name over and over.

"Oh, Swann, how could I have let you go?" he said.

"How could I have gone? Paul, I'm so sorry for all that I did. I didn't mean it to turn out that way. All along I wanted to tell you that I was thinking about writing the book, I needed your cooperation, but you were so secretive and I kept putting it off. I shouldn't have deceived you, darling."

"Are you still planning to write the book?" he asked.

"No, Paul. I've dropped the subject."

"I don't know what to say," he told her.

"Say that you love me," she said.

"I've never told that to anyone before."

"I love you, Paul," she said. "I've loved you almost from the moment I met you."

"And I love you. Oh, Swann, to think that I almost lost you!"

He pulled her close, reveling in the way she fit so perfectly into his arms. This was the way it was supposed to be between them. And he would never let her go again.

"I'm going to live in Philadelphia while I go to med school," he said.

"I'm so glad," she whispered against his cheek. He felt her lips curve into a smile.

It hadn't been so difficult to say he loved her after all; the words had been in his heart all along. There was one more thing he wanted to say, and that wasn't so hard, either.

"Will you marry me, Swann? Please say yes," he murmured.

She didn't hesitate. "Yes, of course," she said, and she smiled, lighting up the room, lighting up his life. He felt her heart beating next to his, and he pulled her closer, inhaling the fresh warm scent of her. She was all he had ever dreamed of, all he had ever wanted. She was someone to love and someone who would love him. They would be married, and there would be no biography; at least, not until he was ready to tell his story. When he did, it would be Swann who wrote it. Swann, whom he had healed so long ago and who, through her love, had recently healed him of so many of the old hurts.

Paul had no idea if The Power would ever return in all its glory. But it didn't matter. It didn't matter! Now he knew that the only power he would ever need for the rest of his life was the awesome power of Swann's love.

He cupped her face in his hands and smiled down at her. "You're not going back home tomorrow. You know that, don't you?"

"I'll stay as long as you want me," she whispered.

"Forever," he said, and he lowered his lips to hers.

Take 4 bestselling love stories FREE

Plus get a FREE surprise gift!

HARLEQUIN Romance®

This April, travel to Greece with Harlequin Romance's FIRST CLASS title #3116, LOVE'S AWAKENING by Rachel Ford.

She was taking a calculated risk.

And Selina knew it when she returned to the Greek islands just three years after that traumatic summer.

She told herself that with the Aegean Sea between them, there would be little chance of meeting Alex Petrides—the man who had so nearly changed the course of her life.

But Alex was the reason Selina had been drawn irresistibly back to Greece. Would she ever be able to break free from him . . . or was she destined to remain always in his power.